Praise for the Cranberry Cove Mysteries

"Author Peg Cochran has a truly entertaining writing style that is filled with humor, mystery, fun, and intrigue. You cannot ask for a lot more in a super cozy!"

—Open Book Society

"A fun whodunnit with quirky characters and a satisfying mystery. This new series is as sweet and sharp as the heroine's cranberry salsa."

—Sofie Kelly, *New York Times* bestselling author of the Magical Cats Mysteries

"Cozy fans and foodies rejoice—there's a place just for you and it's called Cranberry Cove."

—Ellery Adams, *New York Times* bestselling author of the Books by the Bay Mysteries, the Charmed Pie Shoppe Mysteries, and the Book Retreat Mysteries

"I can't wait for Monica's next tasty adventure—and I'm not just saying that because I covet her cranberry relish recipe."

—Victoria Abbott, national bestselling author of the Book Collector Mysteries

Dead and Berried

Peg Cochran

BERKLEY PRIME CRIME
New York

BERKLEY PRIME CRIME
Published by Berkley
An imprint of Penguin Random House LLC
375 Hudson Street, New York, New York 10014

Copyright © 2017 by Peg Cochran
Penguin Random House supports copyright. Copyright fuels creativity, encourages
diverse voices, promotes free speech, and creates a vibrant culture. Thank you for buying
an authorized edition of this book and for complying with copyright laws by not
reproducing, scanning, or distributing any part of it in any form without permission.
You are supporting writers and allowing Penguin Random House to continue to
publish books for every reader.

BERKLEY is a registered trademark and BERKLEY PRIME CRIME and
the B colophon are trademarks of Penguin Random House LLC.

ISBN: 9780425274552

First Edition: May 2017

Printed in the United States of America
1   3   5   7   9   10   8   6   4   2

Book design by Laura K. Corless

Chapter 1

Monica Albertson drove down the hill, away from Sassamanash Farm and toward Cranberry Cove and Beach Hollow Road. It was sunny but dark clouds hovered over Lake Michigan in the distance. The wind was picking up, too, tipping the waves that rolled toward shore with white foam.

As she passed a cottage on her right that had long been abandoned, she noticed a spiral of smoke rising from the chimney and a dusty green Jeep parked in the driveway. She was startled—the place had been unoccupied since she'd moved to Cranberry Cove last August. The shingles were weathered, the grass out front scrubby, and a number of the windows were boarded up.

She wondered who could be living there. The place must need some work after having sat vacant for so long—much like her little cottage at the farm had. She'd scrubbed and spackled and painted for over a month, but now the place looked fresh and cozy, and Monica loved it.

Monica continued on her way into town and Beach Hollow Road, where all the shop fronts along the main street were painted in soft pastel tones. The tulips, which had stood like brightly colored sentinels along the sidewalk in early May, were gone now, replaced by planters overflowing with flowers in every hue. Baskets of red and white geraniums hung from the old-fashioned gas lamps that a previous mayor of Cranberry Cove had had the foresight to convert to electricity.

Monica found a parking space in front of Twilight, a store that sold healing crystals, tarot cards and other new age items. She waved to Tempest Storm, the proprietor, as she got out of the car. Tempest was dressed in one of her usual bizarre outfits—this time a long scarlet dress with bat-wing sleeves. There was a silver belt slung around her waist that made her look like the chatelaine of an old castle.

Monica walked past Twilight and continued two doors down to the pastel pink façade of Gumdrops, the local candy store.

Hennie VanVelsen greeted Monica as soon as she stepped into the shop. She was one of a pair of elderly identical twins who had been running Gumdrops for as long as anyone could remember. Her gray hair was set in precise marcel waves and her peach shirtwaist dress was as demure as something worn in the 1950s.

Hennie normally greeted her customers with a bright smile but today she had an unaccustomed worried look on her face as Monica approached the counter.

"Is everything okay?" Monica asked. Hennie was normally the more unflappable of the two sisters, and it surprised Monica to see her worried. "Where's Gerda?"

Hennie fumbled with a box of Droste chocolate pastilles. "She's in the back." She inclined her head toward the door to the storage room. "Lying down. She's not been feeling well lately."

"I hope it's nothing serious?" Monica asked in alarm.

Hennie turned the octagonal box of pastilles over and over in her hands. "I certainly do hope not. I don't know what I'd do without—" She forced her shoulders back and put the candy box down on the counter decisively. "I'm sure she'll be fine. You know Gerda." She gave an indulgent smile. "Every little ache or pain sends her into a terrible tizzy and she immediately thinks she's about to die."

Monica smiled. She'd been in Cranberry Cove long enough to know that Gerda was something of an alarmist, while Hennie was the stauncher sister. So seeing Hennie worried frightened her, even though Hennie had now put on a brave face.

"I passed that abandoned cottage," Monica said, hoping the topic would take Hennie's mind off of her problems. "You know—the one on the road leading to Sassamanash Farm?"

"Yes, I know the one." Hennie touched a hand to her elaborate gray curls, which were in perfect order as usual.

"I saw smoke coming from the chimney today and a truck—a Jeep—parked in the driveway."

"You don't say?"

"It looks as if someone is moving in. I thought maybe you might have heard something about it."

Hennie looked vexed—as if her sources had, for once, failed her. "I'm afraid I haven't heard a thing. So you think someone is moving in?" Hennie shuddered. "The place must need quite a lot of work."

Monica shrugged. "I suppose someone could be cleaning the place out in order to sell it."

Hennie nodded. "I imagine they have a splendid view of the lake from there—it's set up quite high. A lake view would make the property highly desirable. I'm surprised it's sat vacant for so long." She sighed and fiddled with the antique cameo brooch at her neck. "Someone will probably come in and build another one of those enormous summer homes." She sighed again. "Cranberry Cove certainly isn't what it used to be."

Monica hid a smile. The VanVelsens said that every time a new store opened or someone had the nerve to paint their house a different color.

Hennie slapped her hands down on the counter. "I'm sure we will find out all about it soon enough. You can't hide something like that in Cranberry Cove."

Monica laughed. "That's certainly true."

"Now, is there something I can get you?"

"Do you have any more of those delicious winegums?" Monica said. "My mother's birthday is coming up soon and she particularly enjoyed those the last time she was here."

"You can't go wrong with Katjes winegums," Hennie said, retrieving a bag of the brightly colored sweets from the shelf. "They're imported directly from the Netherlands, you know." She put the bag on the counter.

The influence of the wave of Dutch immigrants that had come to this area of western Michigan in the late

1800s was still strong, and the VanVelsens were carrying that tradition on with enthusiasm.

Hennie plopped the winegums in a Gumdrops bag and handed it to Monica. Monica swiped her credit card and signed the slip Hennie put out on the counter.

"Are you on the committee that has been planning the Vlaggetjesdag celebration?"

Monica must have looked blank, because Hennie gave a smug smile and went on to explain.

"Vlaggetjesdag is Flag Day, and a tradition in the Netherlands. We have our own little celebration here in Cranberry Cove."

Monica vaguely remembered seeing flyers about the event, but she'd been too busy to pay much attention.

"Of course, in the Netherlands, Vlaggetjesdag is also the start of herring season and all the fishing boats crowd the harbor, their colorful flags fluttering in the breeze. And, as you can imagine, everyone eats herring."

"Don't herring live in saltwater?" Monica asked, searching her memory for the very little she knew about fish.

"Yes, so obviously we don't have them here in Lake Michigan. Instead we have a Dutch food festival." Hennie suddenly became animated, clapping her hands together, her eyes glowing. "We have tables and tables of delicious things to eat, games for the children and folk music."

The only Dutch food Monica had sampled so far was the erwtensoep and the Dutch treat known as oliebollen. She couldn't conceive of an entire food festival geared around pea soup and doughnuts.

"We have a fabulous rijsttafel, or rice table. The rijsttafel was adapted by the Dutch when they colonized Indonesia to show off to visitors the variety of dishes served in that part of the world. Gerda and I have always contributed something ourselves." Hennie's face suddenly darkened. "I hope Gerda will be up for it this year. She would hate to miss it." She knitted her gnarled hands together. "She would be devastated, you know."

"Is she that ill? Maybe she should see a doctor?" Monica suggested.

"She's being rather stubborn about it. Dr. VanderWeide retired, you know, and Gerda's terribly suspicious of his replacement—young Dr. Albers—although I'm sure he's perfectly qualified." She frowned. "Even if he does look terribly young."

Monica smiled. She'd been to Dr. Albers for a bout with strep throat during the winter, and he was at least forty years old. "I do hope Gerda feels better soon."

"I'm sure she will," Hennie replied, a smile replacing her frown.

"I'd better be going." Monica tucked her receipt into her purse.

"Have a good day, dear. And if you hear any more about that cottage, you will let me know, I hope."

Monica continued down Beach Hollow Road toward Bart's Butcher. The scent of the flowers spilling out of the planters competed with the smell of frying bacon coming from the open door of the Cranberry Cove Diner. A colorful poster taped in the window of the diner caught her eye and she stopped to read it. It was all about the

Flag Day celebration. She couldn't imagine how she had missed seeing it before.

Of course, she'd been very busy on the farm with all the baking and cooking, but the phrase *time to get a life*, crossed her mind. She would have to make an effort to get out more.

Bart's was empty when she got there. After perusing the case of crown roasts of pork dolled up with paper frills, lamb chops adorned with curly bits of parsley, and skinned and boned chicken breasts, Monica chose a couple of thick porterhouses.

"Good choice," Bart said as he pulled a sheet of butcher paper from the roll. He slapped the steak. "That's a fine piece of meat."

Monica nodded, watching as Bart wrapped up her purchase with practiced ease. "By the way, do you know anything about that abandoned cottage—"

"The one on the road to your farm? Why? You thinking of buying it?"

Monica laughed. "Hardly. I have enough to do keeping up with the farm."

Bart gave her a sly look. "You could fix the place up, you know. You'd have a nice view from there. Perfect for when you and Greg get married. Very convenient, too. It's halfway between the farm and his store."

"What makes you think Greg and I are getting—"

Bart cut her off with a wave of his hand. "Everyone knows he's going to ask you, it's only a matter of when." He chuckled. "They've got a pool going over at the diner."

Monica was momentarily horrified. People were actually talking about her and Greg?

"I think the cottage is already taken," she said, ignoring Bart's last comment. "I saw a green Jeep parked in the driveway, and there was smoke coming from the chimney."

"You don't say?" Bart paused with a piece of string wrapped around his finger.

"You haven't heard anything?"

"Not a word."

Chapter 2

Someone was certainly keeping his or her arrival a very guarded secret, Monica thought as she headed to the Cranberry Cove farmer's market. If a local had purchased that cottage the news would be all over town by now.

Monica looked over the stalls piled with fruits and vegetables and chose a head of lettuce and some zucchini. It was June and a little early yet for Michigan-grown tomatoes—she would enjoy those later in the season. The thought made her mouth water in anticipation.

She walked back to her car, loaded her purchases in the backseat and began the drive back to Sassamanash Farm. She glanced in her rearview mirror and noticed that the heavy, dark clouds hanging low over Lake Michigan were now moving east at a brisk pace. It looked like they would soon be getting some rain. The day had started out mild and sunny, but weather changed quickly as storms blew across the vast waters of the lake.

Monica turned into the driveway of her cottage, the gravel crunching under her tires as she pulled around toward the garage. The trellis outside her back door was dripping with pink climbing roses, bees happily buzzing from flower to flower. She stood for a moment breathing in their scent, feeling the soft breeze against her face. Spring had been a long time in coming, but it had been worth waiting for.

Mittens, her little black and white cat, greeted her at the back door. She was still very young and while she had certainly grown, she was still as playful as ever. She wove in and out between Monica's legs as Monica walked back and forth between the kitchen table and the refrigerator, putting her groceries away.

Monica had invited her half brother, Jeff, for dinner. He was the owner of Sassamanash Farm and the reason she had left Chicago to come to Michigan. He had needed help with his cranberry crop and the small farm store they ran, and Monica hadn't hesitated when he'd called.

She'd also invited Jeff's mother, and her stepmother, Gina. Greg Harper was coming, too. Monica thought about what Bart had said again—about her and Greg getting married. They'd been going out for several months now but so far no commitments had been made on either side.

Greg was busy with Book 'Em, the new and used bookstore he owned in town, and she was busy at the farm. Besides, she wasn't sure she was ready for a serious relationship.

Monica picked up the telephone. She'd better remind

Jeff about dinner. He had any number of stellar qualities but remembering things like dinner engagements wasn't one of them. She dialed his cell phone number, but after ringing a dozen times, the call went to voicemail. She looked at the clock. He was probably out at the bogs. The farm required a massive amount of work and there was virtually no such thing as a day off.

Monica whistled for Mittens who came running up in back of her, skidding furiously on the slick tile floor and finally coming to a halt with her tiny black nose an inch from the refrigerator. Monica opened the back door and Mittens skittered out, peering over her shoulder and looking slightly guilty—like a prison inmate making a break for it.

Monica took the path that had been worn into the dirt out past the pump house, where the equipment that controlled the sprinklers was kept. The grass had turned green again after the long winter and birds were singing in the trees and flapping their wings as if they were spreading the news about the coming storm, which was even more evident now as dark clouds continued to roll in.

The cranberry vines, which had lain shriveled and dormant under a protective coating of ice and sand over the winter, had finally bloomed, creating a sea of delicate pink flowers trembling in the breeze that blew over the bog.

Jeff was standing on the far side of the bog, leaning on a shovel and taking a swig from a bottle of water. Monica felt a rush of affection at the sight of his tall, thin frame and the shock of curly auburn hair that matched her own.

Jeff turned when he heard her coming.

"It's beautiful, isn't it?" He motioned toward the flowers that carpeted the cranberry bog.

"It certainly is," Monica said. They stood quietly for a moment, admiring the scene.

Mittens ran through the grass, batting her paw at a butterfly that had the good sense to stay just beyond the kitten's reach.

"By the way," Monica said turning toward Jeff, "do you know who's living in that cottage down at the bottom of the hill that runs into town? The one that's been abandoned?"

Jeff cocked his head. "No. What makes you think someone is living there? Like you said, everyone has always assumed it's been abandoned."

"I saw smoke coming from the chimney and a Jeep parked in the driveway."

Jeff shrugged. "That's curious. There've been no signs of life around the place for years as far as I know. According to what I've heard, the man that used to own it died and no one ever came to claim it." He took another pull on his water bottle. "I'm sure someone in town already knows all about it—Bart or the VanVelsen sisters or someone at the Cranberry Cove Diner. If there's one thing the residents of Cranberry Cove are good at, it's keeping their ear to the ground."

"I've already asked the VanVelsens and they don't know a thing, and neither does Bart."

"Now that surprises me," Jeff said, chuckling. "Someone is obviously very good at keeping a secret if those three don't know anything about it."

Monica laughed. "You can say that again." She touched Jeff's arm. "Don't forget about dinner tonight."

Jeff rubbed his stomach with one hand. "I won't. I'm really looking forward to a good meal." His expression became serious. "I do appreciate how you take care of me, sis."

Monica strongly doubted that Jeff was taking good care of himself. She suspected that he subsisted on take-out from the Cranberry Cove Diner, microwaveable meals and the occasional dinner at the Cranberry Cove Inn with Gina. It would be good when he was married, assuming his intended bride could cook. Right now his current girl-friend, Lauren, was off in Chicago doing an internship at a marketing firm.

Jeff was worried that Lauren would choose big city life over him and a farm in Cranberry Cove. Monica wasn't so sure, and she certainly hoped not. Lauren had been instrumental in pulling Jeff out of the depression he'd been in after returning from his tour in Afghanistan, and Monica was afraid that all of that would be undone if he and Lauren broke up.

They heard a rumble in the distance and turned to see a truck bumping its way down the primitive path that led to the bog. The open flatbed of the truck was stacked with pallets loaded with unusual looking wood boxes. The boxes were light colored with recessed handles. They were banded together and tied to the pallets to keep them from falling over or sliding off the truck.

Monica looked at Jeff. "What strange looking boxes. What are they?"

"Those are beehives," Jeff said, watching as the truck

made its slow and laborious way down the path, jouncing over the ruts and furrows.

"Beehives?" Monica said. "What on earth are you going to do with them? Are you taking up beekeeping?"

"Hardly." Jeff laughed. "I'm only renting them."

"Renting them?" Monica wondered for a brief moment if something had happened to interfere with Jeff's faculties. He'd injured his arm while stationed in Afghanistan—could something have happened to his brain as well? "Why would you rent bees?"

Jeff seemed to be enjoying Monica's confusion because a dimple formed at the corner of his mouth, which was drawn into a teasing half smile.

"Cranberry flowers aren't capable of self-fertilization. We need the bees to move the pollen from one flower to another. Without the bees, we would be lucky to get fifteen berries per square foot—with the help of the bees those same vines will produce around one hundred and fifty berries."

Monica waved a hand in the air. "Don't we already have bees here on the farm? I swear I heard one buzzing around me yesterday when I was sweeping my front steps."

Jeff pointed toward the bog. "Each flower needs to be visited several times. We don't have enough native bees for such a big job. Plus the nectar in cranberry flowers doesn't appeal as much to bees, so native bees tend to swarm elsewhere."

Monica was amazed by how much she had learned—and continued to learn—since arriving at Sassamanash Farm. Cranberry farming was far more complicated than she'd ever imagined.

The wheels of the truck left a path of flattened grass as it made its way over the field beside the bog. It came to a stop and a man jumped out of the driver's side. He approached Jeff and Monica. He was long and lanky, wearing overalls and a T-shirt, and had thick dark hair that he kept brushing off his forehead as he walked toward them. Monica thought him nice looking—boyish and with an unassuming manner.

He held his hand out to Monica. "Rick Taylor." He jerked his head in the direction of the farm store. "Nora's husband."

Nora worked part-time in the farm store, where they sold the cranberry goods Monica baked along with cranberry-themed kitchen and dining items. Nora talked about her husband occasionally, but had never mentioned what he did—most of her conversation centered around their children.

There was the sound of a motor knocking and a car came into view, headed across the field. It pulled up behind the truck. It was rusted, covered in dust, and it made Monica's ancient Ford Focus look like a late-model luxury car. The driver's side door opened and a woman stepped out.

"Lori," Rick called to her. "Come meet Jeff and . . . ?" He looked at Monica questioningly.

"Monica."

"Monica," he finished.

Lori was in jeans and a T-shirt and had a sturdy, athletic-looking body. She wasn't pretty but was attractive in an outdoorsy sort of way.

"Lori Wenk, my assistant," Rick said when Lori reached them.

The girl did not look well, Monica thought when she got closer. Beads of sweat clustered on her forehead and her skin had an unhealthy pasty color.

The girl smiled at Monica, pulled a tissue from the pocket of her jeans and dabbed her forehead and the back of her neck. Her hand trembled and Monica thought her breath was coming rather fast—as if she'd run rather than walked across the field.

"Awfully hot today, isn't it?"

Monica hadn't found it particularly hot—certainly warm but with a breeze that was developing a cool edge as the clouds continued to blow in.

Rick looked at Lori. "Are you okay?"

"Sure. I'm just a little queasy, that's all. I'm sure it will pass. I think it was that Chinese takeout we had last night." She rubbed her forehead.

"Can I get you some water or—" Monica started.

"No, that's fine." Lori shook her head then winced. She turned to Rick. "What do you think? Should we release the bees?" She put her hand on Rick's arm.

Rick looked up at the sky and scratched his head. "It's quite overcast and there's rain in the air." He looked at Monica and smiled. "Honeybees don't like dark days, and while I've never minded a few drops of rain myself, bees definitely don't like getting wet. It riles them up, and they don't want to work." He turned to Lori. "I think we'd better wait and see if the weather is any better tomorrow before letting them out."

"Whatever you say." Lori slipped her arm through Rick's. "Rick knows everything there is to know about bees." She glanced up at him, a look of admiration on her face.

Rick cleared his throat and gently removed his arm from Lori's. "I don't know about that." He laughed.

Lori swayed and leaned against Rick.

He gently steadied her then moved away, looking more and more uncomfortable.

Monica watched them. It looked as if Lori had an old-fashioned crush on her boss.

"It was nice meeting you," Monica nodded to Rick and Lori. "I'm afraid I've got to get to work."

"See you later," Jeff called out as Monica began to walk away.

"Nice to meet you," Rick and Lori called in unison.

Monica glanced back and saw Lori sway toward Rick again. She turned and headed toward the dirt path that wound around a smaller bog and then toward the building that housed the farm store, the processing room and now, their new commercial kitchen.

The kitchen was small as far as commercial kitchens went, but it enabled Monica to fulfill orders for her cranberry salsa. She'd started selling to Fresh Gourmet, a national chain that had a store on the highway just outside of Cranberry Cove. At first, product had only been going to the local store, but when Fresh Gourmet decided to expand their orders, Monica had had to expand as well. The tiny kitchen in her cottage didn't give her enough room to produce the quantity of salsa she needed. Plus she had to be sure that she met all the health and safety regulations that working on such a large scale required.

The state's aptly named cottage food law allowed for the sale of small quantities of homemade products—like what was sold in the farm store—but not for production of the quantities Monica would eventually be making.

Jeff had agreed on the expansion, and they'd gone to the bank for a loan to build a commercial kitchen. Monica had had butterflies in her stomach signing the papers— what if something went wrong or the grocery store cancelled its order? It had been a leap of faith—faith in herself, Jeff and Sassamanash Farm—to borrow the money.

They'd built the kitchen off of the processing room, where berries were sorted and readied for shipment. The addition had white shingles like the rest of the building, and its own entrance. Monica had painted the door a cheery cranberry red.

She was approaching the kitchen when she saw Nora Taylor standing outside the back door of the farm store. Her head was turned toward where Rick, Jeff and Lori were standing, and her hands were balled into fists at her sides.

She pivoted and waved when she noticed Monica walking toward her.

"You don't look too happy," Monica said as she neared Nora.

Nora slid her round tortoiseshell glasses up her nose with her finger. "I'm not." She gave an unconvincing laugh. "I know it shouldn't bother me, but. . . ." She looked at Monica. "I hate how Lori flirts with Rick the way she does—touching him, taking his arm or leaning on him. Or hadn't you noticed?"

"Oh, I noticed," Monica said. "But frankly, Rick seemed more embarrassed by it than pleased."

Nora sighed and began pleating the fabric of her cranberry-patterned apron with her fingers. "I know Rick would never cheat on me. Still, it gets my goat watching that . . . that hussy come on to him the way she does. And you can't tell me he doesn't enjoy it at least the tiniest bit." She looked at Monica. "What man wouldn't be flattered by the attention of a younger woman?"

Monica found it hard to reconcile the term *hussy* with Lori who, while not unattractive, was dressed in a worn T-shirt, faded jeans, socks and heavy work boots coated with mud. Not exactly the attire of a femme fatale or temptress.

"I really don't think you have anything to worry about."

"I'm sure you're right." Nora looked doubtful.

"I know I am." Monica squeezed Nora's arm.

Nora sighed. "I'd better get back inside. I think I heard a car pull into the parking lot." She turned to Monica again. "We're almost out of muffins—"

"I'm on it. That's the first thing on my list this morning."

"Great. I hate disappointing our customers," Nora said.

"I'll bring them over as soon as they're out of the oven."

"Thanks." Nora smiled and opened the door to the farm store.

Monica walked toward the new building, which formed an *L,* with the farm store being the short part of the *L* and the processing room and new commercial kitchen making up the longer stroke of the letter.

She pulled the keys from her pocket as she approached the door to the kitchen, but realized the lights were already on and the door was unlocked.

"Arline?" she called out as she stepped across the threshold.

Monica had recently hired Arline Loomis, a local girl, to help her in the kitchen. It was another expense that Monica hoped would prove to be worthwhile. Not that she could afford to pay all that much. This was only one of Arline's part-time jobs that she juggled while taking classes at the County Community College.

Arline stuck her head around the door to the supply closet. "In here," she announced.

"Have you started on the batter for the muffins yet?" Monica asked, taking a chef's apron from a hook by the door and tying it around her waist. "Nora says they're almost out."

"I was about to." Arline closed the door to the closet. She was holding her phone in her hand.

Monica looked at her curiously.

Arline held up her cell. "Believe it or not, reception is better in the closet."

"Seriously?"

Arline nodded. "I had a call from my neighbor. She said she was walking past the house with her dog—the most annoying beast you could imagine, barks all the time— when she noticed the front door was ajar. I'm quite certain I closed it. . . ." Arline bit her lip.

"You'd better go then and check on it. I can manage on my own."

"Are you sure?"

"Absolutely."

"I'm just a boarder," Arline explained. "But the owner of the house is an older woman—she spends most of her time in a recliner in the den watching television—and she might not notice the door is open until it's too late."

Arline pulled off her apron, leaving her dark hair in its pixie cut standing out around her head as if electrified. She smoothed it down with one hand while she shoved her phone into the pocket of her shorts with the other.

"I'm sure it's nothing," Arline said as she headed toward the door. "Probably just the wind. . . ."

"Maybe you should call the police?"

Arline shook her head. "If I notice anything amiss I certainly will, but I'm sure it's only a matter of the latch not holding."

Monica smiled. It was well known that no one in Cranberry Cove bothered to lock their door. They all looked out for each other and woe betide anyone who tried to break into someone's home when they weren't there.

"Don't worry about me. I'll be fine," Monica assured her as Arline closed the door behind her.

Monica was used to working alone and doing everything herself. She'd single-handedly made all the baked goods for her now-defunct café in Chicago and had then gone behind the counter and waited on customers. It had made for a terribly long day, and in the end it hadn't been enough to keep the café from going under when a national chain coffee shop moved in across the street.

But if that hadn't happened, Monica mused, she wouldn't be in Cranberry Cove right now, where she was enjoying life in a small town more than she ever thought possible. She certainly wasn't considered a local yet—that took several generations—but she knew many of the people and they had come to accept her presence in what they considered to be their town.

Monica was pouring batter into muffin tins when a hollow knock sounded on the wooden frame of the screen door to the kitchen.

"Come in," Monica called as she opened the oven door. A blast of dry heat billowed out and Monica averted her face momentarily. She slid the muffin tins in and turned around to find Lori standing by the entrance.

She felt herself bristle slightly after having heard Nora's comments, but forced herself to smile as a wave of pity washed over her. The girl really didn't look well.

"Can I help you?"

Lori took a step farther into the kitchen. She looked embarrassed. "Do you have a restroom I could use?"

Her face was still alarmingly pale and the hair around her face was damp with perspiration.

Monica slid off her potholders. "Oh, sure. Right over there." She pointed toward a door that was slightly ajar.

"Thanks. I really appreciate it."

Monica was pulling a bag of cranberries from the freezer when Lori reappeared.

"If it's not too much trouble, could I have a glass of water?" She reached into her pocket and pulled something out that she held in her palm, her hand trembling. "I hope I'm not being a pest, but I'm afraid I must have a migraine coming on." She held her hand toward Monica. "Hopefully one of these will help." She opened her fist to reveal a small pill. "It's the swift change in the weather that's brought it on I'm afraid."

Monica grabbed a glass from the cabinet next to the sink and filled it with water. She handed it to Lori.

"Thanks." Lori tossed the pill into her mouth and took a gulp of water. She swiped a hand across her wet lips. "Hopefully that will head it off before it gets too bad."

Monica smiled. "I hope so." The girl's face was pinched and her breathing was still more rapid than normal. "Are you sure you're okay?"

Lori nodded. "Thanks," she said as she headed toward the door.

The door to the kitchen was closing behind her when the timer on the stove pinged. Monica quickly donned her oven mitts again and pulled out the half dozen tins of baked muffins. She set them on the long counter and whipped off her gloves. She looked around the room.

The appliances were stainless steel, and Monica kept them polished to a high shine. She was proud of what she and Jeff had managed to accomplish together. Although she did miss the coziness of her kitchen at the cottage, she had to admit the extra space and commercial-sized appliances made everything a lot easier.

Monica began work on her cranberry salsa—she would be spending the rest of the morning and afternoon getting the next order ready.

She was chopping peppers when Jeff burst through the door, breathless. "Call nine-one-one," he gasped, a horrified expression on his face. His eyes were wild.

Monica dropped her knife. "Are you okay?"

"No. Yes—I'm fine. It's Lori."

Monica was already yanking off the thin rubber gloves she wore when dealing with the jalapeños. She dug her cell from the pocket of her apron and punched in the numbers with shaky hands.

"What's wrong with Lori?" she asked as she waited for the operator to pick up.

"I think she's dead."

Chapter 3

"Are you sure? What . . . what happened?"

"I went into the shed to grab some tools and when I came out Lori was lying on the ground. I felt her pulse and . . . nothing." Jeff stifled a sob.

The operator finally came on the line.

"We need an ambulance," Monica said, trying to control her breathing as well as the shaking in her hands. The dispatcher would need details—the address, directions to the farm. She had to focus.

Monica did the best she could, although she stumbled over the address of the farm and Jeff had to mouth the information to her. Finally she ended the call.

"They're on their way."

Jeff wiped his hands over his face. "I'd better get outside and wait for the police."

"I'm coming with you." Monica pulled off her apron, balled it up and tossed it on the counter.

She followed Jeff out the door and down the path toward the bog, where Lori's car was still parked. Although she was tall herself, Monica had to trot to keep up with her brother's long strides. Her foot caught on a root that had broken through the surface of the ground, and she gave a cry, nearly falling but catching herself in the nick of time.

Rick's truck was gone, the grass still flattened where it had stood. The wooden hives housing the bees had been unloaded and were placed in even rows on the field bordering the bog.

Lori was lying face down a dozen feet in front of the hives, her hands clenching the grass, her legs splayed.

Monica started toward where Lori was lying when she stopped suddenly. A loud humming was coming from somewhere and it felt as if the very air was vibrating. She grabbed Jeff's arm.

"What's that noise?"

"It's the bees. Someone let them out." He pointed to a twisted and stunted tree near the bog. Hanging from a low branch were hundreds of bees in an angry, buzzing cluster.

Monica stifled a squeal. She wasn't allergic to bees but she remembered well the pain of the stinger the time she'd stepped on one in the grass in her bare feet.

"We can go this way," Jeff said, pointing in a direction that would take them to where Lori was lying but would cut a wide swath around the bees hanging from the tree.

As soon as they reached Lori, Jeff dropped to one knee beside her body. "I've already felt for a pulse, but maybe . . ." He held his finger to her neck for several seconds then shook his head. "Nothing."

"Maybe we should try chest compressions," Monica said. "See if you can turn her over."

Jeff was about to reach for Lori when they heard the bleating of a siren in the distance.

Monica breathed a sigh of relief. "They're here."

The siren ground to a halt as the ambulance bounced its way over the rutted path close to the spot where Monica and Jeff were waiting. A man and woman in navy pants and white shirts jumped out as soon as the vehicle came to a halt.

The man flung open the back doors of the ambulance and began to wrestle a gurney from the interior while the woman rushed toward Lori's prone body.

She knelt down, turned the body over and immediately began CPR.

Lori's face was red and bloated and swollen, especially around her eyes.

Jeff put his arm around Monica and pointed toward Lori. "It looks as if she's been stung repeatedly."

Monica glanced toward the tree where the bees continued to hang in an agitated cluster like a bunch of angry grapes.

They both turned their heads at the sound of a car approaching. A patrol car pulled up sharply in back of the ambulance and two patrolmen got out. Monica thought she recognized the one with the sunglasses—he'd been at the scene the time she'd found a body in the cranberry bog at Sassamanash Farm. He still had the same arrogant look as well as the ever-present wad of gum, which he was working furiously, his jaw going up and down like a piston.

They moved closer as they all watched the EMT continue CPR—her face red and shiny with perspiration from the effort. Her partner wheeled the gurney closer to Lori's body.

"Any luck?" her partner asked.

She shook her head, dropped back on her heels with a sigh and peeled off her gloves. "There's no response."

They both turned to look at Monica, Jeff and the two policemen. The woman stood up, brushed the dirt off her knees and walked toward them.

"I'm sorry," she said. "Is she a friend . . . ?"

Monica shook her head. "Not really."

The patrolman with the mirrored sunglasses reached for his radio. "We have to get the medical examiner out here." He pointed at Monica and Jeff. "Meanwhile, don't move anything, don't touch anything."

"Surely it's an accident," Monica protested. "The bees." She pointed toward the tree where the buzzing had quieted down somewhat.

"Any sudden death like this, we gotta call the ME," the other patrolman explained. "It's up to him to decide cause of death."

"It looks obvious to me," Jeff said, pointing at Lori's body. "She's been stung repeatedly."

The patrolman pushed his cap back, revealing a puckered

line across his forehead where the brim had been. "Like I said. It's not for me to say. You gotta wait for the ME."

"Detective Stevens is on her way," the patrolman in the sunglasses said, straightening his shoulders slightly.

Monica looked from the patrolmen to Jeff and then back again. "Detective Stevens? But surely you don't suspect . . . foul play?"

The one patrolman pushed his hat back a bit farther and scratched along his hairline. "It's routine, ma'am. Only routine. Nothing to worry about."

By now the sun had reached its peak and was shining through a momentary break in the thick clouds. Monica wiped her sleeve across her damp forehead—she didn't know whether she was perspiring from the heat or from a case of shock. The perspiration was certainly at odds with her hands, which were as cold as if she were standing outside in the middle of a blustery winter with no gloves on.

Monica, Jeff and the patrolmen stood around in awkward silence, waiting for the arrival of the ME and Detective Tammy Stevens. Monica had first met Detective Stevens back in October when the detective was nine months pregnant. She'd subsequently given birth to a boy and had gone back to work. Monica knew her to be smart, efficient and fair.

Finally, they heard the whine of a car in the distance, and a red late-model Chrysler Town & Country appeared around the bend. It came to a stop a dozen yards or so from the scene, and a man in gray dress slacks and a rumpled white shirt with the sleeves rolled up got out. He had brown hair cut short and was wearing glasses with dark frames.

The two patrolmen scurried toward him. Monica could see them gesturing toward the scene but couldn't hear what they were saying. They were headed to where Lori's body lay when another car came jouncing down the path, kicking up dust as it came to a stop in back of the ME's van.

Detective Stevens emerged from the second car. She stood surveying the scene for a moment, her hands on her hips, her blond chin-length hair blowing in the slight breeze, before she began walking toward Monica and Jeff. She was wearing a khaki skirt that looked rather tight in the waist and a dark green, short-sleeved blouse.

Monica smiled as Stevens approached.

She greeted Monica and Jeff and jerked her head in the direction of the body. "I'll have a word with the ME, but I want to talk to both of you as well, so please stick around if you don't mind."

Jeff scowled, and Monica knew he was thinking of all the work that needed to be done before the sun went down. He plopped down on a tree stump and ran a hand through his thick hair.

Monica was thinking of work as well. She needed to finish this batch of cranberry salsa and start on another one. The way things were going, it looked like she'd be in the kitchen all day and possibly half the night.

Stevens was gesturing to the two patrolmen. The one had pulled his hat back into position and both were listening attentively. As Stevens finished and turned away, they dashed toward their patrol car and opened the trunk.

Stevens had a brief consultation with the ME then

turned and walked back toward where Monica and Jeff were waiting. She reached them just as the two patrolmen began stringing up black-and-yellow plastic crime scene tape.

Stevens blew a lock of hair off her forehead. "Thank goodness it's cooling down." She glanced at the sky where the sun was now half covered by clouds. She looked back at Monica and Jeff and pointed over her shoulder with her thumb.

The crime scene tape fluttered and snapped in the wind that had picked up considerably since that morning.

Monica motioned toward it. "Surely this is an accident," she said to Stevens.

"It's only a precaution to protect the scene. Right now all we know is that we have a deceased female who is too young to have died of old age. Who knows what the ME will uncover? Quite possibly nothing sinister, but we have to be prepared."

She glanced over her shoulder at the patrolmen then turned back to Monica and Jeff. "What happened here? Can one of you tell me?"

Monica and Jeff both began talking at the same time. Monica motioned for Jeff to go first.

"Rick dropped off the bees this morning, but it was too cloudy so he decided not to let them out." He pointed toward the beehives arrayed on the scrubby grass.

The look of confusion that crossed Stevens's face would have been comical under other circumstances.

"The honeybees are needed to fertilize the cranberry crop," Jeff explained, pointing toward the bog now, where the pink flowers were rippling and bending in the wind.

"Who is Rick?" Stevens tugged at the waistband of her skirt.

"Rick is the beekeeper. We're only renting the bees."

Stevens's look of confusion deepened. She shook her head as if to clear it, opened her mouth then shut it again. "The victim appears to have been stung numerous times," she said finally. "If you didn't let the bees out . . ."

"That's what I don't understand," Jeff admitted. "We'd agreed to wait till tomorrow. Lori knew that."

"Lori?"

Just then Rick's truck came into view, stopping behind Stevens's car. Rick jumped out. He paused for a moment, taking in the scene, before rushing over to where Monica, Jeff and Stevens were standing.

"What's happened? Is Lori okay?" He was breathless and sweating.

Stevens took a deep breath and let it out in a sigh. "And you are?" she asked, pulling a notebook and worn pencil stub from her pocket.

"Rick. Rick Taylor. Those are my bees." He pointed toward the swarm of bees hanging from the tree.

"Is Lori the young woman who—"

"Yes," Rick interrupted. "Is she okay?"

Jeff put a hand on Rick's arm. "I'm afraid not. I'm sorry."

"What happened?" Rick looked bewildered. "She was okay when I left. I know she had a headache, but who's ever died from a headache?" He looked from Monica to Jeff and back again, a puzzled look still on his face. "She said she was about to leave, so why was she still here?"

"It appears she's been stung repeatedly," Stevens said. "Do you know if she was allergic?"

Rick shook his head and his bangs flopped from side to side. "No. She worked with the bees all the time. The occasional sting is an occupational hazard. But I've never known her to have a reaction before."

"But if a person is stung repeatedly . . ."

Rick shrugged. "It's possible that numerous bee stings could release enough venom to kill, but we're talking hundreds, if not thousands, of stings." Rick scowled. "Besides, why were the bees out of the hives?" He looked around as if an answer could be found somewhere in the vicinity.

"She must have let them out herself," Jeff said. "I went back to the shed," he gestured over his shoulder, "to get some tools, and when I came back I found Lori on the ground and the bees swarming in that tree."

Rick shook his head even more vigorously. "She would never let them out—not without the proper protection. At the very least she would have put her hat and face mask on." He made a motion in front of his face. "A sting on the face is especially painful and can cause a great deal of swelling even without an allergic reaction."

The brief glimpse Monica had caught of Lori's face flashed across her mind. Rick was certainly right. Her face was so swollen as to be nearly unrecognizable.

"Officers." Stevens turned and yelled to the patrolmen who were leaning against their patrol car. Both of them now had their hats pushed back, and the one in the sunglasses was patting his forehead with a handkerchief.

They shot to attention and turned to look at Stevens.

"Yes," they said in unison.

"Go check the victim's car. See if you find any beekeeping gear in there."

They both nodded and began walking briskly toward Lori's car.

"Let me get this straight. The victim apparently let the bees out herself," Stevens said.

Rick danced from one foot to the other. "But that alone wouldn't necessarily cause them to swarm the way they did." He pointed toward the cluster still clinging to the tree branch. "Something would have had to rile them up first."

"What sort of something would that be?" Stevens paused with her pencil poised over her notebook.

Rick shrugged. "Any number of things—waving your arms or trying to bat them away, walking in front of the hive. Or disturbing the queen." Rick looked over to where the ME was performing his examination. "Certainly Lori knew not to do any of those things."

"How long had she been working for you?" Stevens asked.

"Not too long—a couple of months maybe. But still, she was a fast learner and certainly knew how to avoid disturbing the bees. That's beekeeping one-oh-one."

Stevens nodded and made a notation in her notebook.

"Can I ask where everyone was when this happened?" She waved a hand toward the beehives. She looked at Jeff. "You said you were in the shed."

"I was in the kitchen," Monica said quickly. "I'd made a couple dozen batches of cranberry muffins, and I was starting on the cranberry salsa."

Stevens turned toward Jeff.

"And when you came back, the victim was already on the ground?"

"Yes."

"And you?" Stevens turned toward Rick.

"Me?" Rick pointed at himself and took a step backward.

Stevens nodded without saying anything.

"I . . . I was . . . I stopped in to say hello to my wife. She works over in the farm store." He pointed toward the white clapboard building. "She's been working there for several months."

"So you walked over there." Stevens jerked a thumb in the general direction of the farm store.

"I took my truck."

Rick stuck his hands in his pockets, and Monica could see his fists were balled.

Stevens looked puzzled.

"I was heading somewhere else right afterward," Rick explained. "And I wanted to leave straight from there. But then I saw all the commotion over here. . . ."

Why did Rick look so guilty? Monica wondered. Surely he didn't have anything to do with this?

"What happens now?" Jeff asked. "This must have been an accident."

Stevens shrugged. "I'm sure we'll know more after the autopsy."

"Autopsy!" Monica said, alarmed. She'd seen murder investigations up close before and wasn't looking forward to being involved in another one. "So you think it wasn't an accident?"

"Most likely it was an accident," Stevens said. "But we'll find out."

Chapter 4

Monica had to really scrub to get the stains from the cranberry juice off her hands. Occupational hazard, she thought, as she ran a nailbrush foaming with soap over her fingers. But she'd finished the salsa for the order from Fresh Gourmet, and she still had time to get ready for the dinner she'd planned for the evening. In her mind, that was a win-win.

Monica wasn't much for fashion and makeup, but since Greg was coming, she did take a few moments to dab some powder on her nose and change out of her jeans and T-shirt—her usual uniform while working in the kitchen.

Her hair refused to cooperate so she pinned it up in a loose knot on top of her head. She glanced in the bathroom mirror. A touch of lipstick and she would be ready.

The dinner she'd planned was a simple one—she didn't have all that much time for fancy cooking. A couple of good steaks, cooked to a perfect medium rare, was always a hit. She had fixings for a salad and she would grill some zucchini and toss it with balsamic vinegar to bring out the vegetable's sweetness.

Dessert would be equally no fuss—vanilla ice cream layered with some store-bought pound cake and cranberry preserves.

Monica was slicing the zucchini when there was a knock on her back door. Before she could even yell *come in*, Gina burst into the kitchen, her arms laden with grocery bags.

Her expensively highlighted blond hair—Gina made regular trips back to Chicago to shop and have her hair done—was in its usual deceptively simple looking twist. She was wearing black leggings and a leopard-print tunic along with leopard-print, pony hair ankle boots.

Gina had come to Cranberry Cove for a visit and had decided to stay, opening an aromatherapy shop called Making Scents on Beach Hollow Road, right next to the hardware store.

"I think I'm finally becoming one of you," Gina said as she put the bags down on Monica's kitchen table.

Monica managed to stifle a snort. "What makes you think that?"

"I went into the Cranberry Cove Diner, and Gus nodded at me. It was a very tiny nod, but I definitely saw him nod." Gina plunged a hand into one of the bags.

Gus Amentas was the rather taciturn short-order cook at the Cranberry Cove Diner. He had no use for the tourists who flocked to Cranberry Cove in the summer and fall, and refused to acknowledge anyone he didn't consider a *local.* To get even so much as a nod from Gus meant you were slowly becoming accepted in Cranberry Cove.

"What's all that you've brought?" Monica said, watching Gina produce items from the grocery bags with the same flourish a magician uses to produce a rabbit from a top hat. "I am planning on giving you dinner, you know."

Mittens, who had been sleeping in the late rays of the sun coming through the window, tired from her afternoon outdoors, jumped onto the kitchen table and pounced on one of the empty grocery bags, knocking it on its side. She then proceeded to curl up inside the bag, purring loudly.

"I thought it would be nice to have a little something beforehand. I went out to Fresh Gourmet and picked up a few things." Gina waved a hand over the items spread out on the table. "I've got some pâté, a few different cheeses and," she paused dramatically, "some champagne."

"Are we celebrating something?" After the events of the afternoon, Monica was hardly in the mood to celebrate. To her mind, champagne was something reserved for New Year's Eve and very special occasions like weddings and notable birthdays.

Gina shook her head. "Not really. But one doesn't need an excuse to pop the cork on some bubbly." She opened the refrigerator. "I'll put these in here to chill."

Monica sliced the last zucchini, spread the slices out on a plate and drizzled them with olive oil.

"Is your boyfriend coming?"

Monica felt herself bristle. "I think I'm a little too old to have a boyfriend," she said mildly.

"Okay, your beau then. Is that better?"

"Yes, he is."

"Good. I always enjoy talking to Greg. When are you two going to move in together?"

Monica felt herself color. "We're perfectly happy the way we are. I live here on the farm, and he has his place over his shop. It's convenient."

Gina snorted. "Love is never convenient." She looked over at Monica. "Your hair looks good like that, by the way. You should wear it up more often."

Monica was relieved when the front doorbell rang.

"Do you want me to get it?" Gina asked.

"That's okay." Monica wiped her hands on her apron and headed down the hall to the living room and the small front foyer.

She opened the door to find Greg on the doorstep, clutching a paper-wrapped bundle of flowers.

He bent and kissed Monica then handed her the flowers. "For my hostess," he said with a smile.

Monica buried her nose in the bouquet and sniffed. "They're lovely." She took Greg's arm. "Come on back. Gina's here."

Monica returned to the kitchen to discover Jeff had arrived via the back door. He'd changed into a clean shirt and pair of jeans and his hair was still slightly damp from his shower.

"Jeff just told me about what happened this morning," Gina said. "That poor woman."

Greg looked from Gina to Monica. "What happened this morning?"

Monica explained about the bees and finding Lori dead from their stings.

Greg whistled. "I had no idea. The village grapevine must be malfunctioning."

"They're performing an autopsy to determine the exact cause of death," Monica said.

She opened the refrigerator and pulled out the steaks she'd bought from Bart's. They were wrapped in brown butcher paper and tied with string. Bart believed in doing things the old-fashioned way.

"An autopsy?" Gina said, mirroring Monica's earlier tone when Stevens had mentioned the word. "Does that mean they suspect it wasn't natural causes?"

Monica undid the paper wrapped around the pieces of meat. "According to Detective Stevens, it's standard operating procedure in the case of any unattended death."

Gina looked slightly disappointed, but then perked up. "Maybe it will turn out to be murder after all. We could use a dose of excitement. And here I thought living in a small town was going to be dull."

"There's nothing dull about it," Greg said, arranging the flowers in the vase Monica had handed him. "I think there's as much intrigue in small towns as there is in big cities."

"You're probably right," Gina said. "Who's up for some bubbly?" She opened the refrigerator and grabbed the bottle of champagne.

"Here, let me open it for you," Greg said, taking the bottle from Gina. The outside was frosted with condensation.

Monica retrieved a couple of mismatched champagne glasses from the cupboard and dusted them off with a towel. She could no longer remember how she'd come by them. Champagne wasn't something she had very often—and when she did, more often than not, it was in a restaurant.

Greg filled their glasses, and they nibbled on the treats Gina had brought.

Monica glanced at the clock. "I think it's time I put the steaks on."

She took the meat outside to the small brick patio Jeff had created for her as a surprise last year. It was bordered by a white trellis covered with pink climbing roses, and was just big enough for her new gas grill, a café table and a chaise longue.

Monica turned on the gas and lit three of the burners. Her parents had had a charcoal grill and her father had always had trouble getting the fire going. Monica had decided she would make it easier on herself and go for gas. She was glad she had—she'd grilled out almost every night since she'd bought it.

Once the grill reached the right temperature, Monica put on the steaks. The meat sizzled and spat and soon good smells were drifting on the air.

When she returned to the kitchen, she discovered that Gina had cleaned and set the table. Monica mixed the salad and tossed it with dressing while the steaks rested.

Finally they were all seated around the table with full plates and a glass of the red wine Monica had bought for the occasion.

"There's another mystery I've been meaning to talk to you about." Monica turned to Greg.

He raised his eyebrows.

"You know that abandoned cottage on the right just before you head into Cranberry Cove?"

Greg nodded.

"I noticed smoke coming from the chimney and a truck parked out front."

"I know the place you mean," Gina said, pointing her fork at Monica. "There was a Dumpster out back last week filled with building materials."

"Well. . . ." Greg leaned back in his chair and folded his hands over his stomach.

"Don't tease us," Monica said, lightly punching him on the arm. "You know something. I can tell."

Greg let out a laugh. "You're right. For once I know something before the VanVelsen sisters do. You'll have to excuse me while I bask in that glory for a moment."

Monica snorted. "Hennie didn't know this morning when I asked her, but I'll bet they know by now."

Greg put on a comically sad face. "Please! Don't puncture my balloon."

Monica felt Gina jiggling her foot under the table.

"I don't think you know anything," Gina said, giving Greg a challenging look. "You're stalling so you can make up some tall tale to tell us."

Greg straightened up and put both hands on the table. "*Au contraire*, madame. I do happen to be in possession of the information you are so desperately seeking."

"Then tell us before I pull my hair out," Gina said, putting her hands to her head threateningly.

"Okay." Greg relaxed back in his chair. "It was almost closing time when this fellow walked in."

"What did he look like?" Gina immediately asked.

Greg held up a hand. "I'm getting to it, don't worry. He was tall and . . . I can only say robust looking."

"Fat?" Gina inquired.

Greg shook his head. "No, not fat. Muscular." He pretended to flex the muscles in his arms.

"Age?" Gina's foot was still going a mile a minute under the table.

Greg held his hands out, palms up. "Middle-aged? He had a full gray beard and thick hair. And very blue eyes. He reminded me of an old-fashioned ship's captain."

Gina raised her eyebrows.

"Which is ironic actually. He's a writer, and he's holing up in that old cottage to finish his latest book. It's going to be on the famous shipwrecks in the Great Lakes like the *Edmund Fitzgerald*."

Gina's eyes widened. "Did he mention his name?"

Greg nodded. "Xavier Cabot."

Gina gave a pretend shiver. "Oooh. I am definitely going to have to meet Mr. Xavier Cabot."

And Monica didn't doubt for a minute that Gina would find a way.

Chapter 5

Monica spent the night tossing and turning. Scenes from the afternoon—Lori lying on the grass, her face suffused with red and hideously bloated—worked their way into her dreams, causing her to wake abruptly, sit bolt upright in bed and gasp for air as if someone was attempting to suffocate her.

She finally managed to catch a scant few hours of uneasy slumber before the alarm went off at six thirty.

Mornings in late June were still chilly, even though the temperatures in the afternoon could climb into the eighties. Monica pulled on a pair of worn jeans, a T-shirt that could use a good bleaching and a sweatshirt with a hole in the elbow. She could remove the sweatshirt later when it finally warmed up.

She made her way downstairs, Mittens weaving in and

out between her legs and making for a rather perilous journey. Yawning, she filled the coffeepot with water and ground beans, and was nearly dozing off, leaning heavily against the counter, when the coffee began trickling into the pot.

The smell jolted Monica awake. She grabbed a thick white mug from the cupboard and waited impatiently as the last of the coffee dripped into the carafe. She poured herself a cup, inhaled deeply as the steam wreathed her face and took a sip.

"Ah . . ." Monica sighed and closed her eyes in rapture. She was still trying to shake off the effects of last night's dream.

With caffeine coursing through her bloodstream, Monica filled Mittens's bowl with fresh water, opened a can of cat food and forked it into the kitten's food dish. While Mittens devoured her meal, Monica microwaved a bowl of instant oatmeal mixed with cranberries that had been harvested in the fall and dried. Thus fortified, she grabbed her keys from the hook by the back door and headed down to the farm kitchen.

Dew sparkled on the grass, reflecting the rays of sun piercing the thin, scattered clouds. Monica followed the well-worn path, enjoying the cool, moist air against her face. She could feel her hair curling in the humidity, and she brushed it back from her forehead and tucked it behind her ears.

She avoided looking at the spot where Lori had been found the day before, but instead focused on the building that housed the commercial kitchen.

Monica slipped the key into the lock, opened the door and flicked on the lights.

Within half an hour she had the first batch of cranberry muffins in the oven and was working on the dough for some cranberry bread with streusel topping. She glanced out the window as she mixed a batch of berries into the dough.

The lights were on in the farm store—Nora had obviously arrived and was setting up for the day. Soon Monica would be able to take her some bread and muffins, still warm from the oven. They had a handful of customers who stopped by on their way to work to add a freshly baked goodie to their morning cup of coffee.

Working with practiced ease, Monica soon had several batches of dough in the oven. While they baked, she wiped down the counters, scooping any random sprays of flour into the palm of her hand and dumping them into the stainless steel sink.

The timer dinged and Monica checked the first batch of bread. It wasn't quite done so she set the timer for another five minutes. Meanwhile, she finished cleaning up. She had her wicker baskets lined up on the counter by the time the timer dinged again. This time the bread was golden brown and pulling away from the sides of the pan. The muffins were done as well, and Monica pulled the pans from the oven.

As soon as everything was cool enough to handle, Monica turned out the bread and muffins and arranged them in the baskets for transport to the farm store.

With the baskets slung over her arms, Monica felt a

bit like Little Red Riding Hood as she made her way down the path toward the store.

Within minutes, she was at the door, the goodies in her basket still warm from the oven, which was one of the reasons she'd been grateful they'd been able to build a commercial kitchen at the farm instead of having to rent one miles away.

"Good morning," Monica said as she pushed the door open with her hip. A bell tinkled overhead, announcing her arrival.

Nora was straightening a stack of cranberry-themed tea towels. "Good morning." She turned around and held out a hand for one of Monica's baskets. "These muffins smell delicious."

Nora went behind the counter and pulled out several of the antique silver trays Monica had found at an estate sale. She covered them with lacy paper doilies and then began arranging the muffins. Monica took one of the trays and arranged slices of cranberry bread, studded with pecans and topped with buttery streusel, on it.

Nora glanced at Monica from under her eyelashes. "You look tired."

"I am." Monica sighed. "I didn't sleep well last night because of. . . ." She waved a hand in the general direction of the cranberry bogs.

"I can understand that," Nora said. "Neither did I. Such an unfortunate accident."

Just then the door to the shop opened and they both pivoted around to welcome their first customer of the day.

The greeting died on Monica's lips when she saw

Detective Stevens standing in the doorway. She was wearing a navy cotton skirt and white linen blouse and had a Styrofoam cup of coffee in her hand from one of the fast food places out on the highway.

"Something smells delicious," Stevens said as she glanced into the case where Monica and Nora had placed the day's baked goods. She held up her cup. "I could use something to go with my coffee. Toby was fussy this morning—he didn't want to eat his cereal—and by the time I finished feeding him, it was too late for my own breakfast."

"We have muffins, cranberry bread, scones. . . ." Monica immediately went into saleswoman mode so she didn't have to wonder why Stevens had stopped by in the first place. She was quite sure it wasn't only for something to eat.

"Those muffins look delicious." Stevens began pulling her wallet from her purse.

Monica held up a hand to stop her. "Please. It's on us." Monica laughed, a little hysterically given her fatigue and nervous edginess. "Or is that considered bribing a police officer?"

Stevens smiled. "I don't think a single muffin would count as a bribe."

Monica grabbed a sheet of glassine, selected the plumpest muffin in the case and handed it to Stevens. "Unless you'd like a bag . . . ?"

Stevens shook her head. "No thanks. I'm eating this right away." She took a bite and rolled her eyes. "Heavenly."

"Is there anything else I can get you?" Monica asked,

hoping that the muffin really was all Stevens had stopped in for, although she sincerely doubted it.

"Just a couple of questions." Stevens wiped crumbs from her lip with the napkin. "The ME performed the autopsy on Lori Wenk yesterday."

"Yes?" Monica had the feeling she wasn't going to like what was coming next.

Stevens was quiet for a moment as she chewed another bite of the muffin, which she chased with a gulp of coffee. "The victim sustained multiple bee stings." She looked at Nora. "I gather that it wasn't the normal procedure to approach the bees without the appropriate protective gear. Am I right?"

Nora nodded. "Rick never does anything with the bees without putting his gear on."

Stevens nodded. "So that was unusual in and of itself."

By now she'd finished her muffin. She crumpled the glassine and was about to stick it in her pocket when Monica took it from her and tossed it into the trash can behind the counter.

"Now I would assume that Lori would have brought her beekeeping gear with her since they planned to release the bees that morning."

"Yes, but Rick said it was too cloudy," Nora added.

Stevens nodded. "Still, those were the original plans. So you'd think the hat with the veil thingie." Stevens twirled a hand over her own head. "You'd think that and the gloves and the other stuff would have been in her car, right?"

Monica couldn't imagine what Stevens was getting at.

"Frankly, I couldn't say. This is my first spring here on the farm, so I've never seen the bee fertilization process before."

"I . . . I know Rick carries his equipment with him in the truck," Nora said timidly.

Stevens nodded again. "That's what I thought. But you know what? When we searched Lori's car all we found were her purse, some fast food wrappers, a brown paper bag with a sandwich and a banana in it and an umbrella with two broken spokes." She tossed back another sip of her coffee. "No beekeeping equipment. No hat, veil, gloves or anything like that."

"Meaning?" Monica said.

"Meaning either she came to the farm unprepared or someone stole her equipment."

"Why would they do that?" Monica looked at Nora, who shrugged.

"I don't know for sure, but maybe so they could wear it themselves."

"Why would they do that?"

"So they wouldn't be stung when they let the bees out and then got them riled up enough to swarm."

Monica thought Stevens was going a bit too far. "Why would someone do that?"

"Maybe they wanted Lori dead for some reason."

"Could they count on the bee stings being fatal?" Monica asked. "After all, it seems pretty unlikely that Lori would be allergic to bee venom and then go out of her way getting a job that required working with bees."

Stevens held up a hand. "I agree with you. That was

my first thought, too. Who would choose to work with bees knowing they were allergic?" She shook her head. "I assumed it was some kind of accident, and I was wasting my time here."

"But it was an accident, don't you think?" Nora said.

Nora suddenly looked unwell to Monica. Her face had lost its usual high color, and her hands were trembling.

Stevens tipped back her coffee cup, frowned and looked into it. "Looks like I should have asked for a large."

"I can put some on if you'd like," Nora said.

Stevens shook her head. "No, thanks." She gave the empty cup to Monica, who had her hand outstretched. "As I said, my first thought when I arrived on the scene was that it had all been an unfortunate accident. But we got the preliminary autopsy report this morning. The ME found a needle mark on her thigh. The area is slightly raised and appears red and irritated."

"I don't understand." Nora ran her hands through her short, dark hair, leaving it standing on end. "Maybe she'd been to the doctor and got a flu shot."

"June isn't exactly flu season," Stevens said.

"Maybe it was a tetanus booster. Or an antibiotic."

Stevens shook her head. "I'm afraid not. The medical examiner made a number of interesting discoveries during the autopsy. Discoveries that led him to believe Ms. Wenk was injected with ricin."

"Ricin?" Nora said.

Stevens nodded. "It's a poison that is extracted from castor beans and is highly toxic."

"But then why release the bees?" Nora turned to look at Monica.

"It could be the killer thought the bee stings would mask the mark left by the hypodermic needle."

"So it wasn't an accident," Monica said.

Stevens shook her head. "No. It was murder."

Chapter 6

Monica and Nora were silent for a long moment after Stevens left. Finally, Monica gave herself a shake and got to work. She went through their stock of kitchen items—the cranberry-themed aprons hanging from hooks, and the placemats, napkins and tablecloths displayed on shelves.

"I think we might need to order some more aprons," Monica said, counting the number on the hooks.

"They're very popular," Nora agreed. "I usually sell at least one a day."

Her voice sounded a bit strained to Monica, but she supposed that was normal considering they'd just been interviewed by a police detective.

Monica straightened some of the pictures on the wall—Nora had suggested they hang photographs of the cranberry harvest, and Monica had thought it a wonderful idea—while Nora fussed over the table of samples of cranberry jelly, salsa and jam.

Suddenly there was a crash and the sound of glass breaking. Monica turned around to see Nora staring at a broken jar of cranberry jam, her mouth in a round *O* and her hands on either side of her face like the figure in the painting by Edvard Munch.

"I'll get the broom," Monica said. She went to the storage closet and grabbed the broom and dustpan.

Nora was picking up the larger chunks of glass and tossing them in a wastebasket she'd dragged over to the table. A shard of glass pricked her thumb, and a bubble of blood formed on her finger. Nora stared at it for a second and then began to cry.

Monica leaned the broom against the counter and went to put her arm around Nora. She could feel Nora's shoulders shaking.

"It's okay. Accidents happen, as they say. Plus we have plenty more jam." She swept a hand toward the jars stacked on the shelves. "And this is easily cleaned up."

Nora sniffed loudly and fished a tissue out of her pocket. "It's not that."

"Oh." Monica was momentarily at a loss for words. "Do you want to talk about it?"

Nora gulped and nodded her head.

Monica waited, patiently, while Nora pulled herself together.

"Yesterday, I assumed Lori's death was an accident," Nora said finally. "And I assumed the police did, too." She sniffed and dabbed at her nose with the tissue. "But now

Detective Stevens is talking possible . . . murder." Nora gave a loud sob.

"I can understand how that's upsetting," Monica said. "Did you know Lori well?"

Nora shook her head. "No, not really. It's not that. . . ." She twisted the damp tissue into a corkscrew. "I do feel sorry for the girl, of course—for her life to end that way . . . even though it made me mad the way she was coming on to my husband."

"I noticed that. But I didn't think you had anything to worry about."

Nora gave a long, drawn-out sob.

"There's something else, isn't there?" Monica said. "What is it? You might feel better if you talk about it."

Nora stared at her shoes. "Lori was a troublemaker. You saw her. She was all over Rick. Of course he told me all about it. After all, he didn't have anything to hide. But when he didn't respond to Lori's advances, she decided to make him pay."

"How?" Monica said. "How could she do that?"

Nora gave a bitter laugh. "It's ironic when you think about it. She was threatening to sue him for sexual harassment. Imagine! Rick said he never so much as looked at her sideways. How could someone do something like that?" She looked at Monica.

Monica sighed. "I don't know. It's despicable."

"So of course I'm afraid." Nora gave a hiccough. "I'm afraid that the police will think Rick had something to do with it."

"But he can't have let the bees out," Monica said, patting

Nora on the shoulder. "He said he was here, at the store, visiting you."

Nora looked startled for a moment. "Oh, of course." She gave a strained smile. "How could I have forgotten that?" she said after a long pause.

Monica made sure Nora was going to be okay, then said good-bye and headed out the door. She could have gone through the processing room and then back to their new kitchen, but the allure of a beautiful summer day was hard to resist. She'd at least get a couple of gulps of fresh air before going back inside.

Monica was reaching for the door handle when she noticed Jeff in the field that bordered the nearest bog. She wanted to remind him that payment on the bank loan was due shortly. The thought quickened Monica's heartbeat, but she reminded herself that they'd been managing okay so far. The contract with Fresh Gourmet for the cranberry salsa was really helping, and Monica was exploring the idea of seeing if they would have any interest in carrying her cranberry streusel bread as well.

As she got closer to the field, she noticed Jeff wasn't alone. Rick was with him, and they had what appeared to be a tarp spread under the tree where the bees had swarmed.

Monica approached cautiously. After what had happened to Lori, she had no intention of antagonizing the bees. Jeff saw her coming and waved her over.

"What are you doing?" Monica asked, stopping well short of the tree. The cluster of bees still hung from the low-hanging branch, buzzing ominously.

"Rick is going to collect the bees," Jeff explained.

"Why not let them go free?" Monica asked.

"Honey bees are rapidly disappearing," Rick said. "Something like one hundred or more major crops are pollinated by bees—apples, cucumbers, pumpkins and many others."

"I had no idea," Monica said.

"Me, either," Jeff replied. "My focus has been on cranberries."

"Sadly, more than forty percent of American bee colonies collapsed last year." Rick swatted at a fly that had flown too close to his face. "It's mainly because of pesticide use, but also because of the loss of wildflower habitats, disease and climate change. Losing wildflower habitats has had an effect on monarch butterflies as well."

Monica frowned and turned to Rick. His face looked as if it had aged overnight. "How on earth are you going to capture the bees though?" She pointed at the mass dangling from the tree branch.

"First I'll put on my protective gear, of course." Rick gave a small smile. "I have a box in the truck." He jerked his head in the direction of the white vehicle with *Rick's Bees* written in dark green on the side that was pulled up onto the grass. "I'll put the box under the tree branch and shake the cluster of bees into it."

Monica couldn't help it—she shivered. "Isn't that dangerous?"

Rick smiled. "Not if I'm wearing all my gear—including the hat and gloves, of course." His expression grew somber, and he looked at Jeff. "I still can't understand why Lori went near the bees without being properly protected."

"I wonder if we'll ever know," Monica said.

"It's too late to ask Lori," Rick said, toeing a clump of weeds. He laughed but there was nothing lighthearted about the sound—it had a raw edge to it.

Monica tapped Jeff on the arm. "I'm off to do some more baking. Don't forget to send that check to the bank."

"I won't, but thanks for reminding me."

Monica would have liked to watch the bee retrieval operation, but she still had work to do. She said good-bye and headed back to the farm kitchen. She was measuring out flour for cranberry scones when the door opened and Arline walked in.

"Good morning." Monica glanced over at Arline.

Like Rick, Arline looked as if she hadn't slept all night—there were inky smudges under her eyes and her face was an unhealthy white.

Monica went over to her. "Are you okay? You don't look well. Would you rather go home?"

"I'll be okay," Arline said in a listless voice.

"But something is wrong."

"It's Lori," Arline said in such a low tone that Monica could barely hear her. "It's terrible what happened. I almost can't believe it. When I woke up this morning I thought I'd dreamt it."

Monica nodded her head in agreement. "I know. I felt the same way. I'm sorry. Did you know each other well?"

"Not well, no, although we lived in the same house. Her mother owns it and Lori lives . . . lived with her. I rent a room there. It's close to college and to both my jobs."

"I imagine you and Lori got to know each other though—living in the same house."

"Oh, sure. On Wednesdays we all liked to watch *Jeopardy!* together. Lori was a whiz at some of the categories." She scratched at what looked like a raised and reddened mosquito bite on her left arm. "And sometimes Lori would make a pot of chili or roast a chicken, and we'd all eat dinner together." She frowned. "But it's not like we went out together or anything. You know, shopping or to a bar. We did go on a couple of double dates, but she spent more time talking to her date than to me."

"Still, I can see this has been terribly upsetting to you. How is Lori's mother coping?"

Arline frowned. "She's a little—you know." She twirled a finger around her ear. "She's got that old-timer's disease. Some days she knows what's going on, and other days . . ." She shrugged. "Not so much. It's a blessing really. She hasn't taken it in that Lori's gone."

Arline reached for an apron from the hook by the door and tied it around her waist.

"Was everything okay yesterday?" Monica asked.

"Oh everything was fine," Arline said, smoothing down the front of her apron. "What are you making?"

"Scones," Monica said.

"Do you want me to start on the sugar glaze then?"

"Yes, that would be great." Monica dumped the last cup of flour into the bowl of the mixer. "It would be a huge help. Together, we'll have these done in no time."

Arline grabbed a bowl from the open shelf that ran down one wall of the kitchen. She measured out confectioner's sugar, then added milk and some vanilla extract.

Monica finished the dough for the scones. She scattered a handful of flour across the counter and on her rolling pin and dumped out the dough. She pressed it into a rough circle, and then rolled it out until it was the thickness she wanted. With a sharp knife, she cut wedges and placed them side by side on a cookie sheet, their edges barely touching each other—that would keep the sides of the scones from getting too crusty.

Monica swept the remaining flour off the counter and wiped it down. She liked to keep her workspace neat, and always tidied up as she went along—she couldn't focus otherwise.

When the timer on the oven dinged, she removed the first batch of scones. Arline brought over the glaze and dribbled some over each of them, leaving their tops glossy with sugar.

Monica thought about Rick and wondered how he was making out capturing that enormous swarm of bees. It certainly wasn't a job she would ever want. But Rick apparently knew what he was doing and probably took the appropriate precautions. That got her thinking about the accident the day before—although according to Stevens it wasn't an accident at all.

"What bothers me about Lori and the bees," Monica said, leaning against the counter and looking over to where Arline was opening a new bag of flour, "is who let the bees out if Lori didn't?"

"I don't know anything about that," Arline said. "But Lori was coming out of the kitchen right when I got here. Her boss came running over and said something about the hives. I didn't know what he was talking about, but it sounded like he wanted her help with something."

"Rick?"

"Is he the guy with the dark brown hair?" Arline asked.

Monica nodded.

"Yes, it was Rick then."

Monica opened her mouth to say something but then closed it again. Why had Rick needed Lori's help? Had he been responsible for Lori walking out into a swarm of bees?

Chapter 7

After lunch, Monica changed, washed her face and brushed her hair, and headed into town for her monthly book club meeting at Book 'Em. She'd debated going—she knew the talk would turn to the incident at Sassamanash Farm. She didn't want to call it murder—not even in her own mind. It was a juicy story and the inhabitants of Cranberry Cove loved nothing more than a good dose of gossip to pass the time. No doubt the story had made the rounds by now.

Monica hoped that by attending book club, she could give those present the true story and possibly quash some of the rumors that were sure to be spreading around town already.

This month they had agreed to read *Brat Farrar* by Josephine Tey. Monica had enjoyed the book and was looking forward to a lively discussion.

She was a bit late, and the members of the book club were already seated in the slightly worn chairs Greg had pulled from all corners of his untidy store. Everyone looked up eagerly when they saw Monica come in.

Monica saw Hennie VanVelsen sitting in Greg's mustard-colored corduroy armchair that had the springs bottoming out. She looked around but Gerda VanVelsen wasn't there. She couldn't recall ever having seen one twin without the other being nearby. She hoped Gerda wasn't really sick this time.

Everyone had plates balanced on their laps with cookies, cake and other goodies Greg had set out at the back of the store on an old gateleg table. Monica helped herself to some coffee and two Dutch windmill cookies.

She slipped into a seat next to Phyllis Bouma, who worked part-time as a librarian. Everyone turned and looked at Monica expectantly.

They were all quiet, waiting patiently, until Phyllis gave an exasperated sigh and said to Monica, "Aren't you going to fill us in on what happened out at Sassamanash Farm yesterday? Donald DeGroot was all agog when he came into the library to pick up the book he'd reserved on Abraham Lincoln. He said he passed a police car and an ambulance heading down the road to the farm. We were all praying nothing had happened to you or your brother." She looked around the small group. "And since you're here, I'm guessing the ambulance must have been for someone else."

Monica glanced around Book 'Em with its crowded shelves and piles of books on every surface, buying time and trying to decide what to say. How much did everyone know already?

"There was an unfortunate accident," Monica said finally, "while releasing the bees that are used to fertilize the cranberry flowers."

That wasn't strictly true, Monica thought. No one knew why the bees had been released, but she thought the story would suffice to satisfy everyone's curiosity.

She was wrong.

Eleanor Mason, a retired schoolteacher with a wobbly gray bun loosely anchored to the back of her head, spoke up. "Who was hurt? How bad was it? Are they dead?"

The questions came at Monica like staccato gunfire. She took a deep breath.

"The young woman who works for Rick's Bees—Lori Wenk—died, I'm afraid." She clamped her mouth shut, determined not to have any more details wormed out of her. But she underestimated the women of Cranberry Cove.

Phyllis put a hand to her mouth. "Oh," she said. "Lori works part-time at the library. I can't believe it." She looked around at the others. "I didn't know her well, but it's still a shock. Her poor mother."

"Harriet Wenk might be too far gone to understand," Eleanor said. "I know her from church—not well—but people have been saying that she's suffering from dementia. I know Wilma Krondyke looked in on her just last week and said it's getting worse."

"It was an accident?" Phyllis asked. She gave Monica a shrewd look.

"Yes," Monica said firmly. She thought about what

Detective Stevens had said about the needle puncture that had turned up in the autopsy along with the ME's suspicions about ricin—details she planned to keep to herself.

"And here I thought that boyfriend of hers had finally done her in," Phyllis said, raising her unkempt gray eyebrows."

"Him!" Hennie said, rolling her eyes.

"If she thought she was going to drag Dale Wheeler to the altar, she had another think coming," Phyllis said. "All he wants out of life is to sit at the bar at Flynn's and drink beer."

"I hope this isn't going to interfere with our Flag Day celebration," Hennie said fretfully.

"I don't see why it should," Phyllis snapped.

"You never know," Hennie said

While they'd been talking, Greg had been in the back room brewing another pot of coffee. He came out carrying the newly filled carafe.

"If anyone wants a refill, I've made a fresh pot," he said, putting the coffee down on the table. He wheeled his desk chair to the head of the circle and sat down. "Shall we get down to our book discussion? Have you all had a chance to read *Brat Farrar*?"

Everyone's head bobbed up and down in assent.

Monica had a hard time concentrating on the lively discussion that swirled around her. She was thinking about Lori and the comment Phyllis had made about Lori's boyfriend, Dale. If this did turn out to be murder, he was a logical suspect.

But so was Rick. The thought flew unbidden into her mind.

Monica tried to turn her attention back to the discussion and felt guilty that she hadn't contributed more. When it was over, and everyone had left, Greg put his arm around her.

"You don't seem like yourself. Is everything okay?"

Monica smiled. Greg had a way of tuning into her feelings.

"Everything is fine. But I can't help thinking about the accident." She hesitated for a moment. "Which appears not to have been an accident at all."

"You're not serious?" Greg perched on the arm of the corduroy chair and stretched out his legs.

"Yes. Detective Stevens said that the autopsy uncovered a puncture mark from a hypodermic needle on Lori's thigh, along with signs that suggested she'd been injected with ricin."

"Ricin! This is beginning to sound more and more like an Agatha Christie novel."

"Only much more real." Monica frowned. "By the way, I noticed that Gerda wasn't here today. I thought she and Hennie went everywhere together. Were they unable to get someone to mind the store for an hour?"

Greg's expression was pained. "Gerda is in the hospital."

"Oh, no!" Monica twisted a loose thread from her shirt around her finger. "I hope it's nothing too serious."

"I don't know. Hennie didn't seem to want to talk about it."

Half an hour later, Monica left Book 'Em and stood for a moment on the sidewalk. The door to the Cranberry

Cove Diner next door was propped open to the fresh summer breeze. The smell of something frying mixed with coffee brewing drifted out.

Monica hesitated then decided she would walk down to Gina's shop. The air outside Making Scents carried the faint aroma of vanilla, lavender and citrus. The scent intensified as Monica pulled open the door and stepped inside.

Gina was behind the counter, organizing small glass bottles of essential oils. She smiled and leaned on the counter when she saw Monica.

"Has there been any more news about the death of that girl?" Gina asked. She picked up a bottle and spritzed some lavender oil into the air.

"Not really," Monica said. "Have you heard anything? I know news travels quickly around town."

"Not a thing. But guess who I met?"

Monica tried to come up with a possibility but failed. "I give up. Who?"

"The mysterious new occupant of that cottage on the road to the farm."

"Did he live up to your expectations?" Monica remembered how avidly Gina had listened to Greg's description of the man.

"He went well beyond," Gina said. She fiddled with the links of her necklace. "Very good-looking."

"Greg did make it sound as if he was attractive."

Gina snorted. "You can never trust a man's assessment of another man's looks. Did I ever tell you about the time . . . well, that's neither here nor there."

"What is the man's name again?"

"Xavier Cabot. Isn't that romantic sounding? And with the looks to match. . . ." Gina sighed and leaned against the counter. "I'm determined to get him to ask me out."

"And I have no doubt that you'll succeed. I'll look forward to learning more about Mr. Xavier Cabot."

"How was your book club?"

Monica started to open her mouth then realized she'd barely been present during the book club discussion.

"I learned something interesting."

Gina leaned farther over the counter. "Really?"

"Lori had a boyfriend named Dale Wheeler, according to Phyllis Bouma. And it sounded like Lori wanted to get married but he didn't."

"Lots of men don't want to get married, but they don't kill their girlfriends over it."

"True. But maybe Dale had another reason for killing her," Monica said. "She certainly can't have had that much in the bank, so it couldn't have been for money."

Gina let her chin rest in her hand. "Have the police said anything more . . . ?"

Monica shook her head. She thought about what Nora had told her and guilt prickled at her skin like hives. She ought to tell Detective Stevens, but she didn't want to betray Nora's trust.

"At least this is one murder you won't have to investigate," Gina said with a laugh. "No one is accusing Jeff or me or your mother. We can leave the detective work to the police this time."

Uneasiness washed over Monica. Didn't she owe it to Nora to try to get some information at least? Nora had been such a huge help to her and Jeff.

"What?" Gina asked.

"Nothing," Monica said sharply.

"Come on. It's not nothing. I can tell by the look on your face."

She really had to work on her poker face, Monica thought with dismay.

"You know Nora Taylor who works in the farm store? Gina nodded.

"There's reason to believe . . ." Monica tried to think of how to put it without revealing the confidences Nora had shared. "Nora is afraid the police will accuse her husband."

Gina looked startled. "Why?"

"Let's say they have their reasons."

"Do be careful." Gina put a hand on Monica's arm. "Last time you almost . . ."

"I will, don't worry. All I plan to do is ferret out some information if I can."

"As long as you're careful," Gina said. She fiddled with three of the glass bottles, arranging and rearranging them. Finally she looked up. "Do you think Jeff has seemed—I don't know—not quite himself these days?"

"How do you mean?" Monica thought back to the last time she'd talked to Jeff.

"Sort of down. I wonder if something is wrong?"

"I imagine his experience in Afghanistan is bound to haunt him at times. No amount of therapy can wipe out the horrible memories."

"True," Gina said briskly. "I'm probably worrying for nothing.

Monica agreed with her but made a mental note to pay more attention to Jeff the next time she was with him.

Chapter 8

Monica left Gina's with a number of worrisome thoughts swirling through her head. She started the Focus and began heading out of town toward the road to the farm when the light on her dashboard reminded her that she needed to get her oil changed. The light had been coming on for a few days now, but she'd been too busy to take care of it. She didn't think it would be wise to ignore it any longer.

Monica had had a friend in college whose driving lessons hadn't included instructions on changing the oil and whose transmission had ultimately seized up. Monica had taken it as a cautionary tale and always made sure to heed all the warning lights on the dashboard of her car.

She made a right turn into a driveway that wound through cornfields toward a house and barn that were invisible from the road. She put the car in reverse, backed out

of the drive and headed in the other direction. There was
a garage a mile or two outside of town near the highway.

Monica pulled into the parking lot of Peck's Garage,
loose bits of macadam crunching under her tires. The
door to one of the bays was open and a Jeep Grand Chero-
kee was hoisted on the lift. Two men in dirty coveralls
with bandanas sticking out of their pockets gathered
underneath it, pointing at various parts of the automobile's
innards.

Monica knew next to nothing about cars and was always happy to leave any tune-ups or repairs to the experts.
Jeff was a whiz with mechanics—he maintained and
repaired all the Sassamanash Farm equipment, changed
the oil himself and could spend hours with his head stuck
under the hood of a car or a truck. And if it was something
he couldn't handle because of his paralyzed arm, he
would direct a crew member how to do it for him.

He had offered to change Monica's oil for her, but she
knew he was busy from dawn to dusk, and she didn't want
to add anything more to his to-do list.

Monica pulled open the door to the small office next
to the garage. The smell of motor oil and gasoline perme-
ated the room and it looked like it hadn't been cleaned
since Jimmy Carter was president. An orange plastic
chair with a triangular-shaped piece missing from the
back was placed in front of a small, scarred wooden table
stacked with magazines that were more than a year out
of date.

The woman behind the desk looked up as Monica approached. She had the hardened face and wrinkled skin
of the habitual smoker. Her steel gray hair was cropped

close to her head, and she had a hoop and a stud earring in each ear.

"I don't have an appointment, but I was wondering if someone could do an oil change," Monica said.

The woman stared at Monica for a second before turning and yelling "Hey, Danny," through the open door that connected the office to the garage. "Anyone got time for an oil change?"

One of the men clustered around the Jeep turned around. "Sure. Tell 'em to pull around up front—second bay."

The woman jerked her head toward the garage. "Bring her up front, and Danny'll find someone to do it for you."

Monica was glad to step back into the fresh air, although gas and oil fumes still wafted from the garage. The door to the second bay went up and Monica pulled the Focus inside as a stocky guy with curly blond hair and a baseball cap worn backward motioned her into position.

He looked familiar to Monica, but she couldn't place him.

"It won't take too long. You can wait in the office if you want," he said to Monica.

He was turning away when Monica caught sight of the name embroidered above the pocket of his shirt—*Dale*.

She was about to ask him his last name—how many Dales could there be in Cranberry Cove?—but he had already walked away.

Monica was glad to escape to the relative coolness of the office, where an ancient air conditioner wheezed in the window, sending clots of dust scampering across the floor. She picked up a dog-eared copy of *Time* magazine that was two years out of date and began to leaf through it, but her thoughts kept returning to the mechanic. He had to be the Dale who was Lori's boyfriend.

She tossed the magazine back on the table and approached the woman behind the desk.

Monica pointed toward the garage. "I noticed the mechanic who is servicing my car is named Dale. Do you happen to know his last name?"

The woman looked up from the invoices she was shuffling around on her desk. "Sure. It's Wheeler." She tilted her hand and looked at Monica. "Do you know him?"

Monica shook her head. "No. I know somebody who knows him."

"One of the bartenders down at Flynn's?" The woman's laugh quickly turned into a gurgling cough.

"His girlfriend," Monica said.

The woman looked up, surprised. "I didn't know Dale had a girlfriend. I thought he steered clear of stuff like that."

Just then there was a shout from the garage. "Hey, Sally, tell the lady her car is ready, would you?"

"Looks like your car's ready." Sally jerked her thumb toward the garage.

"Thanks."

When Monica got back outside she found her car had been pulled out of the bay, and Dale was walking away with his back to her.

Monica didn't want to miss this chance to talk to him.

"Hey," she called, and he turned around. She motioned for him to come back.

"Is something wrong?" Dale asked when he reached Monica.

"No, no. I wanted to know if everything else is alright with the car," she fibbed.

"Yeah. I didn't see anything." He frowned. "Why? You been hearing funny noises or something?"

"Nothing like that, no."

"I'd say she's in pretty good shape."

Monica couldn't think of an appropriate segue so she decided to go for bluntness. If Dale told her to mind her own business, so be it.

"Listen, I gather you knew Lori Wenk."

Dale looked startled. "Yeah." His eyes were wary.

"I heard you were dating." Monica made it more of a statement than a question.

He shifted from one foot to the other. "Yeah? Who said that?"

Monica shrugged and held her hands out, palms up. "Somebody. I don't remember who."

"Yeah? Not dating exactly. We went out a couple of times, sure. But you know—nothing serious."

"I assume you heard she died?"

"Yeah. News travels fast around this town."

"Still. You must have been upset."

Dale looked down at his feet. He rolled a piece of loose macadam back and forth underneath his right shoe.

"Yeah," he said finally, still not meeting Monica's gaze. "No one ought to die that young, you know?"

The sun was still high in the sky as Monica drove back toward the farm. The inside of the Focus was warm, and her hands felt sticky on the steering wheel. The faint scent of motor oil clung to the interior of the car. Monica turned off the air conditioner, which was blasting lukewarm air into her face, and rolled down the windows. Fresh air rushed in, redolent of the scent of hay, grass and dirt warmed by the sun.

Monica decided she would stop in at the farm store. She was worried about Nora and could imagine Nora's panic, thinking her husband had had a motive in Lori's death.

A lone car was leaving the small parking lot as Monica pulled in. Traffic at the store was unpredictable, which made Monica even more relieved that she'd scored the contract with Fresh Gourmet for her salsa. It was a relatively steady source of income until the next cranberry crop could be harvested in the fall.

Nora was running a feather duster over the tops of some jars of cranberry jam when Monica pushed open the screen door to the store. Nora's usually cheerful expression had been replaced by a down-turned mouth and eyebrows drawn together over the center of her forehead.

"Been busy today?" Monica asked, trying to keep her tone light.

Nora shrugged. "On and off. We've sold all the muffins." She pointed toward an empty wicker basket lined with a red-and-white gingham cloth. "I was about to put the basket in the back."

Monica looked at her watch. "We might get some customers yet. There are a few who stop in in the late afternoon to buy something to have for their breakfast in the morning. I'll head over to the kitchen and make up a couple more batches."

Monica reached for the basket and hesitated, her hand on the woven handle. "Are you okay?" She didn't want to pry but she couldn't ignore the distress on Nora's face.

"I guess so." Nora sniffed and swiped a hand across her eyes. She gave a sob and buried her face in her hands. "No. I'm really not okay."

"What is it?" Monica put a hand on Nora's arm.

"I'm still worried that Rick's going to be blamed for that girl's death." Nora looked at Monica, her face tearstained. "It's not fair."

"But you and Rick were together when it happened," Monica said, even as she remembered the look of doubt that had crossed Nora's face when she'd heard that Rick had said that.

Nora sniffed loudly. "I know. But they could claim he was operating his business unsafely." She gave a sob that turned into a hiccough. "We could be sued."

Monica had the feeling that that wasn't what Nora was worried about at all, but rather that she was worried about something else entirely—something far more serious.

Monica was about to leave the shop when the door opened. Both she and Nora jumped to attention but relaxed as Jeff strode in.

"We thought you were a customer," Monica said.

Jeff grinned. "Just a starving farmer." He gave Monica his most persuasive look. "I was hoping my big sister could rustle up some grub for me."

Monica couldn't help but smile. "Of course. I've got some sandwich fixings stashed in the refrigerator in the cottage." She linked her arm through Jeff's. "Come on. I'll fix you a ham and cheese sandwich."

"With pickles?"

"With pickles."

"My mouth is watering already," Jeff said. He waved to Nora. "See you later."

"I'll whip up some more muffins after I feed my starving brother, but if you need anything in the meantime, just ring me and I can come right back down," Monica said.

Nora gave her a smile that didn't quite reach her eyes. "Will do. But I'm sure everything will be fine."

Monica and Jeff walked side by side down the path that wound around the cranberry bogs toward Monica's cottage.

She turned to Jeff. "I went to my book club today," she began.

"Another murder mystery? I'd think you'd have had enough of all that after what's happened here in Cranberry Cove in the last couple of months."

Monica was silent for a moment. "There's a certain appeal to a murder mystery—at least the ones we're reading. Justice prevails in the end, and that's not always the case in real life. Besides, the books are more about the puzzle than the gruesome details of the crime itself."

"I'll stick to the sports page of the newspaper, thanks," Jeff said.

"One of the book club members—Phyllis Bouma—mentioned that Lori Wenk had a boyfriend named Dale Wheeler."

Jeff stopped in his tracks and turned to face Monica. "Dale? He's worked for me a few times during the harvest on his days off." Jeff gave a half grin. "Nearly everyone in Cranberry Cove is happy to make some extra money whenever they can."

Monica flashed back to the harvest that fall and Jeff's crew thigh deep in the flooded blog. There had been a young man with a red cap pulled down over a tangle of blond curls—Dale. No wonder he had looked so familiar this afternoon.

Jeff put out a hand. "Wait! You're not thinking that Dale had something to do with this, are you? He's a good guy."

"Lori told Phyllis that she and Dale were dating. Phyllis got the impression that Lori thought the relationship was a serious one. But according to Dale they only went out a couple of times, and it was nothing much."

Jeff shrugged. "Men are from Mars. . . . Just because they had different views on the state of their relationship doesn't mean Dale had anything to do with Lori's death."

"You're probably right," Monica said. "But there have been cases where someone has murdered their partner because he or she became inconvenient."

They walked in silence for a moment. Monica looked from left to right, enjoying the view. The delicate cranberry blossoms that filled the bogs were swaying slightly in the gentle breeze, their pale pink accented with verdant green leaves. She took a deep breath and, despite everything that had transpired, felt a deep sense of contentment wash over her. This was where she belonged.

Suddenly Jeff came to a stop. Monica looked at him curiously, but his attention was focused on something in the near distance.

"What's that?" He pointed to a group of scrubby bushes alongside the path.

"Where?" Monica stared at the spot where Jeff was pointing.

"That," Jeff repeated, walking toward a scraggly batch of evergreens whose gnarly roots were lifting up the edge of the path.

Monica squinted and looked again toward the spot. She thought she saw something white—some kind of cloth maybe—caught between the bushes.

Jeff approached the evergreens as cautiously as one might advance on a snake or poisonous spider.

Monica joined him, and they both peered between the bushes whose branches had been knitted together over time. She put out a hand, but Jeff stopped her.

"Wait. Don't touch it."

Jeff picked up a stick that was lying alongside the path and, using his good arm, poked and prodded the piece of fabric, trying to pull it through the branches of the bush.

"What is it?" Monica asked.

"I don't know. But I don't think we should touch it in case it's somehow related to Lori's death. Even though it will probably turn out to be an accident after all."

The way Jeff said that made Monica realize he didn't believe it was an accident any more than she did.

Jeff finally succeeded in coaxing the item from between the low-hanging branches of the evergreen. He hooked it with his stick and held it up.

"It's some kind of glove," Monica said, eying the object.

Jeff frowned. "Not just any glove. This is a beekeeper's glove. And if I'm not mistaken, the rest of the outfit is

tangled up in those shrubs. What odds do you want that
this is Lori's missing gear?"

"I guess we'd better call Detective Stevens." Monica
pulled her cell phone from her pocket and punched in the
numbers.

Jeff waved the glove on the end of his stick. "I don't
know what this means, but it could be significant."

Jeff stood waiting for the police while Monica ran back
to the cottage and threw together a couple of ham and
cheese sandwiches for him. She glanced at the clock—he
should have taken a break for lunch hours ago. No wonder
he was still such a long, tall string bean. Given their age
difference, she had been the taller of the two of them until
he'd reached his early teens, when he'd shot up like a
rocket, easily surpassing Monica's five foot eight inches.

Monica grabbed a can of cold pop from the fridge and
a couple of apples and put everything in a wicker basket,
along with a handful of napkins and the remains of a bag
of chips she'd treated herself to and felt guilty about every
time she saw them staring at her in the pantry.

By the time she got to where Jeff was sitting by the
side of the path, guarding their find, she could hear a car
in the distance bumping down the road that led to the
farm.

Jeff had taken the first bite of his sandwich when the
car came into view. It was dusty and looked like it needed
a good wash, and there was a dent in the front right fender.
They watched as Stevens emerged from the driver's seat,
brushed something off the front of her trousers and
headed toward them. She was wearing a white blouse and
as she got closer, Monica could see the rings of perspira-

tion under her arms. She looked as if she'd had a rough couple of days.

Monica smiled sympathetically as Stevens approached.

Stevens ran a hand through her blond hair, brushing it back from her forehead, which was beaded with sweat. She looked up at the sky. "It's awfully hot for late June." She glanced down and picked at what looked like dried, pureed carrot or squash on her top. "You said you found something?"

Jeff pointed at the stick he'd laid down on the ground. "Yes, it's right there."

"What on earth is it?" Stevens looked from Monica to Jeff and back again.

"It's a glove that the beekeepers wear when they handle the hives," Jeff said.

Stevens's expression sharpened. "Where did you say you found it?"

Jeff pointed to the bush. "It was stuck between those two evergreens. It's a miracle I even noticed it."

"Whoa." Stevens got down on one knee and carefully separated the scraggly branches with her hands. She peered between them.

Jeff squatted down next to her. "There's something else stuck in there, see?" He pointed between the branches Stevens was holding apart. "I didn't want to touch it . . . if it turns out to be important. . . ."

"Good thinking," Stevens said. "It might turn out to be nothing, but somehow I don't think that's going to be the case."

Stevens let the branches snap into place again and leaned back on her heels. She stuck her hands in the pocket of her pants and retrieved a pair of latex gloves. They made a snapping sound as she pulled them into place. She reached into the bush and eased out the bundle of white fabric. It caught on one of the branches.

"Ouch," Stevens said, yanking out her arm and staring at the thin scratch that ran from her elbow almost to her wrist.

"I've got some bandages," Monica said, making a move to go.

"Don't bother. I'm fine," Stevens said as she continued to disentangle the bundle of cloth from where it had been shoved.

It stuck on a branch again. "Rats," she said, but finally the object came free and she was able to grasp it. It was obviously a garment of some sort.

Stevens stood up and shook it out. "I'm going to take a wild guess that this is a piece of the protective gear a beekeeper would use."

Jeff nodded. "Yes, but what about the hat and veil? Are they in there, too?" He bent down and peered into the branches of the evergreens. "The hat and veil are the most important parts of the getup. According to Rick, stings to the face can be dangerous and are certainly very painful."

Stevens gave the garment she was holding another shake. "Nothing here." She placed it on the ground, got down on her hands and knees again and peered into the bushes. She even went around to the other side and did the same. "Nope. The hat and veil are missing." She stood up and brushed dirt off the knees of her trousers.

"I suppose we can assume this is Lori's missing gear?" Monica said.

Stevens brushed her hands on her slacks. "It would be quite a coincidence if it wasn't. Still . . ."

"So whoever did this took the hat and veil with them," Jeff said.

"Or dumped them somewhere else." Stevens ran a hand across the back of her neck. She shaded her eyes with her hand, squinted up at the sky and watched a small plane overhead until it was out of sight.

She sighed. "It looks as if someone didn't want us to find this." She pointed at the beekeeper's gear crumpled on the ground. "I'm assuming they wanted to make the whole thing look like an unfortunate accident."

Chapter 9

"What now?" Monica said as she, Jeff and Stevens began walking toward Stevens's car.

"I want to search the property to see if we find anything else," Stevens said. She kicked at a stone in the path. "The trail will be getting colder every hour. I don't want whoever did this to get away with it."

They reached Stevens's car and Stevens stuck a hand through the open window. She pulled out a plastic bottle of water, took a swig and made a face.

"Warm," she said when she noticed Monica and Jeff looking at her. "Excuse me a minute." She yanked a cell phone from her pocket, barked some orders into it and then ended the call. "I'm afraid I'm going to have to ask you to remain inside somewhere while my men canvas the grounds."

Jeff frowned. "It won't take too long, will it? I've got a ton of weeding to do."

Stevens shrugged. "Hopefully not. The men will be complaining. It's not getting any cooler out." She fanned her face with her hand. "I never used to mind the heat, but ever since I had the baby, the heat has really been getting to me."

Monica gestured toward the cluster of buildings in the distance. "Is it okay if I go back to the kitchen? I need to take inventory and order some supplies."

"That's fine," Stevens said, blotting her forehead with her forearm. "We'll try to inconvenience you as little as possible."

Jeff fell into step with Monica as they headed back the way they had come.

"I can keep myself busy in the processing room," he said. "I have to run the sorting machinery anyway and make sure everything is shipshape before the fall harvest." He looked out across the flower-bedecked cranberry bog. "It will be here before we know it."

Jeff never seemed to rest, Monica thought. She was afraid he was going to make himself ill. She remembered what Gina had said about being worried about him. Was he running away from something by working so hard?

"Is everything okay?" she asked as they approached the farm store.

Jeff wiped a hand over his face. "Sure. Just the usual worries about finances, the crop. . . ." His voice trailed off.

"And?"

Jeff's shoulders heaved up and down in a sigh. He gave a smile that disappeared almost immediately. "I can never fool you, can I?" He kicked at the ground with the toe of his boot. "I remember the time I was dating that girl in high school—Carol—and I didn't want anyone to know she'd dumped me. But you managed to work it out of me quite easily."

Monica remembered how angry she had been that some teenage girl with bleached blond hair had dared to hurt her baby brother.

"It's Lauren," Jeff said after a pause. "I haven't heard from her in almost a week. I've left messages, sent texts. . . ."

Monica thought of all the reasons Lauren might not be responding—her phone was broken, lost or stolen—but she didn't mention them to Jeff. She knew he'd probably run through all of them in his head already and had instead decided to believe the worst.

"Maybe a quick trip to Chicago is in order?" Monica said as lightly as possible.

Jeff shrugged. "I wouldn't want her to think I was crowding her. I'm the one who encouraged her to take this internship. I wanted her to consider all her options before settling down in Cranberry Cove. Besides, I have a ton of work to do here on the farm, and I'm probably worrying for nothing."

Monica realized there was nothing she could say that would make Jeff feel any better. That left her feeling frustrated. Why couldn't she wave a magic wand and make all his problems disappear?

"I guess she'll be in touch eventually," Jeff said unconvincingly. He looked at Monica and touched her cheek with his hand. "Don't worry—I'll be okay."

"Let me know when you hear from her," Monica said

as Jeff turned to head toward the processing room. She desperately wanted to give Jeff a big hug but she knew that would only unsettle him even more.

"I will."

Monica stood for a moment and watched as Jeff loped off around the corner of the building, and then she continued on her way toward the kitchen.

Arline was waiting for her when she pushed open the door.

"Are the police here again?" Arline asked. Her hands were coated with flour and a piece of dough was rolled out on the counter in front of her.

Monica really didn't want to discuss it with Arline, but she knew the less she said, the more Arline would persist.

"Yes. They're searching the property. They've asked us to stay inside."

Monica hoped that would satisfy Arline, but she was wrong.

"What are they looking for?" Arline leaned her elbows on the counter.

"I don't know . . . clues." Monica took her apron from the hook and fastened it around her waist.

"So they think it was murder?"

"I don't know. They haven't confided in me." Monica tried to keep her tone from becoming snappish, but she had the impression that this was no more real to Arline than if it were some fictional show on television.

Monica pointed at the dough rolled out on the counter. "If that sits any longer, it's going to get too soft and you're going to have to put it back in the fridge."

Arline poked the dough with her finger. "It's fine." She

flipped it over and dusted it with flour. "I'll bet it was Rick Taylor."

"You don't really think—"

"Lori was always complaining about him. How he kept making these inappropriate advances toward her. She told him she had a boyfriend, but that didn't stop him." She picked up her rolling pin. "I had a boss like that once. I was too scared of losing my job to say anything." She shivered. "He kept putting his hand—"

"I'm quite sure that Rick wouldn't—"

"Lori was different though," Arline interrupted. "Brave. She was going to see a lawyer about suing. She'd read about these women who'd received millions of dollars for their pain and suffering."

The phrase *you can't get blood from a stone* came to Monica's mind. She knew the Taylors were far from wealthy. How did Lori think they would be able to come up with that kind of money?

Monica had had enough. "I'm going to start the inventory. Are those almost ready to go in the oven?" She pointed to the scones Arline was cutting from her dough.

A sulky look settled over Arline's face, but she quickly finished cutting the dough, pulled a baking sheet from the rack on the wall, lined them all up and put them in the oven.

Monica wiped down the counters in the kitchen. She stopped for a moment, blew a lock of hair off her face and rested her elbows on the counter. She was tired and hungry and she didn't have much of anything in her fridge or pantry for dinner. She'd used the last of the ham and cheese for Jeff's sandwiches.

She was resigning herself to tea and cheese toast when her phone rang.

"Have you eaten?"

Greg's voice made her smile. "No. And I'm afraid the prospects are quite grim."

Greg chuckled. "Let me be your knight in shining armor then. I have a couple of lamb chops from Bart's, some fingerling potatoes from that farm over by the water tower and a bag of fresh spinach compliments of the same farm. How does that sound?"

Monica collapsed against the counter. "That sounds heavenly."

"I need to make a run to an estate sale just out of town. The deceased's son assured me there were some real treasures in his father's library. Shall we say in an hour and a half?"

"Perfect. I need to get cleaned up. I've been alternately working and sweating all day. I'm afraid I'm filthy."

Greg laughed. "Don't bother. I like my women that way. Come as you are."

Monica whistled as she clicked off the call. Greg was exactly what she needed right now—a dose of humor, affection and something to take her mind off Jeff's troubles, the farm's finances and, most importantly, the possibility of murder.

She took a quick shower, added food to Mittens's bowl—which was still half full, although the kitten was acting as if she was starving—and put on a pair of fresh white trousers and an emerald green T-shirt that she fancied brought out the color of her eyes. Despite that, she was ready way too early. She decided she would head into town and pop into Gina's shop and say hello. Gina had a way of picking up news, gossip and other information, and might have heard something that would have a bearing on Lori Wenk's death. Monica had no doubt that by now the entire town of Cranberry Cove knew that the police had been back to Sassamanash Farm.

She drove into town with the windows open to the fresh breeze. The sun had dipped a little lower in the sky and the air was cooling down. She wondered if she ought to have taken a sweater with her. This close to the lake, it could get quite chilly at night even in the summer.

Monica thought about Gerda as she passed Gumdrops. Worry about the VanVelsen sisters had been in the back of her mind all day. Hopefully there would be good news next time she stopped in.

There was a space in front of Making Scents and Monica pulled into it. Gina would be closing in a few minutes, but she could see her stepmother through the window, tidying the merchandise on the counters and getting ready for the following day's business.

"Monica," Gina exclaimed when Monica pushed open the door and walked into the shop.

She seemed slightly flustered and knocked over one of the bottles of essential oils, which surprised Monica. But what surprised her even more was finding a man standing in the corner of the shop—she hadn't noticed him when she had glanced through the window.

He was tall—a good bit taller than Monica's five foot eight inches—strongly built throughout the chest and shoulders with remarkable blue eyes and a thick, but neatly trimmed, gray beard. His eyes crinkled with amusement as he watched Gina's consternation at Monica's arrival.

Gina obviously noticed the two of them appraising each other.

"Monica, this is Xavier Cabot." Gina turned to her companion. "Xavier, this is my stepdaughter, Monica Albertson."

"I understand you're Cranberry Cove's writer in residence," Monica said.

"That makes me sound far more exalted than I am," Cabot said.

"I'm sure—" Gina began.

"I'm not producing anything literary, I'm afraid. Merely a chronicle of some of the more famous shipwrecks on the Great Lakes." He made a face. "My deadline is fast approaching, and my editor is becoming more nervous by the minute. I thought that perhaps being in situ, so to speak, would spur my creativity, and the lack of diversions in Cranberry Cove would increase my productivity."

He gave a slight smile. "I hadn't counted on the lovely ladies of Cranberry Cove proving to be such a distraction." He looked at Monica as he said it.

The man was certainly charismatic, Monica thought, even if there was a touch of blarney about him. She was surprised to find herself drawn into his spell in spite of herself. Only the sound of Gina clearing her throat jolted her out of it.

Gina came out from behind the counter and stood next

to Cabot. "Xavier's been telling me all about the wreck of the *John V. Moran*." She looked up at Cabot and linked her arm through his.

"A fascinating story," Cabot said in the tone of an experienced storyteller. "It was early February and the Moran was on its way from Milwaukee to Muskegon across the ice-covered lake. Despite having a strongly reinforced hull, ice managed to pierce the ship and water began pouring in. They dumped their cargo of flour and packaged goods but the ship was obviously still going to go under. A handful of men left the ship to walk across the frozen lake to try to catch the attention of the *Naomi,* which was about three miles away. The *Naomi* managed to plow through the ice and the entire crew was rescued." He paused and stroked his beard. "I'm afraid I could go on forever—I didn't mean to bore you. Lake Michigan is a veritable graveyard, with over three hundred ships lying on its bottom."

"Actually that was very interesting," Monica said.

He gave a slow smile. "Then I will look forward to sharing more stories with you soon."

By now Gina was tapping her foot impatiently. "I'm sure Monica has something to do. . . ." She raised her eyebrows at her stepdaughter.

"I've taken up too much of your time," Cabot said with a smile. "I'd best be getting back to work. Sadly, the book is not going to write itself."

As soon as the door closed behind him, Gina turned to Monica.

"What was that all about? You have a man of your own already—do you have to flirt with mine?" she snapped.

Monica felt her face redden. *Had* she been flirting? She didn't think so.

"I wasn't flirting," she said firmly. "Merely being polite."

"Xavier certainly seemed taken with you."

"Don't be silly. He was only being polite in return."

Gina frowned. "I saw the way he looked at you."

"He probably looks at all women like that." While Monica might have found Cabot charismatic, his manner didn't fool her.

"Hmmmph," Gina said. "Xavier is mine . . . or at least he will be."

Monica held up her hands in surrender. "He's all yours, believe me."

Gina's sulky look lifted slightly. "He is attractive, isn't he?"

"Very."

Gina held her hand out in front of her and examined her hot pink–painted nails. "He's going to be a challenge, but I'm up for it. What's that saying? Nothing worth having is easy?"

"Something like that." Monica glanced at her watch. "I'd better shove off. Greg will be waiting."

Gina's expression turned serious. "Greg is a good man. Don't let him slip away."

"I know," Monica said. "And I won't."

Monica turned right outside the door toward Book 'Em. Bart was in the window of his butcher shop taping a sale sign to the glass. He waved as Monica went by. She smiled and waved back.

She thought about Gina. Monica supposed she was lonely—she wasn't exactly a good fit for small town living and had made little effort to blend in, maintaining her wardrobe of animal prints, high heels and tight tops. She hoped for Gina's sake that this relationship with Cabot worked out.

Greg was watering the planters in front of his shop when Monica got there. She felt a sense of warmth come over her at the sight of his slightly disheveled hair and quick smile.

He gave her a kiss. "My geraniums are doing well, don't you think?" He grinned. "Considering I'm not much of a gardener. Two planters are about all I can handle."

Monica eyed the red and white flowers. "They look splendid. You might want to do some deadheading on the ones over there though."

Greg looked at her blankly. "That sounds very sinister."

"It means removing the dead flowers."

He laughed. "Much better than what I was picturing."

Greg poured the remaining contents of his watering can into the planter on the left and then reached for the door handle.

"You do like lamb, don't you? I'm grilling the chops with a mushroom wine sauce."

"That sounds delicious."

Monica followed him through the shop, straightening a tower of books that threatened to topple off the table they were perched on as she went past.

Greg lived in a small but cozy apartment above the store. It was moderately more tidy than the shop, with comfortable armchairs, a slightly less worn sofa and, of course, stacks of books on every available surface.

Monica followed him out to the kitchen, where he removed a paper-wrapped piece of meat from the refrigerator.

"I heard the police have been out to the farm again," he said as he grabbed a head of lettuce, a tomato and a cucumber from the crisper drawer.

Monica was no longer surprised by the speed at which news spread around Cranberry Cove.

"Jeff found a piece of beekeeper's protective gear—a glove—hidden in the bushes alongside the path that leads to the bogs. We didn't want to touch it in case it was evidence so we called Detective Stevens. She found the rest of the outfit in the tangle of the evergreen's branches." Monica took a sip of the chilled pinot grigio Greg had poured for her. "But the hat and the face veil were missing. The police searched the property and still didn't find it."

"Why hide the beekeeping outfit though?"

"Perhaps it was Lori's, and the murderer didn't want her to have access to it."

Greg nodded. "That makes sense." He retrieved a serrated knife from the drawer and began slicing the tomato. Juice squirted onto the cutting board as the knife bit into the fruit. "But why not dump the hat and veil with the rest of the gear?"

"I don't know. Maybe the murderer wore it when they let the bees out. They had to get them agitated in order for them to swarm like that. Rick—he's the beekeeper—said that stings to the face are the most painful and most likely to cause a reaction." Monica traced a circle in the condensation left on the table by her glass. "The murderer couldn't afford to get stung. It would be a dead giveaway."

"No pun intended, I assume." Greg put down the knife

and leaned against the counter. "And maybe the murderer didn't have time to hide the hat. They'd probably hidden the other gear before they let the bees out."

"Or didn't need to—if they'd only hidden the gear to keep Lori from using it."

"True," Greg said as he placed the lamb chops on the grill pan that had been heating on the stove.

"Stevens thinks the stings were meant to mask the mark left on Lori's thigh by a hypodermic needle."

"That sounds very clever at first, but surely everyone knows that an autopsy and tox screen would quickly uncover the real cause of death if she'd been injected with something lethal." Greg carried the salad to the table. "But then maybe our murderer doesn't watch television or read detective novels."

Greg opened the refrigerator. "More wine?" He held the bottle toward Monica's glass. "From what I've heard, this Lori was a fairly unassuming person—certainly not the sort to get herself murdered."

"Not like Sam Culbert," Monica said, referring to a murder that had taken place shortly after she'd arrived in Cranberry Cove.

"Exactly." Greg removed the lamb chops from the pan, placed them on the plattes and took them to the table.

She nodded. "Lori did have a boyfriend. At least she called him her boyfriend. He insists it wasn't anything serious—nothing more than a couple of dates."

"Aha, the boyfriend did it." Greg laughed. "Don't let anything happen to you or I might come under suspicion." He squeezed Monica's shoulder. "Don't let anything happen to you. Period." His tone was serious.

"I won't," Monica assured him.

"I don't know." Greg leaned against the counter. "It sounds like you're up to your investigating tricks again. That's proved . . . unhealthy, shall we say, in the past."

Monica held her breath for a second. She remembered only too well how she had cheated death the last time she'd been involved in a murder case.

"I'm only doing it because of Rick," she said, trying to keep the defensive tone out of her voice.

"Rick?" Greg raised an eyebrow. "Should I be jealous?" He slid a plate in front of Monica and brought the platter of lamb chops, a gravy boat with the mushroom wine sauce and a bowl of mashed potatoes to the table.

"Everything looks delicious," Monica murmured as she unfurled her napkin and placed it on her lap. "Rick is the beekeeper. No need to be jealous. His wife, Nora, works in the farm store."

Greg sat down opposite Monica.

"That's right. I'd forgotten. You've mentioned Rick. But why would anyone think he was the culprit?" Greg glanced at Monica.

Monica helped herself to a piece of lamb, some rice and salad. Greg picked up his fork and waited until Monica took her first bite.

"Yes." She cut a piece of the lamb and tasted it. "Mmmmm, delicious." She patted her lips with her napkin. "Lori was planning to sue Rick for sexual harassment."

Greg stopped with his fork halfway to his mouth. "What kind of a guy is this Rick?"

"*Not* that kind of guy," Monica said emphatically. "Nora thinks it was a form of retaliation."

"Retaliation for what?" Greg took a sip of his wine.

"Lori had a crush on Rick. She made some overtures but he rebuffed them. And it made her mad."

Greg whistled. "And vindictive it seems. Very Glenn Close and *Fatal Attraction*. Even if Rick is as innocent as you say he is, a lawsuit like that would cost a lot of money just to defend—it might put him out of business or he might lose his house." He speared the last bite of his salad. "If you ask me, it's the perfect motive for murder."

"No," Monica said so vehemently that Greg looked momentarily taken aback. "I mean, I can't see him doing something like that."

"You know him well?"

Monica felt slightly foolish. "I've only just met him. But Nora talks about him all the time and how wonderful he is. . . ."

"Ted Bundy's victims thought he was handsome and very charismatic."

"I know I need to keep an open mind, but . . . I can't picture it. I can't picture Rick as a killer."

"Who, then?"

"I don't know. Dale—he's the sometime boyfriend—seems harmless enough as well."

"Maybe it's someone who hasn't been uncovered yet. You don't know much about the victim, do you, and if you believe Agatha Christie and her fellow mystery writers, it's the victim who is the key to the crime, not the killer."

By now they had finished their dinner, and Greg had stacked the dirty dishes in the sink. He grabbed their glasses and the bottle of wine and they moved into the living room.

They sat on the sofa and batted around ideas as the sun faded, leaving the room in shadows.

Monica stifled a yawn. "Sorry. It was an early morning. And another early one tomorrow." She stood up. "The dinner was lovely. Thank you so much."

Greg walked her to the door. They stopped on the threshold and he put his hands on Monica's shoulders.

"You don't have to leave, you know. You could stay."

Monica hesitated. A million thoughts ran through her mind. She almost said yes but instead said, "Maybe next time." She gave Greg a quick kiss and went out the door before she could change her mind.

Chapter 10

Monica thought about Greg the next morning as she rolled out dough for scones and beat batter for muffins. Why hadn't she taken him up on his invitation to spend the night? She was well over the death of her former fiancé, and it was certainly time to move on.

She sighed as she took off her apron and hung it on the hook. If Greg asked again, she wasn't saying no.

Arline was wrapping small squares of cranberry-printed fabric around the tops of the jars of homemade cranberry jam and affixing them with cranberry gros-grain ribbon. The print matched the cranberry pattern that bordered the Sassamanash Farm label affixed to each jar. Arline had flour on the front of her apron and in her short dark hair, giving the illusion of a broad white streak above her left eye.

"Will you be okay?" Monica asked as she ran a hand

through her own hair—her go-to method of combing it. "I need to run into town to pick up a few things."

Arline looked up from the jar she was concentrating on, the tip of her tongue caught between her front teeth—something Monica noticed she did when she was focusing on a task. "Sure. Go on. I think we're on top of everything."

"Is there anything you need?"

Arline shook her head, and some of the flour in her hair flew into the air. "No, but thanks for asking."

"I'll stop in when I get back."

"Fine." Arline went back to the ribbon she was attempting to secure around the jar.

Although the farm kitchen was equipped with a sophisticated cooking system, it still heated up when the ovens were going full blast, which was most of the time. Monica was grateful to step outside, where it was early enough that a cool breeze was still blowing. She dropped off the batch of baked goods Arline had made that morning at the farm store and headed toward downtown Cranberry Cove.

Traffic in town was beginning to pick up with the warmer weather. Tourists came to spend an afternoon at the lake, although the water was still cold enough to deter all but the hardiest of swimmers or those wearing wet suits, like the surfers hoping for some waves. Soon the summer people would be arriving in full force and all the dark and shuttered cottages would be bursting with occupants, music drifting from porches and open windows, people enjoying their vacation by the shores of the lake.

Monica needed to pick up some shampoo and soap at the drugstore and a paintbrush at the hardware store—she was hoping to finally find time to paint the bathroom. At the moment it was a plain and serviceable white, but she had picked out a color called English Apple Green that she hoped would give the room a spa-like feel, despite the fact that it lacked any of the amenities of a spa and instead boasted an antique claw-foot tub with rust stains around the drain and a small pedestal sink with a chip in the basin.

A large gold SUV with a *Keep Calm and Play Lacrosse* sticker on the back window was pulling out of a space in front of Gumdrops. Monica waited patiently while the car backed out and then pulled her Focus into the spot.

She turned off the engine and got out, ready to head to the drugstore and hardware store. She glanced at the front of Gumdrops and stopped. She hadn't heard anything new about Gerda and she knew Hennie had been very worried. She had been worried herself. Cranberry Cove wasn't the same without a matching set of Van-Velsens manning the counter of the candy store.

Midnight, the VanVelsens' cat and mother of Monica's kitten, Mittens, greeted her at the door, weaving in and out of Monica's legs as Monica approached the counter. Hennie had her back to the store, and the hunch of her shoulders worried Monica.

"Hennie," she said softly so as not to scare the woman.

Hennie whirled around and plastered a welcoming smile on her face—something she had become adept at after running the store for decades now.

"Monica! How lovely to see you. What can I get for you?"

"Nothing right now, thanks. I was wondering how Gerda is?"

Hennie's shoulders sagged a little more. "She's getting better, but it's so hard not having her here." She gave a bittersweet smile. "We've never been apart you know." She waved a hand dismissively. "I know some people find that peculiar and can't imagine it, but for us it's normal." She smiled again, a genuine smile this time. "Having a twin is like being born with a built-in best friend. At least that's how it's been for me and Gerda. Neither of us chose to marry—having each other was enough." A sob caught in her throat. "I don't know what I'd do without her."

Monica spoke softly. "What is troubling Gerda?"

"It's her lungs, as usual. Sometimes with twins, one of them gets short shrift in one area and the other in another area. For Gerda, it has always been her lungs." She looked at Monica. "I'm afraid she's in the hospital, down with pneumonia. With all the antibiotics at our disposal today, people no longer fear pneumonia as they once did, but at our age, and with Gerda's weakness . . ." She shrugged. "You can see why I'm concerned."

"Is she allowed visitors?"

"Oh, she would like that." Hennie clapped her hands. "That would be so dear of you. The only restriction is that the doctor has asked that visitors not stay too long. Pneumonia can cause profound fatigue in the patient, you know."

Monica smiled. "I won't stay any longer than is comfortable for her. Is there something I can take her?"

Hennie gave an abrupt laugh, and Monica was surprised

to see her face turn pink. "She loves those magazines that are all about gossip and the stars even though neither of us recognizes half of the names anymore. None of them can hold a candle to Bette Davis or Doris Day."

"You mean like *Star* and *OK*?" Monica asked.

Hennie nodded enthusiastically. "Exactly. We hardly ever buy them but we enjoy them when we have our weekly set at the beauty parlor."

"I think they sell them at the drugstore, and I'm on my way there now. I'll pick up a couple to take to her."

"She'll be so delighted." Hennie clasped her hands in front of her chest. "And not only because of the magazines, but because of your company. It will mean a lot to her and no doubt will do her a world of good."

Monica said good-bye and left to run her errands—the hardware store first. It still had wooden floors that creaked when you walked on them and the smell peculiar to such stores—a combination of wood and metal.

Monica quickly made her purchases and headed down the street to the drugstore. The magazine rack was full and the current issues ran the gamut from news magazines to the gossip rags Gerda was interested in, along with periodicals about boating, fishing and hunting—a triumvirate of pastimes beloved by tourists and locals alike.

Monica scanned the headlines of the celebrity magazines. It seemed as if everyone in Hollywood was sporting a baby bump—which appeared to be the newest must-have accessory—was getting engaged or divorced or was snapped on vacation in a bikini. She found it hard to picture the staid VanVelsen sisters enjoying these sorts of stories but she supposed everyone had their guilty pleasure.

Monica chose several magazines that she thought would be appealing, picked up her shampoo and the other items on her list and headed back to her car.

She was pleased to see, when she arrived at the hospital, that Gerda was propped up in bed watching a lively game show on television. She was thinner than usual and her cheeks were not as pink, but she didn't look as ill as Monica had feared she would.

Her pale blue eyes lit up when she saw Monica.

"Hello, dear. How nice of you to come by."

"I've brought you something to while away the time." Monica held out the stack of magazines. Gerda's eyes brightened even more and the palest pink blush washed over her face.

"How kind of you. I suppose Hennie gave away our little vice?"

Monica nodded.

"Don't worry. We don't believe half of what they print. But it is fun, don't you think?"

"And perfectly harmless," Monica said as she took a seat in the chair next to the bed.

"I've heard about the excitement out at Sassamanash Farm," Gerda said, her eyes lighting up again.

Obviously being in the hospital wasn't enough to keep Gerda out of the loop, Monica thought.

"I'm not sure I would call it exciting—more like frightening."

"Yes, of course," Gerda said. "And that poor girl—way too young to die. She was always very kind to me whenever I visited the library."

"You knew Lori?"

Gerda nodded and gave a smug little smile. "Between us, Hennie and I know nearly everyone in Cranberry Cove." She frowned. "The permanent residents, of course, not the summer visitors. Although we have gotten to know some of the ones who come back every year for their annual holiday."

"How well did you know Lori Wenk?"

Gerda pulled the blankets up to her chest with her gnarled, blue-veined hands. "Not terribly well really. But over the years I have heard a few things about her."

Monica's heart rate sped up with excitement. "Such as?"

Gerda picked at a loose thread on the blue hospital-issue blanket. "Do you know Charlie Decker?" she asked finally.

"Yes. She runs Primrose Cottage."

Gerda nodded. "Charlie and Lori were about the same age and in the same grade at school. They both started jobs at the Cranberry Cove drugstore at the same time and the next thing anyone knew, they were doing everything together—sitting with each other at high school football games, having sleepovers and walking to school together. They were almost inseparable until . . ."

Gerda paused dramatically and Monica held her breath. Gerda was as adept at keeping her audience in the palm of her hand as a professional entertainer.

"Until?" Monica finally prompted. She realized she'd been holding her breath.

"Until it became obvious someone was stealing merchandise from the Cranberry Cove Drugstore. Things that would be attractive to a teenager—makeup, hair color, nail polish . . . little items like that."

Monica tried to imagine where this was going, but couldn't.

"Obviously the owners—Fred Macgillicutty and his wife, Gladys—kept a keen eye on the store and didn't think customers were pilfering the stock. They were convinced it was a member of the staff."

Gerda began to cough, and Monica waited on pins and needles until her coughing fit subsided and she'd wiped her mouth with a tissue.

"They began questioning the employees who were working there at the time and when they came to Lori, she claimed to know for a fact that it was Charlie Decker who had been doing the shoplifting."

There was a lengthy pause and Monica finally asked, "What happened then?" She hoped she wasn't tiring Gerda unduly with her questions.

"Gladys fired Charlie. Fred tried to convince her to investigate further, but Gladys had had it in for Charlie from the beginning. She'd noticed what an interest Fred had taken in Charlie and how he would look at her whenever she was in the shop."

Monica made a noise, and Gerda held up a hand.

"Fred was a decent man, and he never would have taken advantage of the situation, but he had an eye for the young girls and took pleasure in looking at them."

"Was Charlie really the thief?" Monica asked, thinking of the woman she knew—hardworking, principled and kindhearted.

"Probably not," Gerda said, pausing to cough again, a tissue pressed tightly to her mouth. "The assumption was that Lori was the thief and had thrown suspicion on Charlie to save herself."

Monica's breath caught in her throat. If Lori was responsible for Charlie losing her job, not to mention her reputation, would that still rankle so many years later? Would Charlie murder her because of it? The idea of Charlie Decker being responsible hardly made Monica happy.

"What happened after Charlie was fired?" Monica asked Gerda whose eyes were beginning to flutter and close and whose breathing was becoming more labored.

"Obviously the friendship between Lori and Charlie was over. I'd heard that Charlie vowed to get even, but I don't think she ever did. I don't think it's in her nature."

But maybe it was, Monica thought. Had Charlie waited all this time to get her revenge against Lori?

Chapter 11

Tempest motioned through the window at Monica as Monica went past Twilight.

"Good morning," Tempest said when Monica stepped into the shop.

Unlike most of the people in Cranberry Cove who wore serviceable jeans and T-shirts to go about their day, Tempest had donned a loose, nearly floor-length purple dress with bat-wing sleeves.

Twilight was crowded with merchandise scattered everywhere. The glass counter in front of Tempest was filled with tarot cards, crystals, candles and incense.

"I heard the news about that woman's death out at your farm. This must be so distressing for you and your brother. Do they know what happened?"

"The police are still waiting for lab reports. That should help them to determine if it was an accident or not."

"What do you think?"

Monica paused. "Detective Stevens seems to think some sort of foul play was involved and I'm inclined to agree with her. The facts don't add up any other way."

"I didn't know this girl. Was she the sort someone would want to kill?"

Monica explained about Lori and Charlie.

"Do you really think Charlie would have held a grudge this long?" Tempest fiddled with the ornate medallion necklace she was wearing. "Besides, that doesn't sound like the Charlie Decker we know."

"I didn't think so, either," Monica said.

"Do the police have a suspect—assuming it really was foul play?" Tempest pulled out a pack of tarot cards and began shuffling them.

"Not that I know of. Detective Stevens always gives the impression of being completely candid, but I seriously doubt that's the case."

"Do *you* have any theories?" Tempest smiled as she laid out the cards from the tarot pack.

Monica suspected Tempest was teasing her because of her involvement in the previous murders in Cranberry Cove.

"I'm empty-handed, I'm afraid. There's the boyfriend. . . ."

Tempest raised her dark, arched brows. "That sounds promising."

Monica leaned on the counter. "I don't know. It's the same old, same old—she was pushing for a more serious relationship and he was trying to keep things casual."

Tempest snorted. "Typical male. Still, that's hardly a reason to murder someone."

"That's what Gina said."

"Maybe there's more to it than that," Tempest suggested. "Are there people who knew her that you can talk to?"

"I may have a chat with Lori's mother. Apparently she has some memory issues, but she still might be able to tell me something."

Tempest had continued to lay out the tarot cards while they talked. She pointed to one. "The Lovers. Romance. Of course, eligible men are a little thin on the ground here in Cranberry Cove, but I think I may have found an interesting one."

"Really?"

Tempest nodded. "His name is Xavier Cabot. He's a writer, and he recently moved to Cranberry Cove to work on his latest book."

Monica stifled the words that rose to her lips. Should she tell Tempest she wasn't the only woman in town going after Cabot? She decided against it. Tempest would find out soon enough.

Gina was going to be furious. It looked like Cranberry Cove was in for a match worthy of the WWE.

Monica just hoped no one got hurt.

Monica made a quick call to Arline and Nora to make sure that everything was going well in the kitchen and at the farm store. She'd decided she would visit Lori Wenk's mother before doing anything else. She got the address from Arline and scribbled it down on a piece of scrap paper she managed to find in the bottom of her purse.

Mrs. Wenk lived several blocks in from the lake in a blue house with a three-season porch that faced the street. Despite the mild weather, the glass panels had not yet been exchanged for screens, and they were smeared with fingerprints, splashed with mud and in need of a good scrub.

Monica rang the doorbell and waited. She peered through the smudged glass. She thought she glimpsed a shadow moving around inside the house—hopefully it was Mrs. Wenk.

After a few minutes, a figure came out of the house and stood at the door to the porch. She looked at Monica through the glass. Monica smiled encouragingly.

"Yes?" the woman said as she opened the door a crack. She had dyed brown hair with gray roots that was cut short, and she was wearing faded jeans and a black T-shirt with a Harley-Davidson logo on it.

"I'm Monica Albertson. I knew your daughter."

That wasn't quite true, but Monica thought it would put Mrs. Wenk at ease.

"You might as well come in then."

Mrs. Wenk led Monica into a living room with knotty pine paneling, a brick fireplace and worn but clean up-holstered furniture. A reproduction of a painting of Lake Michigan hung over the mantelpiece.

"I've hardly taken it in," Mrs. Wenk said, her voice trembling slightly. "Lori gone. Sometimes I think it's all been a bad dream."

"I'm sorry for your loss."

"Please sit down," Mrs. Wenk said as she plopped into a floral print armchair.

Monica perched on the edge of the matching sofa.

Mail was scattered across the scratched surface of the oak coffee table. Most of the envelopes appeared to be bills and some had *Urgent!* stamped on them or *Past Due*. Monica wondered whether Mrs. Wenk was short of cash or if paying the bills was something Lori had taken care of for her because she couldn't manage.

"Did you say you wanted to ask me something?" Mrs. Wenk said, pulling on her left earlobe. "I'm afraid I've already forgotten what you said."

"I'm looking for information that might help sort out what happened to Lori."

"Oh, you're with the police then."

"No, I'm—" Monica started to say, but Mrs. Wenk wasn't listening.

"The police have been here already. A nice lady with short blond hair." Mrs. Wenk held a hand up to the level of her chin.

"Detective Stevens?"

"Yes, that's who it was. Do you know her?"

"Yes—"

"She asked me all sorts of questions about Lori. She seemed to take a real interest in her."

Mrs. Wenk was quiet for a moment, plucking at the knees of her jeans. "What was I saying?" She looked at Monica blankly.

"You were telling me about your daughter, Lori."

"She had a boyfriend—did I tell you that?"

Monica shook her head.

A worried look crossed Mrs. Wenk's face. "I can't remember his name, I'm afraid. Maybe it will come to me. Anyway, they were planning on getting married. Lori's been keeping a scrapbook of wedding ideas since she was a teenager." She smiled at Monica. "Most girls dream about their wedding, don't they?"

Monica realized she had never fantasized about her wedding or being married. Was that really so unusual?

"She got herself a real nice young man."

Mrs. Wenk couldn't possibly be talking about Dale, Monica thought. When she'd talked to him, he'd made it quite clear that his and Lori's relationship was strictly no strings attached.

"Lori clips pictures from bridal magazines and posts them on her bulletin board in her room. Turquoise—that is going to be the color. She wants a beach theme—the bridesmaids in turquoise gowns and the tables set with turquoise cloths with white overlays. It's going to be so pretty."

"It sounds like it."

Monica was still trying to reconcile what Mrs. Wenk was telling her with what she already knew about Lori and what she'd learned from Dale. Either Lori had been delusional or she was seeing someone else on the side—someone no one knew about?

"She's even bought her gown. They were having a sale at a bridal shop in Grand Rapids, and she didn't want to miss her chance to get the dress she'd fallen in love with at such a good price." Mrs. Wenk's face brightened. "Would you like to see it?"

"Yes, thank you," Monica said obligingly.

The conversation was giving her a bizarrely unsettled feeling. Mrs. Wenk had acknowledged her daughter's death when Monica first arrived, but now she was talking as if Lori was still alive. Monica felt like Alice must have after falling down the rabbit hole.

With an effort, Mrs. Wenk heaved herself out of her chair, accidentally banging her knee against the coffee table. A number of envelopes slid off it and onto the floor.

"I'll get them," Monica said.

Monica squatted to pick up the scattered envelopes and noticed that one appeared to be a bill from a mortgage company and another a letter from a local bank. She replaced them on the table. Hopefully someone would step in and help Mrs. Wenk with her finances soon. Maybe Arline would be willing to do it?

Mrs. Wenk led Monica down a short hallway to a small bedroom at the end. A twin bed covered in a ruffled pink spread more suitable for a girl than a grown woman was pushed against the wall. A collection of dolls in ornate satin dresses sat on top of a worn-looking dresser and pictures of bridal gowns and wedding decorations were pinned to the bulletin board hanging above it.

The door to the closet was cracked open. Mrs. Wenk made her way toward it. She opened it and stuck her head inside. Monica heard hangers clacking against each other as Mrs. Wenk rifled through the garments hanging on the rod. A moment later she pulled out a large garment bag with a zipper up the front. Monica could see yards of white satin and lace through the clear plastic.

Mrs. Wenk laid the bag down on the bed and began fumbling with the zipper. She finally got it open and managed to wrestle the dress from the confines of the bag. The gown slowly doubled in size as it was released from its protective plastic.

"It's a Disney Princess gown," Mrs. Wenk said as she smoothed out the lace bodice and fluffed the skirt. "It's Belle's gown from *Beauty and the Beast*."

The dress was strapless with a sweetheart neckline and a full skirt that reminded Monica of a tiered wedding cake with ruffled icing.

"It's lovely," she said as Mrs. Wenk looked at her expectantly.

A pleased expression spread across Mrs. Wenk's face. "I've remembered the young man's name finally. It's Dale." She twisted her hands together. "Of course I've forgotten his last name. I'll have to find out from Lori for the invitations."

Mrs. Wenk carefully stuffed the dress back into its bag and hung it in the closet.

"Were Lori and Dale engaged then?" Monica asked as she followed Mrs. Wenk back to the living room and took a seat on the sofa again.

Mrs. Wenk frowned. "I think they had an understanding. It wasn't official yet, and he hadn't given her a ring, although Lori said he would soon. She'd already picked it out. She wanted a marquise cut and a diamond wedding band to go with it." Mrs. Wenk twisted the thin gold band on her finger around and around. "They planned to make the announcement at Christmas."

Monica didn't want to burst Mrs. Wenk's bubble so she chose her words with care.

"I talked to her boyfriend, Dale, and he . . ." She hesitated. "He seemed to think the relationship was actually quite casual—he said that he and Lori had gone out a few times but that was all. He didn't mention an engagement ring or a wedding."

Mrs. Wenk nodded. "I know. That's okay. Lori told me she was positive she could bring him around. She's a smart girl, my Lori." She tapped a finger to her own head. "She said she had a plan."

Monica had a lot to think about as she drove back to Sassamanash Farm. What kind of plan did Lori have to force Dale into marriage? Who would want to do that anyway? She couldn't imagine being married to someone who had dragged his feet down the aisle to the altar. How long would a marriage like that last?

Monica turned into the drive that led to Sassamanash Farm, her tires kicking up dust and gravel as she traversed the ruts and bumps. She pulled into the lot in front of the farm store and parked the car. She thought she'd better check on Nora before heading to the kitchen. She was going to be up to her elbows in flour for the rest of the day.

The shop was empty when Monica opened the door, but she was pleased to see that the trays of baked goods were nearly empty, with only the odd muffin or scone left gracing them.

Nora wasn't behind the counter, but just then the door to the restroom opened and she came out. Her eyes looked as if she hadn't slept well—bloodshot with dark circles underneath—and the tip of her nose was red. Monica suspected she had been crying.

Nora gave a broad smile when she saw her, but it didn't fool Monica. It was plain to see that Nora was upset. Monica didn't want to intrude—while she and Nora had gotten to know each other over the months, they were hardly confidantes yet. But she didn't feel she could or should ignore the fact that Nora had obviously been crying.

"We had a busy morning," Nora said with forced cheerfulness.

"I can see that. I'd better get back to the kitchen and start getting some things going and in the oven."

"I was about to have my lunch," Nora said, pulling a brown paper bag from underneath the counter.

She took out a sandwich wrapped in wax paper and an apple and placed them on the counter. She unwrapped the sandwich and was about to take a bite when she put it down abruptly.

"I guess I'm not really all that hungry," she said.

Monica hesitated for a second. "Is everything okay?"

"Sure." Nora rolled the wax paper from her sandwich into a ball and squeezed it as if it were a rubber stress ball.

Monica didn't want to force Nora to reveal anything she wasn't comfortable with and was about to turn away when Nora blurted out, "Yes, something is wrong. I don't know what to do or think." She buried her face in her hands.

"What is it?" Monica put a hand on Nora's shoulder. She could feel it shaking.

"Detective Stevens," Nora began before she started to cry again. She looked at Monica, her eyes wide and brimming with tears behind her round glasses. "I don't know what to do."

"What to do about what?"

"Rick." Nora unraveled the piece of wax paper, spread it out on the counter and began to methodically shred it into thin strips.

"Why don't you tell me what happened."

Nora took a gulp that turned into a hiccough. "Detective Stevens came to the house to question me. I can't begin to imagine what the neighbors are thinking."

Monica pictured Stevens's car in her mind's eye.

"Her car is unmarked. There's nothing on it to indicate that she's from the police. I'm sure your neighbors never guessed."

"You're probably right." Nora sniffed. "I'm probably worried for nothing."

"What did Stevens want?" Monica asked as gently as possible.

"She wanted to confirm that Rick was with me around the time of the murder." She tugged at her curly brown hair. "Monica, I couldn't lie. I had to tell her the truth—that I had no idea where Rick was at the time because he wasn't with me."

Monica could sympathize, and understood completely. She wouldn't have been able to lie, either.

"And now both Rick and I are suspects again." Nora picked at the crust on her sandwich. "It's even worse for Rick. Arline told Detective Stevens that Rick asked her to tell Lori he needed help with the hives. He denies it, of course, but there's no way to prove it."

"If Rick wasn't here at the farm, he must have been somewhere, right? And that would give him an alibi. Did you ask him where he went after leaving here?"

"That's the problem," Nora said, twisting the paper bag in both hands. "I did ask him. But he refused to tell me."

Monica couldn't imagine what could be so secret that Rick didn't want to tell his own wife. He hadn't been gone from the farm all that long when Lori's body was discovered. He couldn't have gone far. Surely someone had seen him or passed him on the road and would remember?

She said good-bye to Nora and made the short walk around the building to the kitchen. She realized she hadn't eaten yet and was starving. Fortunately she kept lunch fixings in the refrigerator so she wouldn't have to go all the way back to her cottage.

Arline was pulling a baking sheet from the oven when Monica walked in. It was a new recipe Monica had been toying with—chocolate chip cranberry cookies.

"They smell good," Monica said as she peered over Arline's shoulder.

As soon as they were cool enough to handle, she'd taste one. She had her fingers crossed that this would be a successful new product for the store.

Arline removed the cookies from the baking sheet and placed them on a rack to cool.

"How are your classes going?" Monica asked as she tied an apron around her waist.

Arline shrugged. "Okay, I guess. I'll know for sure after I take my finals. I think I'm doing pretty well in nineteenth century English literature, but chemistry"—she rolled her eyes—"is really kicking my butt."

"I saw Lori's mother today," Monica said as she rummaged around in the refrigerator for the container of leftover vegetable soup she knew was in there somewhere. "You're right—she does seem to be suffering from some memory loss, poor thing."

Arline was scooping pale dough dotted with ruby red cranberries and brown chocolate chips into mounds and placing them on a cookie sheet.

"Sometimes she's okay, and other times . . ." Arline shrugged. "Not so much."

"I noticed a stack of bills on the coffee table. . . ."

Arline laughed. "I hope she remembered to pay the mortgage or we'll both be evicted."

"Is there no other family member who can help her?"

Arline opened the oven door and a rush of heat blasted out. She averted her face briefly. The ends of her hair curled slightly from the warmth.

"Not that I know of. I think there's a brother somewhere—Lori mentioned him once or twice—but I know he doesn't live around here. At least he hasn't been to visit since I've been boarding there."

"You've met Dale, the boyfriend, right?" Monica put

the container of soup in the microwave and turned to
Arline. "What did you think of him?"

"I can't say I liked him very much. He couldn't be
bothered to shave before they went out and he was always
wearing that ratty baseball cap turned backward. I guess
he thought it made him look cool or something."

"Mrs. Wenk seemed quite positive that Lori and Dale
were going to get married. She showed me the wedding
dress that Lori bought and talked about all the plans for
the reception."

Arline snorted. "If you ask me, Dale wasn't the marrying type."

"Mrs. Wenk said that Lori had some sort of plan to
entice him into marrying her."

Arline laughed. "Entice him? I think you mean force
him. An age-old technique women have been using to
trap men for years."

Monica was confused. She furrowed her brow. "What's
that?"

"Seriously?" Arline laughed again. She held her hands
out in front of her stomach. "I found a pregnancy testing
kit in the bathroom wastebasket a couple of weeks ago.
Along with the test strip."

"Was it positive?" Monica paused with one hand on
the microwave door.

"Yup. It was as clear as day. I checked the directions
on the box to be sure I was reading it right."

Monica pushed the start button on the microwave and
stared at the turntable spinning her container of soup
around and around as it heated it up. So Lori had been

pregnant. No wonder the girl had looked so ill when she came to the farm that day—she must have been suffering from a bout of morning sickness.

And if she was pregnant, that was surely why she'd been so positive she could convince Dale to marry her that she'd already gone out and bought her wedding gown.

Chapter 12

"What a nosy thing she is," Gina declared when Monica told her about Arline finding the pregnancy kit in Lori's wastebasket.

They were sitting in a booth at the diner having a cup of coffee and sharing a piece of blueberry pie.

Gina stabbed her fork in the air for emphasis. "I mean, I can see glancing into the trash and noticing that the kit had been tossed in there, but she had to have gone digging for the test strip." Gina shuddered. "Imagine! Amongst all those used tissues and whatnot."

"True."

"Does she strike you as the nosy type?" Gina forked up another bite of pie.

Monica stopped chewing while she thought. "I don't know. Not really."

"Well, does she ask a lot of questions?" Gina dabbed at her lips with a paper napkin.

"No. Yes—sometimes."

"Sounds to me like she was living her life through her friend. Does she date or have friends do you know?"

"She's never said."

Monica realized that she knew very little about Arline. The thought made her feel guilty. She ought to take more of an interest in her and take the time to be friendlier. She made a mental promise that she would do that in the future.

"Do you think the pregnancy gives this Dale an even stronger motive for murder?" Gina asked.

Monica put her chin in her hands. "I don't know," she said finally. "He's not the only suspect. There's Charlie Decker, too. Was she still holding a grudge over what Lori had done to her when they were in high school?"

"You know what they say." Gina pulled a tube of lipstick from her purse. "Revenge is a dish best served cold."

"Well this dish is certainly cold. It's practically frozen. It's been years since the episode at the drugstore. Why choose now to exact revenge?"

Gina shrugged as she applied a slick of bright red lipstick to her mouth. "Who knows? Maybe something happened that made Charlie mad?"

"You mean like Lori doing something more recently that heated the whole thing up again?" She paused. "No pun intended."

"Could be. Then again, you might be right and the killer is the boyfriend after all." Gina put the top back on the lipstick tube and dropped it into her cavernous and obviously expensive leather hobo bag.

"Well I refuse to believe that either Nora or her husband Rick had anything to do with it," Monica said with a stubborn set to her jaw.

"I've met Nora, and she does seem like a nice person. Still, you never know."

"True." Monica tried to ignore the sinking feeling in her stomach at the idea that either Nora or Rick could be responsible for such a cold-blooded crime.

"I'm sorry, but I've got to dash," Gina said, digging her wallet from her purse. "The woman I have watching the shop has to leave in five minutes for a dentist's appointment." She tossed a handful of dollar bills on the table. Monica tried to protest.

"My treat," Gina insisted.

Monica had to suppress the uncharitable thought that if it weren't for Gina's alimony from Monica's father, she couldn't afford to be so generous. Sales at Making Scents were picking up, but Gina had recently confided that the store was still operating in the red.

Monica felt a frisson of pleasure when, as she was paying her bill, Gus looked up from his griddle and gave her a quick smile. It was short-lived—barely a second or two—but it was a first, and it meant that she was becoming recognized as *one of the locals*. And in record time, too. It normally took years to elicit a smile, however small and brief, from Gus.

Monica stood on the sidewalk, momentarily undecided. A group of four teenaged girls in tight T-shirts, cutoffs and flip-flops and with brightly colored and patterned tote bags flung over their shoulders parted and went around her, giggling. Monica could see grains of sand stuck to the back of their thighs—they must have come off the beach after a day in the sun. The scent of suntan lotion lingered on the air for several minutes after they'd passed.

Monica's thoughts swiveled from warm, languid days at the beach back to the death at Sassamanash Farm. The fact that Lori was pregnant when she died changed everything. Had she confronted Dale with the fact of the baby? And had he panicked and murdered her after she tried to pressure him into marriage?

Monica wondered if Lori's mother knew about the pregnancy. She would have to pay her another visit.

She didn't want to go empty-handed, so she popped into Gumdrops for a tin of Wilhelmina mints. Hennie was still alone in the shop but Gerda, after having taken a brief turn for the worse, was now much better. Hopefully it wouldn't be long before she'd be released from the hospital and back behind the counter at Gumdrops.

Once again, Monica drove out to Mrs. Wenk's house. She rang the doorbell and stood on the doorstep hoping the woman wouldn't feel as if Monica was hounding her. The flap to the mailbox alongside the door was open and the box was stuffed with mail. Monica pulled out the envelopes.

Mrs. Wenk greeted her with a smile and invited her inside. Monica couldn't tell if she remembered her from her earlier visit or not. Monica refused an offer of iced coffee or a cold can of Mountain Dew and followed Mrs. Wenk into the living room.

Monica handed her the envelopes and the small white paper bag. "Here's your mail. It was in your box. And I brought you some Wilhelmina Mints from Gumdrops."

"Thank you, dear."

The same untidy stack of bills was scattered over the coffee table. Mrs. Wenk added the new mail Monica had just brought in and pushed the pile away from the edge. She collapsed into an armchair while Monica took a seat on the couch.

"It's so nice of you to visit again so soon," Mrs. Wenk said. "I don't get many visitors anymore. It's nice to have a bit of company."

Monica smiled. "I hope you don't mind. I wanted to ask you a question."

Mrs. Wenk slapped her hands down on her knees. "Certainly. Whatever you like."

"Did Lori ever mention to you that she might be . . . expecting?"

"My Lori? No. Although I know she wanted to start a family. As soon as she and Dale were married she said. If she was expecting, I guess it happened sooner than she expected."

"But she never told you about it?"

"Not that I remember. Of course my memory isn't as good as it used to be. Dr. Flikkema keeps trying to fool me—asking me if I know what day it is and who's the president." She shook her head. "I'm a little forgetful is all. Nothing to make such a big deal over."

"Is there someone Lori might have confided in about the pregnancy? A girlfriend maybe? She must have been quite excited about it."

"Let me think. There's the one friend—they've known each other since they were at school together."

"Do you know her name?" Monica mentally crossed her fingers.

Mrs. Wenk looked doubtful for a moment and then her face cleared. "Shannon. I remember thinking it was a lovely name."

"Do you know her last name?" Monica thought it was probably too much to ask of the universe that Mrs. Wenk would remember.

"Sparks it was. Shannon Sparks."

"I don't imagine you would know where I could find her?"

"Sure. She works at Hair Magic. It's near the harbor somewhere."

"I think I know it. Is Shannon a hairdresser?"

"Yes. She does color, too. She always does Lori's hair for free. Lori said they always have a wonderful time talking and gossiping—more like a party than an appointment at the beauty parlor."

Monica was about to get up when Mrs. Wenk began fumbling with the mound of bills on the coffee table.

"Could you do me a favor, dear?"

"Certainly."

Mrs. Wenk handed an envelope to Monica with shaking hands.

"Can you tell me what this means? I've read the letter, but I don't understand it." She clasped her hands tightly and put them in her lap.

Monica cringed. She felt like she was prying as she opened the envelope, but Mrs. Wenk had asked for her help.

She pulled out the piece of paper inside and scanned it quickly.

"This is from your bank, Mrs. Wenk. I'm afraid it says you're overdrawn on your account."

Mrs. Wenk was already shaking her head. "That can't be. My social security checks go right into my account. I don't spend much—my mortgage, the utilities, some food. . . ."

Monica handed her the letter, and it trembled in the woman's hand like a leaf in a strong wind. Mrs. Wenk put the letter back in the envelope and put it beside her on her chair. She went through the remaining envelopes like a dealer shuffling cards before choosing one and handing it to Monica.

"And this one. Can you read it for me?"

Monica was loathe to pry any further into Mrs. Wenk's affairs—didn't Arline say there was a brother somewhere?—but the beseeching look in Mrs. Wenk's eyes persuaded her.

She opened the envelope and wrestled the letter out. It looked as if Mrs. Wenk had already looked it over many times—the paper was wearing at the creases and was a bit grimy as if it had been handled repeatedly.

Monica's heart sank as she read it. It was a notice from the mortgage company that Mrs. Wenk's last few checks had bounced and they would have no choice but to start foreclosure proceedings unless she paid up. Monica had seen the negative balance on the letter from the bank—there was no way Mrs. Wenk would have enough for the amount due. Arline had joked about them being evicted, but it looked as if it was anything but a joke.

• • •

Monica hadn't given any thought to having her hair cut in the near future. It was a tumble of auburn curls that she'd spent her whole life trying to tame and had finally given up on. She examined her reflection in the rearview mirror. Maybe she could use a trim. She held up a fistful of hair and examined the ends—as she suspected, many were split. She did need a trim. And Hair Magic would be the perfect place to get it.

Monica mentally crossed her fingers that Shannon Sparks would be working today as she headed toward the harbor.

Her car rumbled and jolted as she crossed the small wooden drawbridge that spanned the narrowest part of the horseshoe-shaped harbor.

The Cranberry Cove Yacht Club was on the other side of the bridge. As far as Monica knew, virtually no one from Cranberry Cove was a member. The roster was filled with tourists and people who had summer homes along the shore. A handful of cars were in the parking lot— business was picking up now that it was warmer and boaters were anxious to take their boats out of dry dock. Soon all the outdoor tables with their jaunty blue umbrellas would be occupied and the sound of laughter and clinking glasses would float on the air.

Monica passed the dark alley where the sign for Flynn's bar was just visible. Monica shuddered. She'd spent an evening there once when she and Gina were on the trail of a clue. It was a seedy place frequented by hardcore drinkers ordering boilermakers and shots of cheap whiskey.

Hair Magic was down another alley, sandwiched between The Angler, a shop selling fishing equipment, and one that repaired vacuums. Monica found a space for the Focus and pulled up to the curb.

Colorful fishing flies dangled in the window of The Angler, trembling slightly in the draft from the shop's ceiling fan. Monica went past it and stood in front of Hair Magic. She took a deep breath—the place looked clean and respectable. She pushed open the door.

Hair Magic was more reminiscent of the shops Monica remembered frequenting with her mother when she was young than the glossy new ones out at the mall. The air that rushed out of Hair Magic when Monica opened the door was the same though—a combination of hair spray, shampoo, conditioner and the sharp chemical smell of permanent solutions.

The reception desk was empty but a woman soon appeared from the back of the shop. Three old-fashioned hooded dryers stood in a row—two occupied with older women with heads bristling with rollers. Four chairs faced a large mirror on the wall, and a beautician was spraying the hair of the lone woman sitting there.

"Can I help you?" the receptionist asked when she reached Monica.

"I'd . . . I'd like a trim," Monica said, fingering a lock of hair. "I don't have an appointment though. . . ."

The woman paged through a dog-eared appointment book, her long, bloodred fingernail running down the entries.

"Was there someone in particular you wanted?" She looked up at Monica.

"I've heard that Shannon Sparks is very good. I don't know if she's—"

"Shannon is finishing up with a customer"—she pointed over her shoulder to where the beautician was undoing the cape around her client's shoulders—"but if you don't mind waiting a moment or two . . ."

"Fine. That's great. I'm not in a hurry."

Monica quickly went to sit in one of the chairs banked against the opposite wall. She shuffled through a pile of magazines stacked on the table in front of her and was opening one when someone called her name.

She looked up to find Shannon—at least she assumed it was she—standing in front of her. Monica felt her stomach drop. Shannon's smile was warm enough, but her dark hair tipped with blond on the ends and the asymmetrical cut that came to her chin on one side and was nearly shaved down to her scalp on the other rather alarmed Monica.

Shannon held out her hand. "I'm Shannon Sparks. Won't you come this way?" She led Monica over to one of the chairs in front of the mirror.

Monica sat down and Shannon stood in back of her. They both looked at Monica's reflection in the mirror.

Shannon ran her hands through Monica's hair. "What are we going to do today?"

"A trim. Just a tiny, tiny trim." Monica held her fingers barely a quarter of an inch apart.

Shannon frowned at Monica's reflection. "I'd like to see you go a bit shorter to take off some of the weight." She put her hands under Monica's hair and held it up to her shoulders.

What had she gotten herself into? Monica thought. This would teach her to go nosing around!

"Are you giving any thought to color?"

"Color?" Monica repeated blankly. She knew she had a few gray hairs but nothing she needed to worry about yet.

"You've got some nice red tones here," Shannon said, running her hands through Monica's hair. "We could bring those out a bit and maybe add some highlights and a handful of low lights."

"No. No color. Not today," Monica added hastily lest she offend Shannon. "Maybe next time."

"Okay, so only a cut today."

"A trim, but not too much," Monica repeated as Shannon spun her around.

She followed Shannon to the washbasins, trying to convince herself that even if she ended up looking like a French poodle, it would be worth it if she got the information she was after.

Shannon washed Monica's hair and Monica found herself relaxing under the stream of warm water and Shannon's fingers massaging her scalp. But when they returned to the styling chair, Monica felt herself tense up again.

"Just a trim," she said one final time as Shannon reached for the scissors.

Shannon spun Monica around again so she could no longer see herself in the mirror—which was fine since Monica had already squeezed her eyes shut tightly anyway.

"Did someone refer you to Hair Magic?" Shannon asked, her scissors clacking industriously. "I don't think I've seen you here before."

"Yes," Monica said with her fingers crossed under the pink plastic cape Shannon had tied around her neck. "Lori Wenk did."

Shannon stopped what she was doing and leaned over the chair so she could see Monica's face. "It's terrible what happened to her. I just heard. I couldn't believe it."

"Did you know Lori well?"

"Fairly well." Shannon resumed cutting. "We went to high school together and we weren't best friends or anything but we've always stayed in touch. You know, things like girls' nights out and stuff like that. We'd always catch up even if it had been six months since we'd last seen each other."

"Her death must have been very hard for you then," Monica said with as much sincerity as she could muster. "When did you last see each other?"

Shannon's scissors stilled for a moment. "Let me see. She came in for a haircut not too long ago, and me and Lori and some other gals we knew from school went out for a couple of drinks a week or two ago." Shannon paused for a second. "Did you know Lori well? I don't think she ever mentioned you. Of course we usually talked about stuff that happened in the past—like in school and when we were younger. Reminiscing, I'd guess you'd call it."

"No, I didn't know Lori well at all. We'd only just met as a matter of fact. I heard she was expecting—that makes it even more of a tragedy, don't you think?"

"Yeah," Shannon said, yanking a comb through Monica's hair. "Although it was odd. . . ."

"Odd?" Monica prompted. "What was odd?"

"The way Lori acted. The last time we saw her—there were three of us who went out for a night on the town—she told us she was pregnant and getting married to that Dale guy she'd been dating. Dale had never seemed all that keen on marriage in the past, at least the way Lori told it, but this time she'd even gone out and bought herself a wedding dress." Shannon reached for a spray bottle and misted Monica's hair with water. "But the odd thing was she didn't act pregnant, you know?"

Monica didn't know what that meant, not ever having been pregnant herself. "Act pregnant?"

"Yeah. She ordered a rum and cola. Now, I don't have any kids myself but even I know pregnant women aren't supposed to drink alcohol. And she went out for a smoke at one point. I remember my co-worker Janice—we worked together at the same salon before I came here—almost went crazy trying to quit cigarettes when she learned she was having her first."

"That is odd," Monica agreed.

"Misty—she's one of our friends from when we were back in school—has two kids, a boy and a girl. When she mentioned that she really liked her ob/gyn, Lori wasn't even interested. Said she had plenty of time to shop around for a doctor."

A half hour later Monica emerged from Hair Magic with two things—some interesting information and a new hairdo. Shannon had taken a couple of inches off her hair and she was right—it did lighten it quite a bit. She had also used a blow dryer—a tool that Monica had abandoned shortly after the time she dropped it in a sink full of water and had had to turn the electricity off at the breaker—and her hair was sleek and shiny for the first time since her mother had insisted she have her hair done professionally for her graduation pictures.

She also found the information about Lori interesting. Lori hadn't acted pregnant—maybe she wasn't? Maybe it was only a ruse to get Dale to marry her? Monica stopped as she was putting her key in the lock of her Focus. But Arline had found the pregnancy test in Lori's wastebasket along with the test strip showing that the result had been positive.

Obviously Lori had been pregnant but the baby was simply a means to an end. Was it possible for someone to want to be married that badly but care so little for the life she was carrying?

Chapter 13

Monica was on her way back to the farm when the Focus began making strange noises. It sounded as if something was loose somewhere—under the car perhaps? Monica knew next to nothing about automobiles, but she did know that this was a sound she should not be hearing—it wasn't one that a functioning, smoothly running vehicle would be making.

She felt her hands get clammy on the steering wheel. She didn't have the money right now for any expensive repairs and she certainly didn't have the cash for a new car. Perhaps a pebble or small stone had been caught in the undercarriage somehow? She knew she was clutching at straws, but the thought did make her feel better.

The noise suddenly became louder and was alarming enough to warrant a trip back to the mechanic. Monica turned the car around and headed back toward Peck's Garage, where she'd had her oil changed.

The same woman was behind the counter when Monica walked into the office. She'd pushed a pair of half glasses on top of her head, where they were nestled in her short, bristly gray hair. She looked up when she heard Monica enter.

"Yes?" She turned and looked at the clock in back of her.

"I brought my car in the other day for an oil change," Monica began.

The woman nodded. "I remember you. Dale did the change for you, right?"

"Yes."

"You having some trouble with it?"

"Not exactly." Monica devoutly wished she was more knowledgeable about cars—she'd have to make a point of asking Jeff to teach her the basics when he had time. *If he ever had time*, she added to herself.

"So what's the problem?" The woman began shuffling through some invoices stacked on her desk. "I take it you don't have any complaints about the oil change."

"The car is making a funny noise."

"A funny noise," the woman repeated, staring at Monica. "Do you have any idea how many problems a *funny noise* can encompass?"

Monica raised her chin. "I know. But I do think it's rather suspicious that the *funny noise*"—she gave the words extra emphasis—"started right after I had my oil changed."

The woman had been tilting her chair back but now she let it spring forward again as she straightened her posture. "Let me see what the boys can do for you."

She opened the door to the garage and yelled, "Dale," so loudly Monica jumped.

The banging and hammering stopped briefly and one of the men called back, "He's outside, talking to someone."

The receptionist scowled, accentuating the deep furrows crisscrossing her brow. "What's he doing talking to someone? Is it a customer?"

She muttered something under her breath. Monica caught the words *work*, *lazy* and *good-for-nothing*.

The woman pushed her chair back. The wheels squeaked as they rolled across the pitted linoleum floor. She came out from behind the desk and yanked open the front door to the cramped office and waiting room and yelled, "Dale. You got a customer. Her car's making a noise."

Monica stepped outside. Whoever Dale was talking to was getting into their car. The car looked familiar to Monica and so did the driver. It took her a moment before she recognized Detective Stevens. So the police had been talking to Dale—interesting.

Sweat shone on Dale's forehead when he joined Monica. He pulled a grimy rag from the pocket of his jumpsuit and swiped it across his brow, leaving a streak of grease.

"What's up?"

Monica thought she caught the slightest tremor in his voice.

"You changed my oil, and now the car is making a funny noise. It sounds like something is loose and rattling around in the undercarriage."

"Could be a screw loose."

He said it with a straight face, and Monica had to stifle the laugh that immediately rose to her lips. "Can you take a look at it, please?"

Dale glanced toward the office. "Sure thing."

Monica waited outside while Dale got the car up on the lift and began poking around underneath. He called another mechanic over and they both stared up into the bowels of the Focus.

The sun was warm, and Monica was tempted to go back inside, but the ancient air conditioner wheezing in the office window made it hardly any cooler than outdoors.

Finally, Dale came toward her, wiping his hands on the same greasy rag.

"I was right. There was a loose screw. I tightened it up and she should be okay now."

"Was that Detective Stevens I saw pulling out of your parking lot?"

Dale scowled. "Someone must have told the police about me and Lori. I'd like to get my hands on whoever did that."

Monica noticed his fists clench, and took a step backward.

"I told them the same thing I told you. Lori and I went out a couple of times but it wasn't nothing serious."

"Even though she was expecting your child?"

Dale lunged toward Monica, and she took another step back.

"Who told you that?" He raised his clenched fists to his waist.

"A friend of hers."

"Even if it was true, who's to say it was mine?"

"Lori seemed pretty convinced you were going to marry her. She had a wedding gown hanging in her closet."

"She'd have to take one of them paternity tests first. I'm not paying for someone else's brat." He paused to take a deep breath. "And there was no way I was marrying her." He shook like a dog coming out of the water. "She was a real witch. Always complaining. Nothing I did was ever good enough for her."

By now Dale's voice was raised. Monica noticed the woman behind the desk get up and peer out the window.

What Dale had let slip was interesting. It sounded as if he *had* tried to please Lori at one point. As if he'd been as invested in the relationship as she had been. Monica wondered what had happened to change that. And why had Dale lied about it?

Dale was quiet for a moment. He had half turned away from Monica when he whirled around again.

"You!" He pointed a thick finger at her. "You squealed to the police, didn't you? How else would they know about me and Lori."

He moved closer to Monica so that they were standing toe-to-toe. She could feel the heat from his breath.

"Why would I do that? I don't even know you." Monica tried to keep the quaver out of her voice.

"You're trouble, you know that? Sticking your nose in other people's business." He leaned in even closer so that their faces were only inches apart. "Stay out of it, you hear me?" He began to walk away. "Stay out of my business," he shouted over his shoulder.

Monica's hands were shaking in earnest as she turned the key in the ignition of the Focus. She hit the gas a little harder than she should have and shot gravel behind her as she pulled out of the garage driveway.

All she wanted to do was go home and cuddle on the sofa with Mittens. Dale had scared her—the look in his eyes had been evil. It was easy to imagine him killing someone. There was a good chance he was the one responsible for Lori's death.

Monica was halfway back to Sassamanash Farm when a thought occurred to her. What was to have stopped Dale from tampering with her car? It would have been easy enough—he had had it up on the lift. He could have done something to the brakes, and she would never know.

Monica put her foot on the brake pedal and pressed lightly. She felt the car slow and breathed a sigh of relief.

Still, she didn't relax until she pulled into the driveway of her little cottage, got inside and locked the door.

Monica was baking some cornbread to have with her dinner later when someone knocked on her back door.

She jumped and banged her knee against the cabinet door. She wiped her hands on a paper towel, rubbed the spot that was still smarting and approached the door.

Ever since her encounter with Dale, she'd been nervous and jumpy. She eased the curtain aside and peered out. Stevens was standing on the mat outside the door.

"Come in," Monica said as she opened the door.

"I hope I'm not interrupting anything."

Stevens looked tired. Monica was coming to the conclusion that that must be a permanent state during the early parenting years.

She couldn't imagine why Stevens wanted to talk to her, but she soothed her already frazzled nerves by fixing them both glasses of iced tea. It gave her time to collect her thoughts and calm down.

Monica handed the sweating glass to Stevens, whisked her apron off the back of the kitchen chair and offered the detective the seat.

Monica took the chair opposite, wondering if she should have suggested they sit in the living room instead. There was something intrinsically intimate about sitting around a kitchen table that was making her uncomfortable.

Stevens ran a finger around the rim of her glass. "I was at Peck's Garage earlier, and as I pulled out I looked in the rearview mirror and noticed you talking to Dale Wheeler," she said in a matter-of-fact manner. Nonetheless, Monica felt herself bristle.

"Yes. He changed the oil in my car." No need to go into the story of the funny noise, Monica decided.

Stevens gave a small smile. "Look." She held her hands out, palms up. "I'm not here to accuse you of anything. I'm trying to get at the facts—whatever they are."

Monica relaxed a bit.

"We know that Dale and our victim were dating." Stevens took a sip of her tea. "Although he claims it was strictly a casual relationship."

Monica nodded. "That's what he told me."

"But?" Stevens smiled again. "I think you've discovered something we haven't."

Monica heaved a sigh. "My assistant—she helps out with the baking—is a boarder at Lori's mother's house. According to her, she found a pregnancy kit in Lori's wastebasket."

Steven's eyebrows rose dramatically. "A pregnancy kit?"

"Yes. Along with the test strip that showed the result was positive."

Stevens jolted in her chair as if she'd received an electric shock. "It was positive?"

Monica nodded. "Arline thinks Lori was trying to use the pregnancy to force Dale into marriage."

Stevens gave a bark of laughter. "Having a baby doesn't guarantee marriage anymore." She twirled her glass around and around. There was a long pause. "My husband left," she said finally. "He decided he wasn't cut out for family life."

"I'm sorry."

"Better to find out now, right?" She looked up. "It gives me plenty of time to adjust to life as a single parent."

Monica was quiet.

"There's one thing I don't understand though," Stevens said, her voice firm and authoritative again. She ran a finger through the condensation on her glass.

"What's that?"

"Lori wasn't pregnant. I read the autopsy report, and it's there in black and white—no question about it. She wasn't pregnant and had never been pregnant."

Chapter 14

"Are you sure?" Monica asked.

Even as she said it she knew it was a ridiculous thing to say. Of course Stevens was sure—autopsies didn't lie. It was Arline who must have been wrong—she'd obviously read the pregnancy test incorrectly.

"I'm as sure as the ME is," Stevens said. "Discerning a pregnancy during an autopsy is hardly rocket science. Or so I'm told."

Monica went to the refrigerator for the pitcher of iced tea and refilled their glasses.

"Does Dale Wheeler have an alibi?"

"Not that he's willing to admit to." Stevens took the glass of iced tea from Monica. "I asked him where he was when the murder occurred and he said 'nowhere.'" She sighed. "Which is impossible. He had to have been *somewhere*." She took a sip of her tea. "It's obvious he doesn't want to say. He wasn't working that day, so his pals at the garage can't vouch for him, either. Which makes me suspect he was up to something he shouldn't have been. Whether that was murder or not, we'll see."

Stevens wiped at the wet ring her glass had left on the table. "I've got someone looking into Mr. Wheeler's background, but it's slow going. We've got a couple of people on vacation so we're short-staffed at the moment." Steven's cell phone buzzed and she glanced at the number before dropping it back in her purse. "Besides, Wheeler isn't the only one on our radar."

"Oh?"

"It seems more than one person had a beef with our victim."

"Do you think the killer was trying to implicate someone? I mean by using the bees, stealing the beekeeping equipment. It seems as if they wanted to throw suspicion on Rick."

Stevens scowled. "Criminals are rarely that intelligent." She began to get up. "Thanks for the iced tea. And the sympathy." She gave a wry smile. "If you learn anything new, you'll let me know, right?"

To Monica, it sounded more like an order than a question.

Monica washed and dried the iced tea glasses—she'd run the dishwasher but didn't feel like emptying it at the moment. She put the glasses away, hung up the dishtowel and topped off Mittens's bowl of water. The kitten was napping under the kitchen table but began to stir when she heard the metallic *ping* as Monica bumped the faucet with her bowl.

Monica decided she'd walk down to the farm kitchen and store to make sure everything was okay and ready to be locked up for the night. She trusted Nora, but she didn't want to leave anything to chance.

The sun was lower in the sky and the temperature had dropped slightly when Monica stepped outside. The air was cool against her face. The scent of freshly cut grass floated on the breeze, and the roar of mowers vibrated in the distance.

She passed the first bog on her left. It hummed with the activity of the bees as they flitted from one pale pink flower to the next. Jeff was a blur in the distance, still working even though it was after six o'clock.

Monica continued down the path until she reached the farm store. Nora was doing a final tidying up when Monica arrived. She spun around when she heard the door open.

"You gave me a fright," she said, a hand to her chest.

"I'm sorry. I didn't mean to."

"I guess I'm a bit jumpy after what happened the other day."

"I think that's perfectly normal." Monica smiled. She put a hand on Nora's arm. "Has Rick said anything more about . . ."

Nora fiddled with the strings of her apron. "No. He still hasn't told me where he was headed when he left here right before the . . . the . . . right before Lori was killed."

Monica gave Nora a squeeze. "First," she ticked it off

on her fingers, "I'm sure it was something perfectly innocent, and second, there must be a way to find out."

Nora's eyes lit up. "Do you think so?" She gave a bitter laugh. "I might regret this if I find out he was meeting another woman."

"I'm sure he wasn't," Monica said, praying she was right and that she hadn't misjudged Rick.

"But how will we find out?" Nora straightened a stack of cranberry-embroidered tea towels. "He won't talk to me about it."

"Can you check his cell phone? See what calls he's been making lately? Maybe he had an appointment of some sort."

Nora looked doubtful, but then her face brightened. "I suppose I could. He leaves it on the table in the foyer when he comes in from work. He usually falls asleep in front of the television after dinner. I can check it then. He would never know." She frowned. "Should I write the numbers down?"

"Yes. Later we can do a reverse lookup on the computer and find out who the numbers belong to."

Nora reached out and squeezed Monica's arm. "Thanks. Thanks for believing in me. And in Rick."

Monica smiled. "Now you go on home. It's late."

Let's hope we get good news, Monica thought to herself as she began to leave.

Monica had a small plot of land next to her cottage where she'd planted fresh herbs—dill, parsley, rosemary, thyme and basil. Jeff and one of his crew had dug the garden for her, arranging the sections of herbs like the spokes of a wheel, with a narrow brick path between each green triangle.

Monica had a batch of wax beans from the farmer's market that she'd been meaning to turn into a pot of soup. She stopped on her way back into the house to pick a sizeable handful of fresh dill to add to it.

The soup was beginning to simmer when her back door opened and Jeff stuck his head in.

"Can I come in?"

"Do you have to ask?" Monica said with a cheeky grin.

She looked at Jeff but instead of seeing the mature, twenty-five-year-old man, she saw the ten-year-old boy with the dark red hair, cowlick and broken left arm in a sling. Jeff had matured but he'd managed to retain his boyish charm.

Jeff ambled into the kitchen and bent down to pet Mittens, who was rubbing up against his leg, meowing loudly.

"What smells so good?" He lifted the lid and peered into the pot on Monica's stove.

"Bean soup with dill and freshly baked cornbread," Monica said as she emptied the last of the clean dishes from the dishwasher. "Even thought it's June, it's still chilly enough at night out here for a warm bowl of soup to taste good."

Jeff had such a hangdog look on his face that Monica had to laugh.

"And what are you having for dinner?" she teased, knowing full well that Jeff couldn't do much more than fry an egg and that his evening meal usually consisted of something heated up in the microwave or picked up at one of the fast food places out by the highway.

Jeff heaved a dramatic sigh and scratched his head. "I have a couple of those microwaveable dinners in the freezer." He stared longingly at the pot of soup. "Swedish meatballs, a chicken pot pie and turkey with gravy and mashed potatoes, I think."

Monica couldn't bear to tease him any longer.

"Stay for dinner. There's plenty." She gestured toward the stove.

Jeff's face brightened immediately although Monica was pretty sure he knew she was playing with him and would have invited him to dinner in the end.

"There's some cold beer in the fridge."

"Don't mind if I do." Jeff opened the refrigerator, grabbed a cold can of beer, put the can between his knees and, using his good hand, popped it open.

As Monica ladled out bowls of steaming soup and cut slices of cornbread, she told Jeff about her encounter with Dale.

"I'm surprised. I've always thought Dale was a good guy." Jeff bent his head over the bowl of soup and sniffed. "Ah, this smells delicious. Thanks, sis. I wasn't really looking forward to that frozen pot pie."

A man's idea of a *good guy* and a woman's could be vastly different, Monica realized. Men thought someone who paid for a round of drinks when it was his turn was a good guy. Women tended to have slightly higher criteria.

Monica was halfway through her bowl of soup when she decided to tackle the proverbial elephant in the room.

"Have you heard from Lauren?" she asked as lightly as possible.

Jeff dropped his spoon into his bowl, where it landed with a clatter and splashed soup onto his light blue work shirt. He scowled and rubbed at the spot with his napkin.

He glanced down at himself ruefully. "I guess one more spot doesn't matter," he said indicating some of the other stains on the well-worn shirt.

Monica realized she'd touched a nerve. Obviously he hadn't heard from Lauren, or, if he had, the news wasn't good.

"I think I can guess the answer to my question."

Jeff sighed. "No, I haven't heard from her. Now I'm getting worried." He ducked his head in embarrassment. "I even called the Chicago police to see if there were any reports of—you know."

"If anything bad has happened, I suspect her parents would have been notified by now, and they would have been in touch with you."

Jeff bit his lip. "I don't know. Her parents are farmers, too—mostly corn—but I think they wanted something better for Lauren than marriage to another farmer."

"Come on," Monica said, reaching for her glass of water, "I can't imagine her parents not liking you."

"Oh, I'm sure they like me. It's more that they don't want me marrying their daughter." He scowled again. "And the way things are going, it doesn't look as if they have anything to worry about."

The sun was barely above the horizon when Monica unlocked the door to the farm kitchen the next morning. She wanted to get a head start on a new batch of cranberry salsa. An order had come in last night from Fresh Gourmet. They were expanding the number of stores that would be carrying the Sassamanash Farm product, and Monica certainly had her work cut out for her if she was going to deliver on time.

She felt a tingle of excitement as she flipped on the overhead lights. It looked as if their gamble was going to pay off after all. All that had been needed was a little faith . . . and an influx of cash from the bank, she reminded herself with a smile.

Arline would arrive in an hour. Monica was confident that Arline could tackle the muffins, scones and breads needed to stock the farm store for the day.

Monica was chopping the final batch of peppers, her eyes stinging slightly from the heat, when Arline arrived.

Arline's dark, pixie-cut hair was still damp from her morning shower and her T-shirt clung to a wet splotch on her back. She was clutching a large travel mug.

"That smells good," Monica said, pointing at Arline's coffee. She'd been in such a hurry to get started, she hadn't wanted to take the time to put a pot on for herself.

"Haven't you had any?" Arline glanced at the coffee machine that sat clean and silent in the far corner of the counter. "Let me get some going for you."

"That would be heavenly," Monica said, stifling a yawn.

Arline laughed. "Looks like you need it."

A few minutes later, when the gurgling from the coffeemaker stopped, Arline retrieved a mug from the cupboard, filled it and handed it to Monica.

"Down the hatch now," she said with a smile.

Monica took a sip and closed her eyes in pretend rapture. "Heavenly. Exactly what I needed."

Arline laughed and went back to the dough she was rolling out for scones.

Monica took another sip of her coffee and turned toward Arline.

"I almost forgot to tell you," Monica said. "I spoke with Detective Stevens yesterday,"

"Yes?" Arline spun around to face Monica.

"She told me that according to the autopsy they performed, Lori wasn't pregnant like we thought."

"What?" Arline jerked and knocked a shaker of powdered sugar to the floor. She bent to pick it up.

"That's what Detective Stevens said."

Arline straightened up. "I must have read that pregnancy test strip wrong." She smacked herself on the forehead. "I can be a little . . . dyslexic at times, I'm afraid." She frowned. "Maybe the test belonged to someone else? I don't think Mrs. Wenk. . . ."

Monica's laugh cut her off. "I doubt it!"

"I suppose it could have been a girlfriend's. Maybe she didn't want to take the test at home . . . in case her parents or her boyfriend . . ."

"True," Monica said. "That's possible." She went back to mixing the salsa. "No harm done. I thought you might want to know."

Chapter 15

After Monica finished up the cranberry salsa, she was tired and sweating. She felt better after a quick shower and a change out of her work clothes, which were stained with red from the cranberries, making it look as if she had been bleeding. She didn't want to alarm anyone by appearing in downtown Cranberry Cove like that.

She had a couple of library books to return, and there was one on hold she planned to read for Greg's monthly book club—*Cover Her Face* by P. D. James. It was a slight departure from their usual fare of books by the grande dames of the Golden Age, but this author was certainly no less *grande*.

Cranberry Cove's library was near the Central Reformed Church, in an old house that had been repurposed to serve its new function. The mansion had been left to the town by the last son of a family of Dutch furniture makers who had died without a spouse or any heirs.

Large elm trees shaded the house library, so it was always cool inside, and today was no exception. The main room boasted a large fireplace surrounded by antique blue and white delft tiles depicting windmills, wooden shoes, ships at sail and various flora and fauna. It had been converted to gas a number of years ago when a stray spark from a live fire had nearly burned the library down.

Flames were leaping in the large open grate even though it was late June. The quiet section, filled with mismatched desks and chairs, was empty and so were most of the stalls. Even the comfortable and worn sofas and armchairs were largely unoccupied. The library had only recently begun to offer CDs and DVDs—a move that had the older residents of Cranberry Cove tsk-tsking under their breath.

Phyllis Bouma was behind the front desk, a pair of reading glasses dangling against her flat chest. She was wearing a plain white blouse and had a gray cardigan draped over her shoulders.

"Why, hello there," she said when she caught sight of Monica. "I believe your book has come in." She swiveled her chair over to a computer and began clicking the keys.

The library might look old-fashioned, but a forward-thinking board president had seen to it that its equipment, at least, was modern. Several of the older librarians had retired as soon as the first computers were wheeled in, but Phyllis had stuck it out, taking a night course at the high school to learn the ins and outs of the new technology.

Phyllis turned toward Monica and tapped a bony finger

at the computer screen. "Here's your book, right here. It should be on the shelf there." She pointed in back of her. "They're alphabetized by last name."

Monica went over to the pickup shelf to retrieve her copy of *Cover Her Face*. She'd finished the book she'd been reading, and was looking forward to sliding under the covers tonight with this new one.

The library had yet to convert to a system that allowed patrons to check out on their own, although they were holding book sales and other events to raise money for one. When Monica got back to the front desk, a woman was in front of her holding a stack of books, which she handed to Phyllis one by one.

Monica noticed that Phyllis's face looked pinched with disapproval. She handed a receipt to the woman and nodded. She blew out a sigh as Monica approached the desk.

"I really don't think we should be carrying books like that in our library." She gestured toward the woman who was about to leave.

"What sort of book was it?"

Monica couldn't imagine what had thrown Phyllis into such a tizzy—her cheeks were pink and her lips were set in a thin line. Phyllis read murder mysteries—what could have shocked her more than a dead body or serial killer?

"It was that filthy book everyone wants to check out. It's highly inappropriate for Cranberry Cove." Phyllis's color deepened. "*Fifty Shades of . . .* something or other." She tossed her head. "My neighbor, who's old enough to know better, told me about it, and patrons have been checking it out left and right. We had to order a new copy—the original was falling apart."

Monica had heard of the book but it hadn't interested her. However, it wasn't up to Phyllis to decide what the residents of Cranberry Cove should or shouldn't read.

"I caught that Lori Wenk in the stacks one day thumbing through it. She said she was looking for the good parts. Good parts, indeed!" She shook her finger at Monica. "That girl was what we used to call a man-eater back in my day."

"What do you mean?"

"She went after anything in a pair of pants! Even Herbert Mingledorf! He's a sweetheart, but dreadfully naïve. I blame his mother—so incredibly protective. Lori made a play for him and the poor dear was frightened half to death. When he didn't respond—and how could he with his mother looking over his shoulder every minute of the day?—she threatened to sue him for sexual harassment." Phyllis hesitated briefly over the word *sexual*. "Can you imagine?"

Monica nearly recoiled at the vehemence of Phyllis's speech.

"Who is Herbert Mingledorf? I don't think I've ever heard of him."

Phyllis looked momentarily stunned. "He's our program director. A dear boy and terribly nice, but, as I said, terribly naïve, too. He actually went to the trouble of consulting an attorney."

"Do you know which attorney it was?"

Phyllis looked at Monica as if Monica had suddenly sprouted a second head. "Dieter Oostendorp, who else?"

Monica realized, not for the first time, that she was not a native of Cranberry Cove and never would be no matter how many times Gus smiled at her at the Cran-berry Cove Diner. The real natives had so much inside knowledge; it would take her a lifetime to catch up.

"Dieter . . . ?"

"Oostendorp," Phyllis repeated somewhat testily. "A fine Dutch name. And a fine lawyer, too."

"You don't happen to know his phone number, do you?"

Phyllis gave a tinkling laugh and turned toward her computer. She punched some keys and turned back to Monica with not only Dieter's telephone number, but his address and email address as well. She wrote them down and handed the slip of paper to Monica. "Computers are wonderful, aren't they? I know I balked at first, but now I don't know what I'd do without them." She patted her monitor affectionately and then looked at Monica suspi-ciously. "Not in any trouble, are you?"

"Oh, no," Monica reassured her, waving the slip of paper in her hand. "It's for a friend."

Nora was serving a customer when Monica arrived at the farm store. Monica waited for the woman to leave, ar-ranging and rearranging a stack of napkins embroidered with cranberries. Finally the door clicked closed behind their customer, and Monica and Nora were alone.

"Did you get the list of phone numbers from Rick's cell?" Monica asked as soon as she heard a car start up in the parking lot.

"Yes." Nora blushed. "I felt bad going behind Rick's back like that. Once I thought he was waking up—he had dozed off in his chair in front of an episode of *NCIS*—and

I was so startled I nearly dropped the phone. Imagine! That would have been hard to explain. But it was only Dexter, our ringtail cat." She laughed. "That cat is so big he sometimes sounds like a person walking."

Monica held her breath while Nora fished around in the pocket of her jeans. She pulled out a piece of paper and handed it to Monica.

"These are the calls he made the day before the murder, the day of and the day after." She frowned. "Do you think I should have written down more of them? A lot of the numbers were repeats, and some days the only calls were to our home phone or my cell."

Monica dug around in her purse and pulled out the slip of paper Phyllis had given her at the library. She was operating on a hunch, and her fingers were crossed that she was right.

She put the two pieces of paper side by side on the counter and went through the numbers, running her finger down them one by one. She nearly shouted when one of the calls made from Rick's cell phone matched the telephone number for Dieter Oostendorp, the lawyer Phyllis had told her about.

"Look." Monica jabbed the piece of paper with her finger. "This is the telephone number for an attorney in town."

"What would Rick want with an attorney?" Nora's face had gone so white that the freckles scattered across the bridge of her nose looked as if they had been drawn on with a marker.

"Let me explain."

She told Nora about poor Herbert Mingledorf at the

library and Lori's allegations of sexual harassment, which had forced Herbert to consult an attorney.

The more Monica talked, the more Nora's lips tightened. She finally let her breath out in a furious exhale. "The nerve of that woman!" A confused look shadowed her face. "But how does this help Rick?"

"It's a long shot, I agree. But if Rick contacted that lawyer and made an appointment to see him—would he want the police to know that?"

"I don't . . . oh, you mean they would learn about Lori's suit and that would give him a motive for murder."

"Yes. If Rick told them about a meeting with the lawyer—assuming he had one—they'd want to know why, and it would all come out."

"But why didn't he tell me that? I wouldn't have said anything. . . ." Nora's voice trailed off and she gave an abrupt laugh. "You're right. I would never have been able to lie to the police. I'm no good at it."

Monica put a hand on Nora's arm. "Neither am I." She thought back to the time Jeff had refused to tell her where he was for fear she wouldn't be able to keep the knowledge from the police.

"Now we know he contacted that lawyer." Nora stuffed the slip of paper with the phone numbers on it back into her pocket. "But how do we find out if he made an appointment?"

Monica picked at the cuticle on her left thumb. "I'm not sure. . . ." She realized she hadn't thought that far ahead—she'd only been focused on finding out if Rick had been in contact with Dieter Oostendorp.

"Can you ask Rick? Now that you know this much, perhaps he'll tell you the truth."

Nora shook her head, her curls bobbing back and forth. "Then he would know I'd been . . . spying on him." She shook her head again. "I don't suppose we can call the attorney's office and ask?"

The same thought had crossed Monica's mind. But would they give out information like that? Wouldn't it be privileged?

"I don't suppose there's any harm in trying."

Nora pulled her cell phone from her pocket and held it out to Monica. "Here, can you do it, please? I know I can't. I'll mess things up."

Monica felt her palms get damp as she took the phone from Nora. It took her two tries to enter the telephone number correctly. Finally she was connected with the receptionist at the law firm.

"Who did you want to speak to?" the woman asked.

"Dieter Oostendorp, please."

There was a rustling sound and the woman came back on the line. "I'm sorry. I'm filling in today for Mr. Oostendorp's secretary. The agency sent me. Can I ask what this is in reference to, please?" Her voice became more businesslike all of a sudden.

"I . . . I'm checking to see if someone had an appointment with Mr. Oostendorp." Monica gave the woman the day and date. "His name is Rick Taylor."

Nora tugged on Monica's sleeve. "Richard. He might have used his formal name."

"Richard Taylor, I mean," Monica said to the woman.

"I'm not sure I'm supposed to tell you that." A sigh came over the line. "Like I told you, the agency sent me, and they stuck me at this desk with a phone and a computer and no instructions."

Monica heard rustling again and held her breath.

"I don't suppose there's any harm in giving you that information. I have the appointment book right here. This guy is pretty old-fashioned. Most of the people I've temped for use a calendar on their computer."

Monica waited some more, trying to curb her impatience.

"Okay, here it is. Yes. He had an appointment with a Richard Taylor, just like you thought."

Monica felt herself break out into a smile. She put a hand over the phone and whispered to Nora, "That's it!" She turned back to the phone. "Thanks for your help."

She could barely keep herself from jumping up and down. She gave Nora an impulsive hug.

"Obviously your husband was meeting with that attorney."

"And if he was meeting with this lawyer, it proves he couldn't have killed Lori." Relief flooded Nora's face, but it swiftly clouded over again. "There's one thing, though."

"What's that?"

"I still don't have an alibi. And I had as good a reason for killing Lori as Rick did."

Chapter 16

Monica was in the kitchen, fixing herself a late lunch, when Gina pulled into the driveway with her traditional flourish that included spraying gravel into the herb garden that Monica would have to pick out later.

"Yoo-hoo," Gina called as she opened Monica's back door.

"I'm making myself a turkey and cranberry sauce sandwich. Would you like one?" Monica asked as Gina settled into a kitchen chair with Mittens purring in her lap.

Gina was wearing a low-cut sundress and high-heeled strappy sandals. Somehow she managed to maintain her expensive highlights and French manicure despite the fact that the places that could provide such services were nonexistent in Cranberry Cove.

"No, thanks. I stopped by to see how Jeffie is doing. He's been working awful hard lately, and I can't help but think of that time he came down with mono after studying so many hours for his SATs." Mittens lifted her chin, and Gina scratched underneath it. "He wasn't home so I imagine he is out on the bogs somewhere. That boy doesn't know when to take a break."

"Running Sassamanash Farm is a full-time job." Monica carried her sandwich over to the table. "But I know what you mean—I wish Jeff could afford to hire some more help." She took a bite of her sandwich. "Not that he would. He likes doing everything himself."

"He's something of a control freak," Gina agreed. "Like his father." Her foot, which was already jiggling, began to move even faster. "I'm having dinner tomorrow night with Xavier Cabot, that new writer in town."

"Oh."

"I'm meeting him at the Pepper Pot. They do a great lemon drop martini there. Although I don't imagine that would be up Xavier's alley. I'm sure he'd go for something more manly, like Macallan straight up."

Gina dumped Mittens from her lap and stood up. "I'd better be off. Keep an eye on Jeffie for me, would you?"

Monica saw Gina out and then sat down to finish her turkey sandwich—no mean feat with Mittens attempting to swipe it out of her hand even when she was down to the last bit of crust.

She thought about what Gina had said. Jeff *was* working very hard. Monica suspected he was still out on the bogs and hadn't stopped for lunch or anything to drink. She had some roast turkey breast left and some cold pop in the fridge—she'd make him a sandwich and take him a cold drink.

Monica packed a sandwich, a can of cola and a couple of her cranberry chocolate chip cookies in a basket. Mittens followed her outside, where she immediately became engrossed in chasing a fly. Monica glanced into her herb bed and stooped down to fish out a few pieces of gravel and toss them back onto the driveway.

The skies were a clear blue but the birds were twittering in the trees—did that mean a storm was brewing, Monica wondered? She saw Jeff in the distance as she rounded the bend near the pump house where she left the path to cut across the field. The grass was rough and prickly against her bare ankles and a couple of times she had to swat some bees away.

"You look hungry and thirsty," she said as she approached Jeff. He was standing in one of the ditches that would be running with water come the fall harvest.

His eyes lit up when he saw the contents of Monica's basket. He put down his hoe, yanked off his work gloves with his teeth, pulled a handkerchief from his pocket and wiped it across his forehead.

"You sure are a sight for sore eyes."

"I thought you might need a little something to eat and drink." Monica pointed at the hoe Jeff had let drop to the ground. "What are you doing now?"

"Cleaning up the ditches so they'll be free-flowing when we need them." He motioned to the ditch. "Sometimes the vines start growing across the edge of the ditch and those need to be cut back." He pointed to a man in a sweat-stained white T-shirt a couple of dozen yards ahead of him. "Lance did the trimming, and I'm following up with the hoe to gather the debris together." He pointed in back of him. "The rest of the crew will use pitchforks to scoop up the debris and put it alongside the ditch where it can be collected."

"Can you manage the hoe with one arm?"

"I've figured out a way to do it. It isn't pretty, and I'm not very fast, but it works.

"Why not let one of the crew do it?"

Jeff's face dissolved into a stubborn mask. "When I got out of the hospital, I decided that if I could figure out how to do something with one arm, I was going to do it. I don't like being dependent on someone else."

He sat on the ground beside the ditch and unwrapped the turkey sandwich Monica had made him. He took a bigger bite than Monica thought humanly possible.

"These berries are Early Blacks." Jeff gestured toward the bog with his sandwich. "The vines aren't as thick or as heavy as the Stevens berries, for instance," he mumbled around the food in his mouth. "They're a lot easier to trim."

Jeff popped the top on the can of cola and took a long swig. He put it down and wiped his hand across the back of his mouth. He finished the rest of his sandwich and reached for one of the cookies.

He bit off half of it in one bite. "Delicious. Are these new?"
Monica nodded. "Yes. An experiment."

Jeff grinned. "These are definitely going to be a hit."

He downed the rest of the cookies, drained the can of pop and picked up his hoe again. He looked behind him. "The team's going to catch up with me if I don't get moving." He grinned at Monica. "Thanks for the grub. I appreciate it."

Monica gathered the empty plastic wrap and pop can, put them in her basket and headed back toward the path. She was halfway there when she heard Jeff shout.

Had he hurt himself? Monica began to retrace her steps, running back the way she had come through the grass that had been flattened by her earlier footsteps.

"What's the matter?" Monica asked breathlessly when she reached Jeff.

Jeff was standing beside the ditch, staring into it, leaning slightly on the hoe he held in his good hand.

"What is it?"

Monica peered into the ditch and saw a gnarled ball of weeds, cranberry vines and other debris.

"What's the matter?" she asked again.

Jeff poked at the collection of debris with the hoe, tearing the ball apart into its separate components.

"I was raking up what I thought were the usual weeds and dead vines when my hoe caught on something. It's not unusual for it to catch on a vine so I tried to pull it free. When I did, I found this."

He continued to untangle the tumble of weeds and vines, revealing the veil from a beekeepers hat.

Jeff looked out across the bogs. "What do you want to bet the rest of the hat is out here somewhere?"

"But the police searched very carefully."

Jeff snorted. "There's acres and acres of hiding places here. And this veil was tangled up in the vines—I wouldn't have noticed it myself if my hoe hadn't caught on it and gotten stuck."

"What's that?" Monica pointed to a scrap of yellow

paper that had been tangled up in the snarl of weeds and vines.

Jeff crouched beside the ditch and, stretching out his good arm, managed to retrieve the slip of colored paper. He handed it to Monica.

She unfolded it carefully. "Looks like a withdrawal slip from the bank. There's an account number on it but no name."

"Probably one of my guys pulled a handkerchief from his pocket and this came along with it." He gestured toward the paper in Monica's hand and sighed. "He should have picked it up but obviously couldn't be bothered."

Monica shoved the slip into the pocket of her jeans. She would throw it in the trash when she got back to the cottage.

"I suppose we should call Detective Stevens," she said, pointing at the beekeeper's veil. "This could be important."

Jeff looked toward the field where they had stacked the pallets of bees. "We know someone stole the protective gear from Lori's car and then had to get rid of it."

"But why ditch part of the outfit in one place and part of it in another? They must have stolen the gear from Lori's car so she wouldn't have access to it. But they needed the hat to at least protect their face—the most vulnerable part when it comes to bee stings—so they saved that. But ultimately they had to get rid of it as well." Monica looked around. "You're right, the rest of the hat must be here somewhere."

Jeff laughed. "Good luck finding it. It's a miracle the veil didn't get bundled up with the rest of this mess in the ditch." He jerked a head toward a crew member coming up behind him. "Skip would have pulled this tangled jumble out with his pitchfork and then Joe and Pete would have carried it away to be gotten rid of. And no one would be the wiser."

As they expected, Stevens advised them not to move anything when they called her on Monica's cell phone. Fifteen minutes later she pulled up with a squeal of brakes.

"Well, well, well," she said when Jeff showed her the beekeeper's veil hidden amidst the weeds and vines in the ditch. "Whoever our killer is must have taken off across the fields and dropped this in the ditch, thinking it wouldn't be found."

"It almost wasn't," Jeff said.

"The veil obviously came loose from the hat which must be here somewhere."

Stevens pulled out her cell phone and barked some orders into it. It wasn't long before several cars pulled up and a team of police was methodically crawling through the ditch looking for the rest of the hat and anything else the killer might have dropped.

"It would be great if they cleaned out the ditch while they were at it," Jeff quipped.

Stevens shot him a dirty look and Jeff shrugged.

Monica was hanging laundry on her clothesline—she loved the smell of sheets dried in the sun and fresh air—when she noticed Rick's truck go past. He pulled up to the edge of the field, parked and jumped out.

"Hello," Monica called as she headed over toward

where Rick was standing. When she got closer, she noticed his face had lines on it that Monica didn't think had been there before. This murder was taking its toll on both Rick and Nora.

"Are you looking for Jeff?"

Rick leaned against the dusty side of his truck. "No, Detective Stevens asked me to come by."

Monica heard rustling and turned around to see Stevens making her way across the field to where they were standing. She had a plastic bag in her hand. Monica couldn't see what was in it, but she suspected they had found the beekeeper's hat.

Perspiration beaded Stevens's forehead and she fanned herself with her free hand.

"It's hot out there in the sun."

"We could go inside," Monica offered. "I have a pitcher of lemonade in the refrigerator."

"That's very tempting, but I don't want to waste any more of your time," Stevens said, brandishing the plastic evidence bag. "We've found the rest of the hat." She turned to Rick, whose eyebrows had gone up, nearly disappearing under the fringe of hair flopping down on his forehead.

"The rest of the hat?"

"The veil was in one place and the hat in another, although not all that far away." She jerked a thumb over her shoulder. "I imagine the veil must have come loose for some reason."

"Lori said she couldn't stand the traditional beekeeper's hat like the one I wear. The veil comes down to my chest and is kept in place with elastic straps that go around the shoulders. She said the getup made her feel claustro-phobic."

"Is the veil attached?" Stevens asked.

"On my hat, yes. But Lori ordered something online that came in two pieces—a hat with a wide brim and a veil that went over it. Frankly, I wouldn't feel adequately protected in something like that, but it didn't seem to bother her. Besides, she'd rarely ever been stung so—" Rick stopped abruptly.

"Exactly," Stevens said. She stared at Rick until Rick finally looked away. "Have you remembered where you were at the time of the murder?" she asked after a long pause.

Rick's face shut down—even his eyes took on a blank look. "No. I don't remember. I wasn't anywhere." He waved his hands in the air, his voice taking on a desperate tone.

Monica wasn't sure what she should do. Should she tell Stevens about Rick's visit with the lawyer? The decision was made for her when Stevens turned to leave and Rick got back in his truck.

Monica decided she would urge Nora to talk to Rick, and to tell Stevens herself if he refused. It was their story after all, not Monica's.

Chapter 17

Arline was giving the farm kitchen a final cleaning when Monica arrived, slightly breathless. She knew Arline would be waiting for her. She opened the door to the smell of disinfectant in the air and all the stainless steel appliances gleaming brightly.

"I'm sorry you had to do that all by yourself," Monica said, noting the martyred look on Arline's face. "I got held up, I'm afraid."

"No problem. I'm glad to be of help." Arline wrung her sponge out in the sink. "I saw the police were here again. I hope they didn't find another dead body." Arline gave a bark of laughter.

"Nothing like that, thank goodness. They found Lori's beekeeping hat."

"Imagine that," Arline said as she pulled off a length of paper toweling and dried her hands. "That was lucky.

It couldn't have been easy with Sassamanash Farm being so big."

Monica explained about Jeff and his crew cleaning the ditches. "I suppose they were lucky, as you said. It could have been easily missed."

"I wonder if the hat will tell the police anything?" Arline took a sample-sized bottle of hand cream from her purse and squeezed a dab onto her palm.

"I don't know," Monica admitted. "Maybe there will be some trace of DNA? From a stray hair or something?"

"I always thought that only happened on those television shows," Arline said, returning the tube of hand cream to her purse. "I still wonder if it wasn't that Dale Wheeler who did it. Dale felt cornered by Lori and her insistence that he marry her. And you know how savagely a cornered animal will fight."

"You've met him," Monica said. "Did you get the impression he might be dangerous? He certainly scared me."

Arline ran a hand through her short dark hair. "There was something unsettling about him, although I can't put my finger on exactly what it was. Maybe it was because he had a drinking problem."

"What?" Monica whirled around. "How do you know? Did Lori tell you that?"

For a brief moment Monica wondered if Arline wasn't fabricating things to make them sound more dramatic than they really were.

"He had one of those Breathalyzer thingies in his car. I saw it when he picked Lori up one time. You know—you have to blow into it and the car won't start if it senses you've been drinking."

"Why would someone have one of those—"

Arline laughed. "Well you can be pretty sure no one would willingly install one of those Breathalyzers themselves."

Arline brushed at a spot on her T-shirt. Monica feared it was juice from a cranberry and not likely to come out in the wash.

"Usually people have to install them as part of a deal with the courts when they've been hit with a DUI."

"Oh," Monica said. That did make it sound as if Dale had a drinking problem. Had he been drinking when he killed Lori?

Monica couldn't wait to get back to her cottage and her computer. Once she did, Mittens seemed determined to thwart her efforts—strolling across Monica's keyboard, her tail swishing back and forth under Monica's nose.

Monica gave Mittens a kiss and put her down on the floor. Seconds later, Mittens was on the table again, batting at Monica's *Q* key. Monica was about to put her down again when Mittens became bored of the game and dashed off to chase a tumbleweed of cat fur being blown across the floor by a breeze coming in the window.

Monica went to her favorite search engine and put in Dale Wheeler's name. Some of the results weren't relevant—like the obituary for a Dale Wheeler in West Virginia who died twenty-three years ago. She scrolled through the entries, wondering if she was wasting her time, when she came to a link to a newspaper story.

The story was brief and contained few details, but

there was enough information for Monica to glean that her Dale Wheeler had been arrested for drunk driving. He looked younger in the grainy picture that accompanied the article, but it was definitely the Dale Wheeler who worked at Peck's Garage and who had been dating Lori Wenk.

Monica went back to the search engine and put in Dale's name again, only this time she added the date of his DUI. A new list of results popped up when she hit *enter*. At the top of the list was a link to another news story. Monica clicked on it and was taken to a story from the local paper. This report was about Dale's trial and subsequent sentencing. Apparently a man had died in the crash that Dale had caused. His attorney was obviously very adept because Dale got away with several years' probation and was restricted from using or being around alcohol for the duration of his sentence. It was also stipulated that a Breathalyzer be installed in his car.

Had Dale been out drinking when Lori was killed and that was why he couldn't give the police an alibi? Monica remembered something the receptionist at the garage had said—about Dale being a regular down at Flynn's. Of course it would do nothing to help Nora or Rick if Dale turned out to be innocent.

Monica bit her lip. She hoped it wouldn't come to that. She had nothing against Dale but she could picture him as a murderer far more easily than either of the Taylors.

Maybe the bartender would remember if Dale had been at the bar when Lori was killed.

Monica did not relish the thought of another trip to Flynn's bar. She'd been there once before—in the interests of chasing down a clue—and the experience hadn't been particularly pleasant. Flynn's was located by the harbor, down a dark, seedy alley. She certainly wasn't going to go there alone. The thought made her shiver. Maybe Gina would be up for an adventure—she usually was.

Gina was closing up Making Scents when Monica called her. She was more than thrilled to join Monica on a trip to Flynn's as soon as she'd gone up to her apartment and changed.

Monica suspected that Gina's attire was fine the way it was, given that the male patrons of the bar were usually in jeans with flannel shirts in the winter and stained T-shirts with risqué sayings on them in the summer. But Gina never missed an opportunity to dress up if there was even the remotest possibility of meeting a man. Monica didn't think she'd find any likely candidates at Flynn's, but as Gina always said, *you never know*.

Back at her house, Monica gave a quick glance in the mirror and was pleased to see that her new smooth hairdo still looked good. She ran a brush through it, washed her face and hands, dabbed on some lip balm and was ready.

A well-tuned roar—far different from the dissonant sounds Monica's Focus made as it chugged along—announced Gina's arrival half an hour later as she flew down Monica's driveway and brought her Mercedes to a halt inches from the garage door.

"Oh," was all Monica could say when she opened the front door.

Gina's expensively highlighted blond hair was in a casual updo that was almost more down than up, giving the impression she had just rolled out of bed. Thick applications of eyeliner and mascara made her eyes look heavy and sleepy. To continue the illusion, her sundress was more negligee than dress, with a wispy handkerchief hem that ended a good few inches above her knees.

If Gina was dressing like this for Flynn's, where she already knew she wasn't going to meet any eligible men, Monica couldn't help but wonder how she dressed when she was really on the prowl.

Scenery sped by at an alarming rate as Gina shot down the hill toward the town of Cranberry Cove. She negotiated the turn onto the bridge by the harbor on two wheels, causing Monica to hold on for dear life. As much as she was dreading the visit to Flynn's, Monica was relieved when they pulled up outside its windowless front door.

"Is this a parking space?" Monica glanced at the lines painted on the street, her eyebrows raised in concern.

"Probably not, but it will do," Gina said. "I don't want to walk too far. The night air is getting damp, and it will ruin my hairdo."

Monica put a hand to her own hair.

Gina must have noticed the gesture. "Your hair looks great, by the way. You ought to wear it that way more often."

Sure, Monica thought. But first she'd have to get on a first name basis with a blow dryer. Not to mention set her alarm clock earlier so she would have time to wrestle with the thing.

Gina pulled open the door to Flynn's and paused at the entrance. Monica couldn't tell whether she was assessing the situation or waiting for her eyes to adjust to the dim light.

Flynn's hadn't changed since the last time Monica had

been there. It certainly hadn't changed for the better. It smelled of spilled beer and industrial disinfectant—an unsavory combination.

It was fairly crowded. The men must have escaped from home as soon as the empty dinner dishes were whisked off the table. Most of them chose the stools lining the bar but a few sat at tables by themselves, tilting their chairs back along with their glasses. Two men were throwing darts at a board pockmarked with holes.

The bartender flicked his eyes over Gina and Monica then went back to polishing the glass in his hand with a dingy looking rag.

Gina sidled up to the bar and caught the bartender's eye. He ambled over to her, still polishing the same glass.

"Listen, I don't want no trouble," he said, his eyes on Gina.

"Trouble?"

"With the cops. You know what I mean. I'd rather you ladies took your business outside."

At first Monica couldn't imagine what he meant, but then it dawned on her. She tugged at Gina's arm and whispered in her ear.

"He thinks we're ladies of the night."

"Wherever did you pick up that quaint expression?" Gina said sourly as she gave the bartender a look that stopped him in his tracks.

"I'm going to ignore that remark," Gina said imperiously. "We're here to ask you a question."

The bartender looked momentarily nonplussed but quickly regained his composure. He put the glass down on the bar and leaned his elbows on either side of it.

"Shoot."

Gina looked at Monica.

Monica cleared her throat. "Do you know Dale Wheeler? He works at Peck's Garage right outside of town."

The bartender gave a laugh that ended in a wheeze. "Sure I do. He's a regular. Or he used to be before he got nailed with that DUI."

Monica's ears perked up. "So he hasn't been in recently?"

"I wouldn't say that." The bartender smiled, revealing a gold tooth. "He gets his buddies to drop him off by the back door—down that alley over there." He pointed toward the wall of the bar. "That way his probation officer—nasty fellow always looking to catch Dale out—will be none the wiser if he spends the occasional night or afternoon knocking back a few with the guys."

"Do you happen to know if he was here on Monday, June 21?" Monica asked.

"That was this Monday, right?" He frowned.

"Yes."

"I think so." He rubbed his chin. "Monday, you said?"

"Yes."

"Let me check something. Give me a minute, okay?"

The bartender ambled off, leaving the polished glass behind on the bar. He disappeared through an archway into a back room.

One of the men playing darts began to walk in Monica and Gina's direction, but Gina shot him a look and he shrugged, turned around and rejoined his buddies.

"What's taking him so long?" Gina complained, one eye on her watch, the other on the men playing darts.

The bartender finally reappeared. "Yup," he said, as he reached Monica and Gina. "Dale was in that morning."

"Awfully early to be drinking," Monica said.

The bartender laughed. "I could stay open all day and all night and still have customers."

"How can you be so sure Dale was here on that particular morning? You must get a lot of people through here in a week."

"It's like this, see." The bartender leaned on the bar, and Monica pulled back, away from his sour breath. "I had a delivery of beer. I've been having trouble with my back lately," he put a hand to his lower back, "and Dale gave me a hand with the boxes. So, yeah, he was here late Monday morning."

Chapter 18

Monica was still thinking about Dale Wheeler the next morning. With Dale out of the picture thanks to the alibi the bartender at Flynn's was able to give him, Monica didn't know where to go next. Rick had an alibi—he was at his lawyer's—and she couldn't believe Nora would so much as swat a fly let alone kill a person in cold blood. It wasn't conceivable.

Monica leaned her left elbow out the window of the Focus. She was headed into town to check on Gerda and to get some takeout chili from the Cranberry Cove Diner. It was only ten o'clock in the morning, but she'd been up for ages already and was craving some of the Diner's most secret and famous dish. It wasn't on the menu—if you were a local, you already knew about it, and if you weren't . . . well, it was best you steered clear of the diner in the first place.

The sun was warm on her arm and her hair fluttered in the breeze as she sped down the hill into town.

She nabbed a spot right in front of Gumdrops. She hoped that was a good omen.

Hennie greeted Monica with a smile when she walked into the candy store. Monica was tempted to read something positive into that, but she knew that Hennie made it a point to smile at all of her customers no matter how she herself was feeling that day.

"I hope it's good news about Gerda," Monica said immediately, her fingers mentally crossed.

Hennie gave a genuine smile as she smoothed the pleats in her pink linen skirt. "Gerda got out of the hospital earlier this morning and is resting comfortably at home." Hennie dashed at her cheek where a solitary tear glistened like a raindrop. "It's so good to have her home again. It will be a while before she can come back to the shop full time, but she's definitely on the mend."

"That is good news." Monica found herself breaking out in a grin almost as wide as Hennie's.

"And she's home in time for the Flag Day celebration. We haven't missed a one since we were out of our cribs. We used to go with our parents, then we used to take them, dear things, when they needed walkers and canes, and now we've come full circle."

Monica was pleased. She'd come to feel as if the people in Cranberry Cove were family—even cranky old Gus at the diner. When they hurt, she hurt, too.

"Can I get you anything, dear?" Hennie gestured toward the counter filled with colorful candies.

"Not today, thanks. I wanted to check on Gerda."

"That's terribly kind of you. Gerda will be pleased to hear it."

"I'm headed to the diner. Is there anything I can get you?"

Hennie shook her head and her tidy gray curls bounced with the motion. "No thank you, dear. I brought some leftover erwtensoep for my meal."

By now Monica had been in Cranberry Cove long enough to be able to translate *erwtensoep* as Dutch pea soup. It was a staple in the sisters' diet. It was a thrifty meal but also very tasty.

"I'll be going then. Have a good day," Monica called over her shoulder as she left Gumdrops, the bells on the door tinkling softly as it shut behind her.

Monica paused in front of the window of Danielle's—a high-end boutique that catered to the summer crowd with their fat wallets and gold credit cards. One of the mannequins sported a pale, celery green sundress that caught Monica's eye. She would love to own something like that, but would she have the nerve to wear it? She'd spent so much time recently in jeans and T-shirts that a dress felt like an exotic costume.

No matter—it would certainly be too expensive for her.

The delicious smells from the open door of the diner pulled Monica down the sidewalk. She was already anticipating the taste of the chili—spicy with a hint of smokiness from what Gus claimed was a secret ingredient but what Monica suspected was chipotle peppers, jalape-ños that had been smoked and dried.

Monica was about to enter the diner when something down the street caught her eye. She squinted—it was Gina waving madly at her. Monica began walking in the direction of Gina's shop. She hoped nothing was wrong. The thought made her quicken her steps until she was nearly running by the time she reached Making Scents.

Gina was pacing back and forth in front of her shop, her backless sandals smacking against her heels with each step. Her carefully undone updo was now more down than up, and her cheeks were flaming red.

"What's wrong?" Monica asked as soon as she reached her stepmother.

"Some people!" Gina fumed, her hands clenched at her sides.

"What's happened? Tell me." Monica kept her voice low and soothing.

"I'll bet it was Tempest," Gina said, gesturing down the street toward Twilight. "I should never have told her I was having drinks with Xavier."

Uh-oh, Monica thought. It looked as if something had hit the fan. She'd been afraid this was going to happen from the minute she'd found out both women were setting their sights on the same man.

"What did she do, and why do you think it was Tempest?"

"It stands to reason, doesn't it? Why would anyone else do something like this?"

"Do what?" Monica had to restrain herself from screaming the word in frustration.

"Someone let their dog use my front mat as a bathroom." Gina gestured toward her shop. "I've spent the last ten minutes cleaning it up."

Monica noticed a bottle of bleach and a roll of paper towels alongside the mat.

"But Tempest doesn't even have a dog."

Gina looked alarmed. "If it wasn't Tempest . . . maybe someone is trying to frighten me?"

"I don't honestly see anything frightening about it. Disgusting, maybe, but frightening, no," Monica said in the confident voice of a parent reassuring a child.

Gina grabbed Monica's arm. "What if someone is trying to get me to leave town?"

Monica sighed. While the townspeople of Cranberry Cove had certainly been wary of Gina at first—the flamboyant out-of-towner who had landed in their midst—they'd come to accept, or at least tolerate, her in the same way they had Tempest.

"I'm quite certain no one did it to try to get you to leave."

"Then Tempest must have done it," Gina insisted stubbornly.

"Not necessarily. It's far more likely to have been a careless dog owner. Besides, what did Tempest say when you told her you were going out with Xavier?"

"She wished me luck." Gina tossed her head, nearly unraveling the rest of her hairdo. "She made it sound as if I would need it."

Monica laughed to herself as she headed back down the street toward the diner. Gina and Tempest sounded like two high school girls fighting over the same guy. She hoped they could work things out without jeopardizing their friendship.

Delicious smells spilled from the open door of the diner, and Monica felt her stomach rumble. There was the ever-present lingering scent of bacon, the smell of hamburgers sizzling on the grill and the occasional spicy note of cumin and chili powder from the pot of chili simmering on the back burner.

Monica gave her order to the harried woman behind the takeout counter and stepped away as another customer approached. She'd asked for two orders of chili—she decided she would take one of them to Nora to cheer her up. Several minutes later, the woman gestured toward Monica and held out a white paper bag.

Monica took a deep breath of the delicious scents emanating from the bag and joined the line at the checkout.

Someone tapped her on the shoulder and she whirled around. It was Greg.

"Hey, stranger," he said, giving her a quick hug. "I've been meaning to give you a call, but I've been so busy tidying up the shop and getting ready for Flag Day. When everyone has had their fill of Dutch food, music and games, they often wander down Beach Hollow Road to shop."

Monica raised her eyebrows, and Greg laughed.

"I know. Tidying the shop is a Herculean effort. So far I've barely made a dent in the job. I'm concentrating on showcasing my first editions in case there are any interested out-of-town buyers. I have a Margery Allingham—*Police at the Funeral*—that should elicit some interest in anyone who is a collector."

Gus was behind the grill watching everything that was going on in the diner while simultaneously flipping the burgers that were almost ready and turning over some potatoes that had browned sufficiently on one side.

"Hey, Gus," the man in front of Monica shouted. "Are you going to have a booth at the Flag Day celebration?"

"Yes." Gus looked in the direction of the man wearing overalls and a white T-shirt with *Grateful Dead* written across the front. "I'm going to have Greek food. Dolmades— stuffed grape leaves—baklava, spanakopita, souvlaki."

Monica was startled. She didn't think she'd ever heard Gus do more than grunt before. Greg looked at her and raised his eyebrows.

"Who's going to eat that stuff?" the fellow in the overalls called back, and several people laughed.

Gus shook his spatula at them. "It's good stuff. You'll like it."

By now Monica had moved to the front of the line. She fumbled in her purse for her wallet, pulled out her money and handed it to the cashier.

Greg squeezed her arm. "I'm going to grab that empty seat at the counter. I'll call you later. It's time we had dinner at the Pepper Pot. We haven't been there since the grand opening, and I thought it was pretty good then."

Monica waved good-bye to Greg, scooped up her change and headed out the door.

Nora was finishing up with a customer when Monica got to the farm store. She checked the cases and the cooler while she waited, making a note of what was running low.

Finally the customer left with two bakery bags full of muffins and scones.

"I've brought you something." Monica put the containers of chili on the counter. "I thought you might enjoy some of Gus's finest."

Nora's eyes welled with tears. "That's so kind of you. I didn't have a chance to put together anything for my lunch." She gave an indulgent smile. "The boys were almost impossible to corral this morning. It took them forever to finish their breakfast."

They pried the lids off the containers, and Monica handed Nora a plastic spoon. The air in the farm store quickly became redolent of spices mingling with the scents of sugar and cinnamon.

"What do you have arranged for the kids this summer?" Monica asked, blowing on her first spoonful of chili.

Nora stirred her chili around and around in her cup. She didn't look at Monica.

"I don't know what I'm going to do. I don't make enough money to warrant hiring a sitter, and all the other options are sort of hit or miss—Bible camp for a week; their grandparents will be here visiting another week." She looked at Monica. "I don't know."

Monica felt a moment of panic. Nora was a wonderful employee—how would she manage without her. Maybe Arline could mind the store while Monica did all the baking?

"Listen." Nora stopped stirring for a moment. "I'll figure out something. I love working here."

They were quiet for a moment, concentrating on their containers of chili.

"Have you spoken with Rick about the lawyer—that you know that's where he was when Lori was killed?" Monica asked after several minutes.

Nora dropped her spoon into her container and blew out a puff of air that fluttered her short, curly bangs.

"I did. A lot of good it did." She balled her fists. "He can be so stubborn sometimes."

"What do you mean?"

"He refuses to go to the police even though it would give him an alibi." Nora's shoulders drooped. "I wish there was someone who could talk him into it. I'm certainly not having any luck."

"Does he have a good friend maybe? Or a brother or sister? Someone he might listen to?"

Nora was already shaking her head. "We don't want anyone else to know about this whole . . . nightmare."

"I can understand that." Monica spooned up the last of her chili.

Nora turned toward Monica so suddenly she nearly knocked over her container. "What if you talked to Rick? Maybe he'd listen to you."

"Me?" Monica pointed to herself. "I hardly know him. Maybe Jeff—"

"No, you would be perfect. You're so calm and rational."

"So is Jeff . . ."

"I think Rick would be more likely to listen to a woman."

Monica tried to quell the sigh that rose to her lips. The whole thing seemed . . . awkward. What if Rick got angry with her for interfering? She could hardly blame him.

"Please?" Nora clasped her hands together. "I have this feeling he would listen to you."

This time Monica did sigh. "Okay. I suppose it can't hurt. But I can't promise anything."

The chili Monica had so looked forward to felt like molten lava in her stomach as she drove out toward Rick's Bees. She rehearsed possible openings over and over again in her head but they all rang false. She'd have to trust her instincts once she was face-to-face with Rick.

The farm was down a rutted dirt road with fields of clover on either side. A wooden sign with *Rick's Bees* and a caricature of a bee on it stood outside the entrance. A chain-link fence bordered the farm. The front gate hung open, and by the rust on the hinges, Monica guessed it was rarely, if ever, closed.

A truck with *Rick's Bees* on the side was pulled up outside a weathered white building. The fields beyond were dotted with square wooden boxes holding the beehives.

Monica knocked on the door. She hoped the presence of the truck meant Rick was in.

The door opened so abruptly, Monica had to stifle a startled gasp. Rick was wearing jeans worn to a pale blue, a white oxford cloth shirt with the sleeves cut off and work boots encrusted with dried mud.

"Is everything okay?" he said. A look of alarm passed over his face. "Nothing's happened to Nora has it?"

Monica hastened to reassure him. "Nora is fine. I wanted to talk to you."

"Come in then. I'm afraid the place is a bit untidy at the moment. Lori was the one who used to fuss about straightening things."

"Thanks."

Monica followed Rick into a small office with two desks separated by worn cubicle partitions. He grabbed a desk chair from each of the spaces and arranged them so they were facing each other.

"Please. Have a seat."

Monica sat down on the edge of one of the chairs. It wobbled slightly. Rick took the other seat. Their knees were almost touching, and Monica pushed her chair back a few inches.

"Nora sure enjoys working with you," Rick said, leaning back and giving an easy grin. "She's always talking about it."

"I'm glad." Monica cleared her throat. How to broach the subject she'd come here to discuss?

"What can I do for you?"

The phone rang, and Rick swiveled his chair around toward the desk, glanced at the number on the caller ID and shrugged.

"I'll call them back later." He smiled at Monica.

"Nora asked me to speak to you," Monica began.

Rick frowned. "About what?"

Monica took a deep breath. She thought of how her father had taught her to plunge boldly into the cold lake instead of inching her way in a foot at a time.

"Nora doesn't understand why you won't go to the police with your alibi. She knows you had an appointment with a lawyer—Dieter Oostendorp."

Rick sighed and his face relaxed slightly.

"And here I thought I was being so discreet. I didn't want to worry Nora. She can make a mountain out of a molehill faster than a magician can pull a rabbit out of a hat."

Monica held out her hands, palms up. "But don't you see? The meeting with the lawyer gives you an alibi. If you tell the police, they'll leave you alone."

Rick concentrated on picking a speck of dirt off the knee of his jeans. After several seconds, he finally looked at Monica.

"There's only one problem. I didn't go to the lawyer. I changed my mind at the last minute. It seemed like a waste of time and money. I thought I'd be better off trying to convince Lori to drop the suit."

Monica let out her breath in a sharp exhale. This wasn't good. They were back to square one—neither Rick nor Nora had an alibi.

"Please don't tell Nora." Rick held his hands out in supplication. "She's already worried enough as it is."

Monica was about to say something when there was a knock at the front door.

"Hang on a sec. Let me see who that is. I'm expecting

a delivery of containers. We've started selling honey and royal jelly over the Internet."

Rick spoke briefly to the man at the door, then turned to Monica.

"I'll be right back. I need to show Shep where to put the boxes."

Monica felt a sense of defeat settle over her. What was she going to tell Nora? Nora had been so hopeful that Monica would be successful.

She pushed her chair back and leaned her elbow on the edge of the desk. It must have been Lori's desk. Tacked to the side of the cubicle were numerous photographs. Monica wheeled her chair closer for a better look.

There was a black-and-white strip of photos of Lori and Dale that looked as if it had been taken in one of those photo booths they often had at fairs and carnivals. Lori was smiling broadly, her arms wrapped around Dale's neck. Dale was scowling in each of the pictures.

Some of the photographs were of Lori and a group of girlfriends—at the lake, at a rock concert and some taken in various bars with the girls holding up drinks topped with maraschino cherries and miniature paper umbrellas. In one of the pictures, a blond girl was wearing a sash that had *Bride* written on it. Monica might have been imagining it, but she thought the look on Lori's face was half wistful, half jealous.

She was about to pull out her cell and check her email when a last photo caught her eye. Lori was sitting on a man's lap, and the man wasn't Dale. He looked familiar. Monica leaned closer. It was Mauricio who was Charlie Decker's boyfriend and who used to work for Jeff.

Had Charlie found out about Lori and her boyfriend? Lori had done Charlie wrong once already—was this the final straw that had ripped the bandage off that old wound?

Chapter 19

On impulse, Monica removed the photograph of Lori and Mauricio from its place on Lori's cubicle and slipped it into her purse. She didn't know what she was going to do with it, but she had the feeling it could be important.

Rick came back from dealing with his delivery. He didn't sit down but stood by his desk, his lanky frame looming over Monica.

"I'd rather Nora didn't know about our conversation, if that's okay with you." He ran a hand around the back of his neck. "It would only worry her."

"Sure," Monica said wondering what she was going to say when Nora asked her about the meeting. She'd have to cross that bridge when she came to it.

Rick hooked his thumbs in his belt loops. "Is there anything else I can do for you?"

"No. No, thank you." Monica stood up and the swivel chair she'd been sitting in shot backward, nearly tripping her.

Her shirt was stuck to her back with perspiration—the makeshift office wasn't well air-conditioned and her nerves hadn't helped any.

Rick stood by the door and watched as Monica walked toward her car. She noticed the dust on the wheels and the dried mud on the side of her Focus and vowed she would make a point of washing it as soon as she got the chance.

She sensed Rick was still standing at the door as she reversed, turned around and headed back down the long driveway.

She breathed a sigh of relief when she reached the main road. From her vantage point, she could see the increased activity down by the harbor in preparation for Flag Day. More boats than usual bobbed in the bay, their decks festooned with colorful flags. According to the VanVelsen sisters, boats would be cheek-by-jowl by Saturday when the celebrations officially got under way.

Monica's thoughts went back to the photograph she'd stolen from Lori Wenk's cubicle. She didn't know what she was going to do with it—show it to Charlie? That would only upset her and make her mad. Besides, what good would it do? Charlie would hardly admit to murdering Lori because she wanted to even old and new scores.

What about Mauricio? she wondered. Maybe she could ask him if the photo actually meant anything. Maybe he and Lori had only been fooling around. Maybe they were friends. Then she could feel him out and see if either of them had an alibi.

In her heart of hearts she didn't think that was the case, especially given Lori's reputation as a man-eater. She had the feeling Lori had wanted something from Mauricio and the picture had been part of her plan.

Monica was loathe to face Nora after her conversation with Rick—how was she going to tell her that Rick didn't have an alibi after all? What she'd prefer to do is talk to Mauricio first, but it would have to seem like a casual encounter. She didn't want to raise Charlie's suspicions. Monica shivered. She'd had run-ins with a few murderers already, and while she sincerely suspected Charlie was innocent, she didn't want to willingly put herself in danger again.

She was driving past Primrose Cottage—Charlie's bed-and-breakfast—when she noticed a ladder leaning against the side of the shingled cottage. A dark-haired man was standing on it, methodically swiping a paintbrush back and forth across the shutters.

It looked like Mauricio. Monica quickly switched on her blinker and pulled into the parking lot. By now she knew she could trust Arline with the baking that needed to be done—nothing would happen if she stole a few more minutes away from the kitchen. Hopefully she would soon find out what Mauricio's relationship with Lori had actually been—a moment of fun in a photo booth or had he really been cheating on Charlie?

Monica parked her car and walked up the path that was bordered with pink, purple and white primroses. Mauricio was headed down the ladder, a bucket of paint in his hand, when Monica reached him. He smiled when he saw her.

"Good day," he said. "How is Jeff? I miss working on his crew but Charlie needs help now that the season is picking up."

"Jeff's fine. I'm sure he misses working with you, too."

Mauricio jerked his head in the direction of the cottage. "Are you looking for Charlie? I think she's in the office."

"No. Actually, it's you that I wanted to talk to."

Mauricio gave Monica a quizzical look. "Me?" He pointed a finger at his own chest.

Monica noticed the shadow of worry that passed over his face. She knew that Mauricio still didn't have his papers and lived in fear of being deported. She felt vaguely guilty for causing him alarm.

"Do you know Lori Wenk?" she asked, trying to keep her tone light and non-accusatory.

"Who?" Mauricio made a big show of scratching his head.

"She's the woman who was killed out at Sassamanash Farm."

Mauricio's shoulders lifted up and down. "I don't know. The name is somehow . . . familiar?"

Monica reluctantly pulled the picture of Lori and Mauricio posing together in the photo booth out of her pocket where she'd stashed it. She held it out toward Mauricio.

Mauricio recoiled as if the picture was radioactive. "What's that?" He frowned, drawing his eyebrows into a deep *V*, wrinkling his normally smooth forehead.

Monica put the picture in his hand.

He held it hanging at his side, not looking at it.

Monica motioned toward the picture. "Where was that taken?" she asked.

Mauricio glanced at the sepia-toned photo briefly. His entire face collapsed like a soufflé abruptly snatched from a hot oven.

"Where did you get this?" he asked.

"Lori had it pinned to her cubicle at work."

Mauricio drew his lips back in a grimace and stomped his foot, kicking up a clod of moist earth. "She . . . she made me do it." He glanced at the photo in his hand again. "She saw me with Charlie at the tulip festival in May. They were friends when they were in school, but they had a fight." He wiped a hand across the back of his neck.

"I heard about that."

Mauricio nodded. "Charlie didn't like her at all. When she saw Lori at the festival, she took my arm and pulled me in the other direction."

"So how did you end up . . ." Monica motioned toward the photo Mauricio still held in his hand.

Mauricio bit his lip and looked at the ground. "Charlie had to come back here, to the cottage, because guests were coming later that day. I stayed at the festival—I was going to meet Jeff and some of the crew for a beer."

Monica waited as Mauricio angrily toed the tufts of grass alongside the path.

"Then that woman caught sight of me. Charlie said her name is Lori. All of a sudden she was all over me—trying to get my attention, touching my arm, offering me a bite of her ice cream." He shuddered. "I didn't want to have anything to do with her—not after what Charlie told me, and anyway. . . ." He blushed slightly. "I mean, Charlie and I are together." He held up two fingers side-by-side. "I don't want anything to come between us."

"And then what happened?"

"She saw the photo booth." He waved the picture at Monica. "Where this picture was taken. She asked if I would pose with her. She wanted to make her boyfriend jealous." He shook his head. "She said she wanted to get married." He spread out his hands, palms up. "I don't understand. Who wants to marry someone like that?"

"Why did you pose for the picture?" Monica asked gently. "Obviously you didn't want to."

Mauricio's shoulders sagged. "She said she would tell the immigration authorities that I didn't have the proper papers if I didn't do it."

"How did she know that you don't have your papers yet?"

Mauricio shrugged. "I think everybody in Cranberry Cove knows." He gave a brief smile. "You know how this town is."

Monica smiled back. "I certainly do." She thought back to her early days in town—when she'd just arrived to help Jeff. "People knew who I was before I even introduced myself."

Mauricio kicked at a clod of dirt he'd loosened. "Then you know how I feel. I feel . . . exposed. I never know when someone might turn me in to the authorities. Maybe I make them mad without realizing it, or they just don't like me. So you understand, right?" He looked at Monica with pleading eyes.

She nodded. She did understand.

"Did Charlie know about the picture?" Monica gestured toward Mauricio's hand.

He hung his head. "I told her." He looked up at Monica, his dark eyes earnest.

Monica was startled. "You did? Why?"

Mauricio shrugged again. "Why not? If Charlie knew about it, it couldn't do me any harm." He held his hands out toward Monica. "I love Charlie." He touched his heart with his fist. "I don't want to have secrets from her." He scowled. "That woman," he brandished the photo of Lori, "does not know what real love means. It is sad, don't you think?

"Yes, I do." Monica hesitated. "I imagine Charlie must have been quite angry when you told her about the photograph."

Mauricio was already nodding. "She was. She was furious. Especially because of what Lori had done to her when they were in school. She said this was too much and she wanted to get even with her somehow."

He must have noticed the look on Monica's face because he held up both hands, palms out. "No. Charlie wouldn't do something like that. Never. Someone else killed Lori. Maybe that boyfriend she was chasing after. You have to believe me."

Monica was quiet.

"Besides, she was with me when it happened. We were painting the bathroom on the third floor. The one in the Primrose Suite."

Monica smiled and put a hand on Mauricio's arm. "I didn't mean to imply I thought Charlie had anything to do with Lori's death." Monica mentally crossed her fingers. No need to upset Mauricio.

Mauricio let out a deep sigh and his shoulders relaxed. He smiled. "I'm sorry. I was afraid that that was what you were thinking."

Monica shook her head. "That's okay." She looked at her watch. "I'd better be going.

Mauricio said good-bye, picked up his paint can and headed toward the cottage. Monica stood for a moment, thinking.

Mauricio may have said that Charlie was with him, but Charlie had lied for Mauricio once—giving him a false alibi when he'd been suspected of murder. Wouldn't it make sense that now he would lie for her?

Chapter 20

Monica noticed traffic had increased on Beach Hollow Road and more people than usual crowded the sidewalk as she drove back toward the center of town. Flag Day was the unofficial start of the summer tourist season in Cranberry Cove and soon the cash registers would be ringing, the restaurants would be full and men and women in boat shoes would be relaxing with drinks on the deck of the Cranberry Cove Yacht Club.

Monica glanced at the clock on her dashboard. She had time to make a trip to the bank before it closed. Nora had said that they were running low on change at the farm store.

The bank was a few blocks removed from the main part of town. It was a small brick building with pillars flanking the front door and only two teller windows and a walk-up cash machine. The fluted white pillars always made Monica smile, as if someone had been attempting to dress it up—they looked like fancy trim on a plain cotton shift.

The bank was rarely busy so Monica was surprised to see several people lined up along the velvet rope that separated them from the tellers' windows and provided those doing their banking with a modicum of privacy.

She took her place behind a young woman in her twenties who was wearing very short cutoffs, rubber flip-flops and a T-shirt with a deep V-neck. Every few seconds she gave an impatient sigh as she checked the texts on her cell phone.

Monica assumed she was a tourist used to the fast pace of a larger city and wasn't accustomed to waiting in line at the bank—especially when the two elderly tellers moved at a snail's pace, wetting their finger and carefully counting out the money two or three times before handing it over.

Monica was thinking about Mauricio and Charlie when she heard a raised voice. She glanced toward one of the windows where a woman was standing, her back to the waiting customers. Something about her was familiar. Monica recognized the short gray hair but at first she couldn't place its owner.

The woman turned to the side, gesturing frantically, and Monica realized it was Mrs. Wenk. Her voice was loud and was getting even louder and had a plaintive edge to it.

"I should have money in my account. What are you

telling me?" Mrs. Wenk leaned closer to the teller as if that would help the teller to understand.

Monica couldn't hear the teller's response—only Mrs. Wenk's querulous voice—as she continued to argue.

"But I can't be overdrawn. My social security check should be in my account," she said, her tone pleading.

Monica wasn't sure what to do. It was obvious that Mrs. Wenk was in distress, and from Monica's previous encounters with her, she knew that Mrs. Wenk was easily confused. She hesitated for a few more seconds and then stepped forward, going up to Mrs. Wenk and gently touching her on the arm.

"Perhaps I can help."

Mrs. Wenk's face brightened. "Would you, dear? That would be wonderful." She tilted her head to one side. "You look familiar."

"I knew your daughter, Lori," Monica said.

"Yes, of course—Lori. She should be home any day now." She smiled at Monica.

Monica didn't have the heart to correct her. At least her memory loss was protecting her against the harsh reality that she'd lost her daughter. Maybe in this case it was for the best.

Monica leaned across the counter toward the teller. The women's posture was ramrod straight, her mouth set in a tight line and her thinning brown hair sprayed into place.

"What seems to be the problem?" Monica asked.

The woman hesitated, her fingers plucking at the pearl buttons on her long-sleeved lace blouse.

"We're not supposed to reveal information about our customers." Her face took on a brighter look. "Unless your name is on the account." She looked at Monica expectantly.

"I'm afraid it isn't." Monica held out both hands. "I'm not asking you to reveal anything, but surely it's okay if Mrs. Wenk doesn't mind. I only want to help."

The woman continued to fuss with the buttons on her blouse, her mouth working.

"I don't know. We have rules, you know."

"I realize that," Monica said with as much patience as she could muster.

The woman lowered her hands, and they hovered over her computer keyboard for a few seconds before she began clicking the keys. She frowned at the screen and looked at Mrs. Wenk.

"You withdrew all the money from your account last week." She tapped the monitor with a bony finger. She looked at Monica. "I suspect she's forgotten."

Mrs. Wenk twisted her plain gold wedding band around and around on her finger. "I didn't take the money out. I didn't come to the bank last week. I would remember."

"Would you, dear?" the teller asked.

Monica felt her neck stiffen. The teller had no need to be so snarky to the poor woman just because she was a little befuddled.

"If you didn't take it out yourself," the clerk said, her pointed nose still in the air, "then you must have given someone else permission to do it for you." She clicked off the screen on her computer and folded her hands on the counter as if to say that was that. "Because the money isn't there, and that's all I can tell you."

Monica felt a thrill of anticipation as she waited for Greg to pick her up. She was looking forward to a good dinner and Greg's warm and interesting companionship.

She'd taken extra care with her hair—fumbling with the new blow dryer she'd purchased at the drugstore—and had spent more time than usual in her closet choosing an outfit.

Finally she was standing in the living room in her coat, looking out the window, waiting for Greg to pull up.

Right on the dot of six forty-five, she heard the sound of a car coming up the driveway. Monica smiled. She appreciated when people were on time.

Monica gave Mittens a final scratch under the chin, checked her hair in the mirror in the foyer and headed out. Greg immediately ran around to the passenger side of the car to open the door.

"You look lovely tonight," Greg said as he put the car in drive.

Monica felt a blush color her face and was glad Greg's eyes were on the road.

The drive into town was quick, and they managed to secure a parking spot a few doors away from the Pepper Pot. Greg took Monica's arm as they strolled down the sidewalk. A light breeze blew in off the lake and Monica caught a whiff of the spicy scent of the geraniums in the planters hanging from the light posts.

Enticing smells wafted from the restaurant as soon as

Greg pulled open the door to the Pepper Pot. Monica recognized notes of garlic, onions and herbs, and her mouth watered.

Greg looked around the crowded room. "Good thing I made a reservation."

"I think summer tourist season is almost in full swing."

"You're probably right."

"If you'll come this way, please." A hostess in a long, gauzy white skirt and tangerine top breezed up to the podium and grabbed two large, leather-bound menus.

They followed her through the wood-paneled room, skirting occupied tables, dessert carts and bussing stations overflowing with dishes headed for the kitchen.

"Here you are." She pulled a chair out for Monica and handed them the menus.

Before opening hers, Monica looked around. A planter with a silk flower arrangement sat on the grate of the stone fireplace that reached to the wooden beamed ceiling. Most of the tables were occupied, lit by small lamps that lent a rosy glow to the room.

A waiter appeared at their table. "What can I get you to drink?"

"I'll have a glass of chardonnay, please," Monica said.

Greg ordered a Scotch and soda, and the waitress headed off to fill their order.

Unlike the Cranberry Cove Inn, where the waitstaff wore formalwear, the servers at the Pepper Pot wore black shirts and pants and tan canvas bib aprons with *Bon Appetit* written on them in red script. Monica knew the owner had wanted to create a warm, welcoming atmosphere that would complement the menu, which consisted of elegant takes on hearty fare like chicken pot pies with a puff pastry crust, meatloaf with a balsamic glaze and macaroni and cheese embellished with chunks of lobster.

The waitress appeared with their drinks and set them down on the table.

"Here's to a bright future," Greg said, taking a drink of his Scotch.

Monica took a sip of her wine and breathed in the delicious smells. She felt her shoulders slowly relax.

"This is just what the doctor ordered," Monica said.

Greg looked up from his menu, his eyebrows drawn. "This murder is getting you down, isn't it?"

Monica ran her finger around and around the rim of her glass. "It is casting a shadow over things."

"What are your thoughts so far?"

"My thoughts are in a jumble, to tell you the truth. I was convinced the culprit was Lori's boyfriend, but he has an alibi. Of sorts. I suppose he could have convinced the bartender at Flynn's to lie for him. But then why wouldn't he tell the police where he was?" She paused and took a sip of her wine. "That leaves Nora, who works in the farm store, or her husband Rick. They both seem like nice people."

"Nice people sometimes do surprising things when cornered. And it sounds like Rick, at least, was cornered by the victim."

Monica didn't want to believe that. She fiddled with the edge of her cocktail napkin. "Then there's Charlie Decker. Mauricio gives her an alibi, but he would, wouldn't he?"

Greg nodded. "Tit for tat, I guess."

Monica was about to open her menu when she heard someone calling her.

"Yoo-hoo, Monica!"

Monica swiveled around in her seat to see Gina making her way toward them through the crowded tables. She was wearing what could only be described as a bandage dress with stiletto-heeled sandals. She had Xavier Cabot by the hand and was dragging him along behind her. Xavier was wearing a black polo shirt with a sport coat over it and had a look of bemusement on his face.

"This is wonderful," Gina said when she reached their table. "We don't have a reservation, and they said it's going to be an hour wait." She feigned a pout. "You know how I hate to wait. But now we can sit with you."

"There's not much room. . . ." Monica began but Gina had already signaled to the waitress who was bearing down on them, a concerned look on her face.

"Can you bring us two more chairs? We'd like to join our friends."

The waitress bit her lip, opened her mouth and then closed it again. She obviously recognized that there was no point in arguing with Gina.

"Monica, you know Xavier," Gina said when they were finally all crowded around the small table. "And Greg?" Gina put her hand over Xavier's.

"Yes, we've certainly met." Xavier raked a hand through his thick gray hair. "He's helped me track down some volumes that have been invaluable in my research."

Gina put her arm around Xavier's waist and drew him toward her. "Xavier is so intellectual, don't you think?" She cupped a hand under his chin and smiled at him.

Monica took a deep breath and exhaled quietly. She'd been looking forward to dinner with Greg—just the two of them. She glanced in his direction to see how he was taking the intrusion. He didn't look as if he minded, but Monica knew his innate good manners would prevent him from showing any signs of irritation.

Gina flagged down the waitress as she flew past their table. She turned to Xavier when the waitress came to a halt by their side. "What would you like to drink?"

Xavier turned an appreciative glance on the waitress whose Pepper Pot apron couldn't disguise her ample curves. "What single malts do you have?"

"We have Macallan."

Xavier stroked his beard. "I'll have that."

"Water or soda?"

"Neat, please."

The waitress made a note on her pad and turned to Gina, her eyebrows raised.

"A glass of champagne, please. Veuve Clicquot, if you have it."

"We only sell that by the bottle."

Gina waved a hand in the air. "Fine. Bring the whole bottle then." She turned in her chair. "And four glasses," she called to the retreating waitress. She swiveled back toward the table. "Isn't this cozy?" She linked her arm through Xavier's.

Monica hoped her smile didn't look too forced.

"Tell us about your book," Greg said to Xavier. "Which shipwreck are you researching at the moment?"

"Several, actually." Xavier put his hands behind his head and tilted his chair back slightly. "Six boats went down in the Armistice Day Blizzard of 1940. Three of these have already been well documented—the *SS Anna C. Minch*, the *SS William B. Davock* and the *SS Novadoc*. Two smaller ships were also lost between Little Sable Point and Pentwater."

The waitress reappeared with Xavier's drink, a silver bucket of ice with a champagne bottle sticking out of the top and four champagne flutes. She deftly uncorked the champagne, which gave a satisfying pop, and poured Gina a glass. She glanced at Monica, who was nearly finished with her chardonnay. Monica nodded and the waitress poured her a glass of the bubbly. She held the bottle out toward Greg, but he was still nursing his scotch and soda.

"I've read about the Armistice Blizzard of 1940," Greg said when the waitress moved away. "The temperatures were unseasonably warm—into the sixties that afternoon. But then they dropped precipitously."

"The perfect atmospheric conditions for a big storm," Xavier said, taking a sip of his whiskey and leaning back in his chair. "The blizzard that ravaged the Midwest. Two ships lost all hands but some of the crew from the *SS Novadoc* were rescued by an intrepid fisherman named Clyde Cross." Xavier chuckled. "Some called him a hero and others called him crazy. No matter. He saved quite a number of lives that night."

"Do we want to order?" Gina said. She'd been perusing her menu while Xavier was talking.

They quickly decided what they wanted, Monica settling on the chicken potpie, although it had been tough to choose between that and the beef stew.

"You mentioned a sixth ship," Greg said when the waitress had finished taking their order.

Xavier leaned toward Greg. "It was a smaller ship and much less is known about it. It was called the *SS Pegasus*. She was carrying a load of hardwood lumber to Chicago. I've unearthed a couple of interesting facts."

Greg raised his eyebrows. Xavier took a deep breath as he launched into the story.

"It seems that one of the sailors on board, Patrick Boudreaux, had had a run-in with another member of the crew, a young man by the name of Jacob Spindler. Some notes about their set-to were found in a journal one of the sailors had been keeping but which he'd left behind on this particular voyage—thus it survived. A fellow at the Michigan Shipwreck Research Association has been most helpful."

Xavier paused and took a sip of his Scotch. Gina leaned over and brushed aside a lock of hair that had fallen onto his forehead.

"It was about a woman, of course. Most of these things are."

Monica started to protest, but Xavier continued on.

"It's conjectured that Patrick, who had been seen near the telegraph machine on board the *Pegasus*, intercepted a telegram warning the captain of the raging blizzard. Again, this is all conjecture, but it is thought that instead of delivering the correct message, Patrick told the captain that it was safe to embark—the storm was letting up— consequently sending the ship directly into the eye of the storm."

"But wasn't he putting his own life in danger?" Monica asked.

"That's the interesting part—and the reason this story has been put forward. A crew member from another ship saw Patrick standing on the dock as the ship pulled away. And records indicate that a Patrick Boudreaux lived a long and healthy life, dying in 1998 at the age of eighty-six."

Chapter 21

"That was an interesting story Xavier told," Greg said later as he and Monica were leaving the Pepper Pot. "As a matter of fact, he has a lot of interesting stories. I can't wait to read his book."

"It was interesting. Also slightly frustrating," Monica said. "I've been thinking about the story since Xavier related it, and something about it seems . . . important somehow, but I can't grasp exactly what."

"That is frustrating," Greg said. "Maybe if you relax, it will come to you."

He took Monica's arm.

"That wasn't exactly the intimate dinner I'd been planning," he said as they strolled down Beach Hollow Road.

"I'm sorry, but you know Gina. There's no stopping her."

"No need to apologize." Greg reached for Monica's hand. "It was an entertaining evening. And the food was excellent." He squeezed her hand. "How about a nightcap at my place? We didn't have much of a chance to talk."

"I'd like that," Monica said.

They continued hand in hand down the street. The night air had turned cooler and a soft breeze was blowing in off of the lake. The shops were shuttered for the night and the gas lamps created pools of light on the sidewalk.

Greg stopped just short of Book 'Em and fished a tangle of keys from his pocket. He opened the windowless door next to the shop, and he and Monica mounted the stairs to his apartment.

It looked to Monica as if he'd made an effort to clean up. Books were arranged in neat piles instead of being scattered helter-skelter over every available surface, and the papers that had been stacked on top of them had been whisked away somewhere.

Monica smiled at the thought of Greg tidying up in hopes that she would come upstairs for a nightcap. She was glad she'd said yes.

"I've got a lovely bottle of merlot breathing on the counter." Greg laughed. "My, how pretentious that sounds. But the fellow at the Purple Grape said it would enhance the flavor and the bouquet of the wine. I'm going to take his word for it." He turned toward the kitchen. "I'll bring the bottle and some glasses out here."

Monica settled on his slightly lumpy but comfortable sofa and picked up a book sitting on the table in front of her. It was a Ruth Rendell she hadn't read yet. Greg returned with the wine and some glasses on a tray as she finished reading the back cover copy.

Greg nodded toward the book as he settled the tray on

top of a stack of hardcovers. "Have you read *Dark Corners* yet? I highly recommend it." He gestured toward the book again. "Take it with you, if you'd like."

Monica put the book down beside her on the sofa and reached for the glass Greg held out to her.

He picked up his own glass and clinked it with Monica's. "'Let us be grateful to people who make us happy, they are the charming gardeners who make our souls blossom.' Marcel Proust," he added.

Monica felt a rush of pleasure. She took a sip of her wine.

Greg settled on the couch beside her. "Are you going to the Flag Day celebration tomorrow?"

"Yes. I'm going to try to get away for a bit. What about you?"

Greg shook his head. "I'd better man the store. The town will be crawling with tourists and perhaps I can lure some of them into my shop. It's a fun festival—you'll enjoy it."

Monica's free hand was in her lap, and Greg picked it up in his. He ran his fingers gently over her palm and slipped his fingers through hers.

Later, Monica was surprised when she noticed the time. They'd finished the bottle of wine while discussing a wide range of topics from books to music to pop culture. The conversation never lagged and was always interesting and stimulating.

She stretched, put her empty glass down on the table and stood up. She hesitated, wondering if Greg would try to get her to stay. She knew what her answer was going to be.

Monica looked at her watch. "I didn't realize it was so late."

Greg stood up with her. He put his hands on her shoulders, his gaze level with hers.

"Do you really have to go?"

This time Monica didn't hesitate. She smiled. "No. You're right. I don't have to go. Not if you don't want me to."

"I don't," he said, his lips hovering over hers.

Greg was already in the kitchen making coffee when Monica woke up the next morning.

Despite the closeness she and Greg had achieved the evening before, she felt slightly awkward now. Greg had set the table with placemats, napkins, silverware and glasses of juice, and the scent of bacon cooking wafted on the air. It immediately made Monica think of the Cranberry Cove Diner, so accustomed had she become to associating that smell with the restaurant.

"You're up," Greg said. He went to Monica and gave her a kiss.

Suddenly everything seemed right and natural about her being there. She felt her stomach grumble. She was surprised to find herself quite hungry.

Greg opened the oven door and more delicious cooking aromas drifted on the hot steam from the oven.

"I've made a frittata," he said, pulling out a baking dish and placing it on a hot pad in the center of his small table.

As Monica watched, the puffy egg concoction sank slightly in the dish. The top was golden brown and studded with tomatoes, peppers and mushrooms.

"It looks delicious," Monica said as she pulled out a chair.

Greg sat opposite and served up the frittata.

Monica suddenly felt like giggling—a truly unaccustomed feeling. She glanced at Greg to see his eyes dancing with merriment, his lips curved into a smile that was just short of bursting into a laugh.

They ate in silence for a few minutes. Monica felt as if they were wrapped in their own unique bubble of intimacy—sharing breakfast after having spent the night together.

She was astonished when she looked up and noticed the time on the clock.

She put down her knife and fork and pushed back her chair. "Let me help you with the dishes, and then I have to get going. Hopefully Arline has already started the baking without me."

"I wish you didn't have to go," Greg said as they filled the dishwasher with the dirty dishes. He turned and took Monica in his arms, nuzzling his lips against her neck. "I hope that someday you won't have to."

Monica's breath caught in her throat. She didn't know what to say, but she could feel her heart speed up and a wide grin spread across her face.

Greg gave Monica a final squeeze, letting go of her reluctantly. She gathered her things together, and he walked her down the stairs and stood at the open door, watching as she went down the street.

Beach Hollow Road was quiet and hushed, the sun hanging low on the horizon. The air had a slight morning chill to it. Bart was outside his shop, a clean apron tied around his waist, putting up the metal shutters that he pulled down every night over his plateglass display window. Breakfast smells were already wafting out of the propped-open door of the Cranberry Cove Diner.

"Good morning," Bart called to Monica as she went past. The shutter rattled and groaned as it went up, revealing the empty window. "Any news on the murder out at your brother's farm?"

"No," Monica said. There'd been no more news from Detective Stevens, and she was as much in the dark as anyone else.

"It's strange, don't you think?" Bart stuck his thumbs in the apron strings encircling his waist. "A young girl like that. Hardly old enough to have made many enemies."

"I don't know," Monica said. "Some people manage to collect enemies the way other people collect coins or stamps."

Bart nodded. "True. There are those who rub everyone the wrong way without even meaning to or even knowing they're doing it."

Monica thought the situation with Lori Wenk was a little more complicated than that, but she didn't say anything.

"I'd best be going," Bart said. "I've got a side of beef that needs butchering."

Monica shuddered. She loved nothing more than a fine steak or some juicy chops, but she didn't like thinking about the process of getting the meat from the hoof to her table.

She waved good-bye to Bart and continued down the street. Gina was standing in front of Making Scents, her

keys in her hand. She stopped and turned when she saw
Monica coming down the sidewalk.

She looked as surprised as a kid on Christmas morning. A grin spread across her face and she waggled her
eyebrows comically when Monica reached her.

"You're either out awfully early, which makes no sense
since everything but the diner is still closed . . ." She
paused dramatically. "Or you never went home," she finished triumphantly.

Monica willed herself not to blush and was only par-
tially successful.

"You were at Greg's," Gina stated without waiting for
Monica's explanation. "It's about time."

Monica bristled. "I wanted to be sure. Ted hasn't been
gone all that long."

"Pooh, your fiancé died almost two years ago. It's time
to move on. Listen to mama Gina, don't let this fish slip
off the hook."

Monica was about to protest the fishing analogy and
that she hardly wanted to hook Greg—that made it sound
so Machiavellian—but she knew it was useless. Gina's
view on male-female relationships was based on the be-
havior of animals in the wild—the male stalked the female until the female was captured and subdued.

Monica let Gina prattle on, only half listening because
she was thinking about what Greg had said—how he
hoped there would be a time when she didn't have to go.
Without thinking, she blurted it out to Gina.

Gina stopped midsentence, her hand flying to her
mouth, her eyes wide with excitement.

"He proposed!"

Monica was so taken aback she actually took a step backward. "No, no," she protested. "It wasn't a proposal."

"It's as near to one as makes no difference," Gina insisted, clapping her hands. "What did you say?"

"It wasn't a question," Monica insisted. "I didn't say anything."

"Well, then it's only a matter of time before he pops the question officially. Is he going to pick out the ring or are you going to do it together?"

No amount of protesting on Monica's part could convince Gina that Greg's words hadn't been a proposal, tacit or otherwise.

By the time she said good-bye to her stepmother, she had started wondering herself—what exactly *had* Greg meant by saying that?"

In contrast with Beach Hollow Road, the harbor hummed with activity. A number of small boats adorned with colorful flags bobbed in the calm waters of the lake, while off in the distance, others headed toward shore, sails aflutter. Canopied food stands were being set up on the grounds of the Cranberry Cove Yacht Club, this being the one time when the tourists mingled with the locals. A white paneled truck with *Van Veldhuizen's* on the side in black lettering was backed up to one of the stands, and a blond-haired young man was unloading a huge stainless steel steam table.

Monica thought of the traditional Dutch rijsttafel Hennie

VanVelsen had described to her, and felt her mouth water. She was looking forward to the festival, but first she had to get some work done.

Monica headed back toward the farm. She had the windows open and relished the sweet breeze blowing in. She passed the once-abandoned cottage. Xavier's green Jeep was missing from the driveway, replaced by a blue pickup truck carrying several large, framed windows. A man in baggy overalls and a red baseball cap was standing on a ladder leaning against the side of the house. Monica noticed that the boards had been removed and replaced with a new window.

It looked like Xavier planned on staying awhile. That was good news for Gina.

Monica pulled into the driveway of her cottage and parked around back. She planned to change her clothes— she didn't want to take any chances on anyone else recognizing that they were the same ones she'd worn yesterday and drawing the obvious conclusion. Besides, even with an apron on, she was sure to get something on her good slacks and blouse.

Mittens greeted her at the door. Monica picked her up and they rubbed noses, Mittens purring loudly with satisfaction. She let Monica stroke her head a few times and then, wriggling with impatience, leapt from Monica's arms and scampered toward a sunbeam coming in the kitchen window, where she proceeded to chase the dust mites hanging in the air.

Monica checked Mittens's water bowl and added another half cup of food to her dish.

Mittens scampered after her as she went upstairs to

change into jeans and a T-shirt. She brushed her hair and pulled it back into a loose ponytail. She glanced in the mirror—that would have to do.

By the time she headed down the path to the farm kitchen, the sun was higher in the sky and the air warmer. The sky was blue and cloudless—a perfect day for the Flag Day celebration, assuming the mercurial Michigan weather didn't change within the next couple of hours.

Monica quickened her pace as she approached the farm kitchen. There were a number of cars in the farm store parking lot, which meant they might be running out of stock soon. But she would shortly have a warm batch of baked goods fresh from the oven to take down to Nora.

Monica was surprised to see that the windows of the farm kitchen were dark. Arline should have been there by now. Monica felt a twinge of annoyance as she inserted her key in the lock and opened the door.

She immediately knew something was wrong. The overpowering smell of natural gas nearly gagged her as she walked in. The door to the oven was open and all the burners on the stove were on, although Monica couldn't see a flame from where she was standing. She suspected there was none.

It was obvious someone had done this deliberately. It might be possible to leave one burner on, not realizing it hadn't lit, but not all of them—and the oven, too.

Monica backed out immediately and moved a safe distance away. She pulled her cell phone from her pocket and dialed 911.

"What is your emergency?"

Monica was surprised to find her voice shaking as she

relayed her discovery. The operator promised help would be on the way and warned her not to go near the kitchen until they arrived. Monica was tempted to dash in and at least turn off the gas, but she agreed to wait until help came.

A police car, followed by a Michigan Gas Utilities truck, soon rumbled down the path, much to Monica's relief. She knew it wouldn't take more than a single spark to send the farm kitchen flying sky-high. And although they had insurance, there would be the deductible to be covered, not to mention the time lost. The thought made her feel sick.

She wasn't surprised to see Jeff running down the path moments later. He stopped in front of Monica panting, his face creased with concern.

"What's happened?" he asked when he'd caught his breath.

"Someone turned on all the burners in the kitchen and blew out the flames. The oven, too."

"Someone had to have done it on purpose."

Jeff looked around. "Where's Arline? Did she—"

"She's not here yet. I don't know where she is. Someone obviously took advantage of the fact that no one was here."

Jeff pushed his cap back and scratched his forehead. "But why?"

"To frighten me?" Monica guessed.

"But why?" Jeff asked again. "Why you? What kind of a sick jerk would want to do that?"

"I may have asked the wrong questions of the wrong person," Monica admitted reluctantly.

"You mean about Lori's murder?"

"It's the only thing I can think of. It can't have been an accident. I wouldn't be so careless and neither would Arline. This had to have been done deliberately."

"If that's true then you've got to go away," Jeff said, grabbing Monica's arm. "You could have been killed. The killer might try again. You won't be safe until they're caught."

The idea was tempting—Monica *was* scared, even if she would only admit it to herself.

"I can't. There's too much to do here at the farm. Besides, where would I go?"

"You could visit your mother in Chicago."

Monica made a face.

Jeff laughed. "It wouldn't be that bad."

"I don't like the idea of running away. It smacks of cowardice."

"It wouldn't be running away," Jeff said, looking Monica in the eyes, his own pleading. "It would be the safest thing to do. At least until the police have this wrapped up. Until then, you'll be in constant danger."

Monica was about to say something in rebuttal when they heard someone shout in the distance.

"What's going on?"

Monica turned to see Arline running down the path, waving frantically. She skidded to a stop in front of them. She was panting and her short dark bangs were plastered to her forehead.

"What happened?" she said. "What's wrong? I heard the sirens. . . ." She bent over and put her hands on her knees, her breath coming in gasps.

Monica explained about the gas being left on. Arline began to shake.

"It's my fault." Her words ended in a sob.

"You mean you . . ."

"No," Arline protested. "I didn't leave the gas on—I would never do something like that. It's Bruce. It has to be. He works with Dale at the station. We double-dated with Dale and Lori a couple of times, but we didn't hit it off. At least I didn't. Even after I'd turned him down for a third date, Bruce kept calling me." Arline put trembling hands over her face. "Sometimes I'd come out of the house and he'd be standing on the sidewalk across the street, waiting for me. Or I'd be in the grocery store, and he'd be there watching me." Arline shivered. "It was so creepy. I told him to stop but he said I was going to have to pay for turning him down."

At that point Arline began crying in earnest, her small shoulders heaving as she buried her face in her hands again.

Monica put an arm around her. "Why didn't you tell someone about this? The police would have helped you."

"I was too scared. I didn't think anyone would take me seriously. And I didn't know what Bruce would do if he found out. He warned me not to say anything."

"Of course you would have been believed." Monica squeezed her shoulders.

Jeff smiled over the top of Arline's bent head. "I guess this settles it. They were after Arline, not you, and you don't have to go visit your mother after all."

Monica managed a small smile, although her neck still

ached with tension. She massaged the muscles with her hand. "You're right. That's one good thing at least."

Monica glanced toward the open door to the kitchen. The windows were open, too, and two workmen in dark blue pants with *Michigan Gas Utilities* in white on the back of their dark blue shirts stood talking to the two policemen who had come screeching down the drive in their patrol car.

One of the workmen began walking toward Monica. He had intense blue eyes that peered out from under the brim of his cap. He jerked a thumb over his shoulder toward the farm kitchen.

"We've turned the gas off and opened all available doors and windows. Still, I'd give it some more time to air out. It doesn't take much gas to cause an explosion."

"I have things that need to get done," Monica said, clenching her hands together. "When do you think . . . ?"

"Give it another half an hour to clear. And if you don't smell gas anymore, it will be okay for you to go back inside."

"Look, sis," Jeff said. "Let it go for today. We'll close the farm store early if need be. It's not worth the risk."

"But if we close early, people will think we're unreliable and they'll stop coming around."

Jeff shook his head. "No, they won't. Besides, everyone is going to be at the Flag Day celebration. I'd be surprised if we had more than one or two more customers today."

Monica sighed. She didn't like it. Unreliability was death to a business. She'd seen it happen with the small boutique that had been down the street from her café in Chicago. The owner, a young woman with dyed purple hair, had been quite sketchy about her opening and closing times. At first, there had been a steady demand for her stock of vintage clothing, but eventually business had died off. Monica couldn't bear to see that happen to the farm store.

She looked longingly toward the open door of the farm kitchen and sighed. "I suppose it will be okay to wait half an hour. That will still give me time to get a couple of batches of muffins and scones in the oven."

Jeff threw his good hand in the air. "Have it your way." He grinned. "I see we've both inherited the Albertson stubborn gene, so there's no use arguing. But you're not going in there a minute before the half hour is up. As a matter of fact, I'd feel a whole lot better if you gave it forty-five minutes."

"Fine. I'll do it your way."

"I'm glad you've seen the wisdom of my reasoning."

Monica punched Jeff on the arm. "Don't kid yourself. I'm humoring you, little brother. Nothing more."

Chapter 22

It took all of Monica's self-control to wait the forty-five minutes she'd promised Jeff. She spent the time going over the farm's accounts—something she'd planned to do later in the week anyway. When she finally did return to the farm kitchen, she sniffed carefully for any lingering odor of gas but couldn't detect any. Still, when she turned the oven on to preheat it, she found herself cringing in spite of herself. She let out a sigh of relief as the flame caught and lit the heating element.

Monica set about measuring her flour and sugar and retrieving a bag of frozen cranberries from the stainless steel freezer. She'd told Arline not to bother to come back—the poor girl had been badly shaken by the events of the morning. Monica hoped Arline was right, that turning on the gas had been an act of revenge by the fellow she'd spurned for a date, and not something Lori's killer had done to frighten Monica. Monica didn't want to think about the fact that filling the kitchen with gas had more likely been done to silence her for good than to simply frighten her.

Her hands were trembling as she began patting out the dough for cranberry scones, but the longer she worked, the steadier they became, taking up the familiar and soothing rhythm of rolling dough, measuring flour and stirring batter.

Monica might have been present in the Sassamanash Farm kitchen, but her mind was elsewhere. Her brain went around and around with thoughts of Lori's murder and who the culprit might be. There was no proof that Rick or Nora hadn't committed the crime, but Monica refused to believe either of them capable of such violence—even thinking about it was a waste of time.

Dale had been ruled out, but perhaps he'd bribed the bartender at Flynn's to give him an alibi. But if he had, then why hadn't he told the police about it? Certainly being caught violating his probation carried a lesser penalty than cold-blooded murder.

Charlie? She'd lied to protect Mauricio once so there was no reason to think he wouldn't lie to protect her. Monica didn't want to think Charlie capable of murder, either—she liked and admired the woman—but Monica did have to admit that there was a ruthless streak to Charlie that might have made it possible for her to commit murder.

Then again, the killer might be someone Monica hadn't even thought of yet—a colleague of Lori's at the library or someone she had dated other than Dale.

Monica finished the last batch of muffins and gave the kitchen a cursory cleaning. She'd come back later and do a more thorough job. Excitement about the Flag Day celebration had been in the air in Cranberry Cove for several weeks, and Monica had finally caught the bug herself. She couldn't wait to shed her worries and get down to the lake to see all the boats in the harbor and sample the delicious foods Hennie had told her about.

Having finished in the kitchen, Monica headed back to her cottage to change. Mittens was exceptionally playful, and Monica spent several minutes wielding the laser pointer, much to the kitten's delight.

"Sorry, but game's over," Monica said, replacing the pointer in the kitchen drawer. "I have to get ready."

Monica headed up to her bedroom, Mittens either on her heels or dashing ahead through her legs.

Monica peeled off her jeans and T-shirt and lifted the lid of the bulging laundry basket. If she didn't do some laundry, the only thing she'd have to wear tomorrow would be her good slacks and silk blouse.

Monica changed into a light blue cotton sundress with a halter neck, fitted waist and full skirt. Her white sandals would complete the outfit. Monica enjoyed dressing up on occasion, but there were few occasions in Cranberry Cove that called for it.

She tipped the laundry basket over and quickly sorted the dirty clothes into lights and darks. She carried the bundle of dark clothes—consisting mainly of pairs of jeans in various degrees of shabbiness—down to the first floor.

Before tossing them in the washing machine off the

kitchen, she checked the pockets for tissues. She was notorious for forgetting to do that, and more often than not, her clothes came out of the dryer with bits of lint clinging all over them.

She stuck her hand into the front pocket of the final pair of jeans and pulled out a crumpled piece of paper. She was about to toss it in the trash basket when she changed her mind. She took it over to the counter and smoothed it out.

It was a withdrawal slip from the bank. For a moment she couldn't remember why she had it in her pocket—she hadn't withdrawn any money recently—then she remembered having found it in the ditch along with the bee-keeper's hat and veil.

She nearly crumpled it up again before she changed her mind. She thought about Mrs. Wenk and her insistence that she hadn't taken any money out of her bank account. Maybe Lori had gone to the bank for her and this withdrawal slip had fallen out of her pocket while she was at the farm?

If that was the case, it might reassure Mrs. Wenk. She'd been quite fixated on the idea that someone had stolen her money.

Monica was grabbing her purse from the chair where she'd left it when the doorbell rang.

Who could it be? She wasn't expecting anyone. Maybe Detective Stevens had stopped by with some news? Although from past experience, Monica knew Stevens was more likely to be there to ask questions than give answers.

Mittens bounded onto the back of an armchair and watched as Monica opened the front door. Charlie Decker was standing on the doorstep. For a moment Monica was at a loss for words.

"Come in," she said finally.

Charlie was wearing cutoffs, a T-shirt with *Primrose Cottage* across the front and she had her ponytail pulled through the back of her pink baseball cap. She looked as if she'd been working in the garden—there were grass stains on her shorts and a smear of mud on the sleeve of her T-shirt.

"I had to come and see you," Charlie said, "after what Mauricio told me."

So Mauricio had told Charlie that Monica had been around, asking questions. Monica tried to hide her embarrassment.

"I was only trying to—" she stammered before Charlie interrupted.

"I suppose you heard that old story from someone— the VanVelsen sisters? Bart? Old Mrs. Macgillicutty at the drugstore?" Charlie shrugged. "It doesn't matter. Some people refuse to let sleeping dogs lie—especially where I'm concerned."

"I'm sorry—"

Charlie waved a hand. "No need to apologize. You're not the first and I'm sure you won't be the last to dig up old dirt."

"Won't you sit down? Would you like some iced tea or a cup of coffee?"

"No, thanks. And I'd better not sit down." She gestured to the dried mud on the back of her shorts. "I didn't want to take the time to change. I came as soon as Mauricio told me." She gave a small smile. "Although I did have to worm it out of him. He didn't want to upset me, he said." Charlie fiddled with a loose thread on her cutoffs. "But I could tell something was wrong."

Monica nodded.

"He told me he said he was with me at the time of Lori Wenk's murder. He said we were painting. That's not true."

Even though Monica had suspected that Mauricio had lied to cover up for Charlie, she was still taken aback.

"It's true Mauricio was painting, but I had an appointment. I didn't want to tell him where I was going because I was afraid it would worry him." Charlie scraped a bit of mud off her shorts with her fingernail.

"Where did you go?" Monica finally asked when Charlie didn't say anything.

Charlie looked up. "You know my mother died of cancer?"

"Yes, I'm sorry."

Charlie dashed a hand across her eyes. "I was having symptoms. Just like the ones my mother had had right before the doctor diagnosed her with cancer. I freaked out. I called my doctor, and he gave me the earliest appointment he could. Still, there were quite a few sleepless nights."

"I'm so sorry." Monica leaned against the back of the armchair and stroked Mittens's silky fur. The kitten closed her eyes and purred loudly.

"The good news is it's not cancer but common, garden-variety gastroenteritis. Still, I didn't want to tell Mauricio. I didn't even want to put the thought in his mind that I could get cancer. There would be no end to his worrying."

Charlie stuck a hand in her pocket. "I know you talk to that policewoman a lot, and I didn't want her to hear that old story about me and Lori and jump to the wrong conclusion. Because I do have an alibi." She pulled a creased and folded piece of paper out of her pocket and handed it to Monica. "Open it."

Monica unfolded the sheet. *Kenneth P. Johnson, MD PC* was written at the top. Charlie's name was entered on the line where it said *Patient*, along with the date and time of her appointment, both of which proved Charlie couldn't have been at Sassamanash Farm when Lori was killed.

Monica folded the paper and handed it back to Charlie.

"I didn't really think you could have had anything to do with the murder."

"No problem," Charlie said briskly as she pocketed the sheet from her doctor's office. "That old story about me and Lori made me a strong suspect, although I don't believe in carrying a grudge. What's that saying? 'Holding on to anger is like taking poison and expecting the other person to die.'" Charlie gave a halfhearted smile. "Anyway, it looks like you're about to go out, so I won't keep you."

"I'm headed to the Flag Day celebration. Are you going?"

"No time. We're booked full at the Cottage and I have to turn some rooms this afternoon."

Monica's conversation with Charlie hadn't taken that long. It was still fairly early—the Flag Day celebration was scheduled to run until ten o'clock that night, when it would finally be getting dark enough for fireworks over the lake. Monica had plenty of time to pay a quick visit to Mrs. Wenk on her way into town.

The washer was still going in the small laundry room off the kitchen. She decided not to wait for the load to be done—she could toss the clothes in the dryer later that night when she got home.

Mrs. Wenk's car wasn't in the driveway when Monica arrived, and Monica wondered if she had gone to the harbor for the celebration. She didn't feel particularly sanguine as she got out of the car and went up the path to ring the doorbell.

She was surprised when Mrs. Wenk almost immediately flung open the door. Her blue eyes were much clearer than the last time Monica had seen her, and her hair was neatly combed.

"Hello, dear," she said as she led the way into the living room. "How kind of you to stop by."

"I was afraid you might not be home—I didn't see your car in the driveway. I thought perhaps you'd gone to the Flag Day celebration."

"I don't enjoy crowds anymore. I find them . . . confusing." She shook her head. "That young lady who is renting a room from me—Arline—asked to borrow my car. I really didn't want her to, but she got me all turned around, and in the end I said yes." She rubbed a hand over her face. "At least I think I did." She frowned. "It worries me when I can't remember things."

"Do you remember the last time we met, at the bank,

and you told me about the money missing from your account?"

"If you say so, I suppose I must have." She gestured toward the bills that were still scattered across the coffee table, their envelopes marked *Urgent* and *Past Due*. "I still need to pay all those bills."

Monica pulled the withdrawal slip from her purse. "I found this slip at the farm where I live. I wondered if it might belong to you. Maybe it fell out of Lori's pocket?"

Mrs. Wenk frowned at the piece of yellow paper in Monica's hand. "I don't know, dear."

"Can we check the bank account number on here against your checking account number?"

Mrs. Wenk's face brightened. "Good idea. I never was any good at remembering numbers."

She got up, went into another room and returned with a slim, blue leather-bound checkbook. "The number should be on here, isn't that right?" She handed the book to Monica.

Monica took it, flipped the pages past the register and opened it to the first check. She put the checkbook down on the coffee table and put the withdrawal slip next to it. Mrs. Wenk watched Monica, her expression drawn into a frown that furrowed the skin between her eyebrows and drew them together.

"Do they match?" she asked before Monica had even finished.

Monica bit her lip. "One second. I want to make sure."

She compared the numbers a second time and they matched perfectly.

"Yes," she said twisting around to look up at Mrs. Wenk, who was leaning over Monica's shoulder. "They're the same account."

"So that means someone did take money out of my account," Mrs. Wenk said triumphantly, her face flushing. "I knew it." She shook her index finger at Monica. "People say I'm crazy and that I'm losing my mind, but it's not true. I am a bit forgetful at times, but I hope I still have my wits about me."

"I imagine you must have withdrawn the money yourself and then forgotten about it," Monica said, closing the checkbook and pushing it toward Mrs. Wenk.

Mrs. Wenk picked up the withdrawal slip and stared at it, her mouth moving.

She lowered it and looked at Monica.

"What would I be doing with this amount of cash?" She waved the slip in the air. "When I have all these bills to pay?" She swept a hand toward the stack of envelopes on the table then peered more closely at the withdrawal slip. She slapped it down on the table. "That isn't my handwriting," she said, pointing to it.

"Could it have been Lori who withdrew the money for you? And then she lost the slip while she was out at our farm?"

Mrs. Wenk knitted her gnarled fingers together and a worried look came over her face.

"I don't know," she finally admitted after a long pause. "I'm afraid I don't remember."

Monica left Mrs. Wenk's house more puzzled than ever. She had hoped to set the poor woman's mind at rest regarding the money that had disappeared from her account, but it seemed as if she had done anything but.

Lori must have been the one to withdraw the money from the bank. But what had she done with it? Had she used the money for herself?

The thought made Monica feel slightly sick. How could someone take advantage of their own mother like that—especially a parent afflicted with memory problems like Mrs. Wenk?

Monica was standing in the driveway, her hand on the door of the Focus, when she heard someone come up in back of her.

"Everything okay with Mrs. Wenk?"

The woman was middle-aged and wearing shorts that were a bit too short for someone her age. She had straight, slightly greasy dark hair, parted in the middle and held back with bobby pins on either side of her face.

She pointed behind her. "I'm Harriet Wenk's neighbor. I check in on her from time to time." She snorted. "I was always told it was wrong to speak ill of the dead, but that daughter of hers was good for less than nothing. She was more interested in men than in taking care of her mother."

A loud blast of rock music came from the open window next door.

The woman swiveled around, cupped her hands to her mouth and yelled, "Turn that down this instant, Dom!" She shook her head. "Kids," she said as if that explained everything.

They heard the window slam shut and the music became muted.

Monica smiled. "Mrs. Wenk seems okay. But I do wonder if she should be alone."

"There's that boarder that lives with her. But she's out most of the day."

"Arline?"

"You know her?" The woman bent down and scratched at a nasty looking bug bite on her ankle.

"She happens to work for me. Out at Sassamanash Farm."

"That the place that sells cranberries?"

"Yes."

"She seemed to care more for Mrs. Wenk than her own daughter did." She fiddled with the bobby pin in her hair. "Maybe that's what the two of them argued about the other day."

"The two of them?"

"Yeah. Lori and Arline. Their kitchen window was open and I was out on my patio having a cigarette."

"What were they arguing about?"

"I could hear them yelling but I couldn't make out the words. Something to do with money, I think." She gave a bark of laughter. "But then isn't that always the case?"

Chapter 23

Monica's thoughts continued to go around and around as she drove away from Mrs. Wenk's house. She couldn't figure out what or if any of this had anything to do with the murder. The fact that Lori had dropped the withdrawal slip at the farm was probably completely unrelated. But she felt sorry for Mrs. Wenk and she certainly would like to get to the bottom of the mystery of the missing money.

Monica was headed toward the harbor but she couldn't get Mrs. Wenk's crestfallen face out of her mind. It wouldn't take her more than a few minutes to stop in at the bank. Maybe one of the tellers or even the bank manager would be willing to tell her whether or not someone else had privileges on Mrs. Wenk's account. If that was the case, then Lori most likely had access to her mother's money and had taken it for reasons of her own. And there wouldn't be much Monica could do about it.

Monica pulled into the driveway of a small, well-kept bungalow, reversed, and headed back toward town and the Cranberry Cove Bank. Three cars were in the bank parking lot. Monica pulled in next to a silver Equinox and turned off the engine.

Saturday mornings were often busy at the bank, it being the only time people with full-time jobs could get there. Monica was relieved to see only two people waiting for the lone teller and one person sitting in the manager's office.

The line moved quickly, and soon it was Monica's turn. She was grateful that the teller was a different one from the last time she'd been to the bank. This one was very young—probably only just out of high school—with blond hair in a ponytail that swung with every movement of her head.

Monica showed her the withdrawal slip. "Can you tell me if someone other than Mrs. Wenk has privileges on this account?"

The girl frowned at the slip then slowly entered the account numbers into her computer. She looked up. "Mrs. Wenk?"

Monica was tempted to say *yes*, but she couldn't bring herself to lie. "No, I'm a friend of hers."

The girl frowned. "I don't know. . . ."

"You don't have to give me any names. I only want to know if someone besides Mrs. Wenk is allowed to take money out of that account."

The teller looked doubtful.

Monica thought that maybe if she explained things, the teller would relent.

"Mrs. Wenk has memory problems. Money is missing from her account, and she doesn't remember withdrawing it. It's possible she made the withdrawal herself and then forgot about it and perhaps hid the money somewhere in her house. But if someone else has their name on the account, then they might have been the one to withdraw the money."

The teller looked confused. Her eyes darted from Monica's face to her computer monitor and back again.

"I suppose it's okay. There is another name on this account. It's—"

"Patty!" one of the older tellers said sharply.

She strode toward Patty's station and stood next to the girl. She gave Monica a stern look.

"I'm afraid that is privileged information that we are not at liberty to give out."

Just as Monica had suspected. She apologized for any inconvenience and headed toward the exit. She could feel the older teller's eyes on her until the door had eased shut behind her.

So someone else could withdraw money from Mrs. Wenk's account, she thought as she started the Focus. That someone was most probably Lori. And with Lori dead, Mrs. Wenk shouldn't find any more money missing. Monica would encourage her to call her mortgage company, explain the situation and ask for a grace period to pay back the amount of money overdue. Hopefully they would be willing to work something out.

She was about to head to the harbor at long last when she thought of Mrs. Wenk's worried face and the stack of past due bills sitting on her coffee table. Maybe she should reassure the woman that, from now on, things would be okay.

Mrs. Wenk didn't seem surprised to find Monica on her doorstep again. Monica wondered if she'd already forgotten her earlier visit. She would have to talk to Arline about contacting Mrs. Wenk's brother. The woman really shouldn't be alone anymore.

"Would you like a cup of tea?" Mrs. Wenk asked as she headed into her living room.

"No, thank you. I don't want to keep you."

Mrs. Wenk gave a sad smile. "You're not keeping me from anything, I'm afraid."

"It's about your checking account. According to the bank, someone else has withdrawal privileges on it. Meaning they're allowed to take out money without asking you."

Mrs. Wenk frowned. "Who would that be?"

"I don't know. They wouldn't tell me."

"I know I signed some sort of paper from the bank, and I think it had something to do with the account, but I can't remember." She pressed a hand to her forehead.

"Was it your daughter who gave you the paper?"

"I don't know. Maybe. I'm afraid I can't recall."

"It had to have been Lori, so I don't think any more money will go missing now." Monica put a hand on Mrs. Wenk's arm. "Everything will be okay."

"That's wonderful, dear. I don't know how to repay you."

It had to have been Lori taking the money, Monica thought again as she headed—finally—toward the lake and the harbor where the festivities were taking place. She drove through downtown Cranberry Cove, where the sidewalks were clogged with tourists and every parking spot along Beach Hollow Road was taken with a line of fancy cars from out of town waiting impatiently for a space to open up.

Monica planned on leaving her car in the Central Reformed Church parking lot and walking back to the harbor and the Cranberry Cove Yacht Club.

Traffic made slow going of the trip through downtown but Monica was able to see the harbor now and was enchanted with the view of the many small boats bobbing in the water, their colorful flags standing at attention in the stiff breeze. She was so enchanted, as a matter of fact, that she didn't notice the cars in front of her had pulled forward until the person behind her leaned on their horn to get her attention.

She muttered a silent *Sorry about that*, and stepped on the gas. The Focus sprang forward and soon Monica was through downtown and a block away from the church. The last few yards were tortuously slow but eventually she was pulling into a vacant space and shutting off the engine.

The walk back to the path that led to the harbor was pleasant, with the sun warm on her arms and a sweet breeze cooling her face. She brushed at the tendrils of hair blowing across her forehead. Delicious smells drifted on the air currents and Monica could distinguish something spicy overlaid with the tantalizing aroma of baked sugar.

Crowds mingled on the grassy slope leading down to

the Cranberry Cove Yacht Club, some standing, others sitting on picnic blankets holding cold drinks. Red, yellow and green umbrellas created inviting canopies over the food carts and stalls. The rijsttafel that Hennie had told Monica about was set up on the lower patio of the Yacht Club, while the upper patio was reserved for club members who lounged on canvas deck chairs with sweating glasses of wine, beer or pop.

Monica felt her cell phone buzz in her pocket and pulled it out. There was a text from Greg.

How is the Flag Day celebration? Business at the store has been modest. I hope to get away soon. I'll call you. Love you.

Monica couldn't suppress a smile as she slipped the phone back into her pocket and continued down the hill toward the food carts lining the waterfront. Monica wandered along the path examining the wares of each stall, plotting just what she was going to go back and sample. Rieka, who worked as a secretary at the Cranberry Cove Health Department and was well known in town, was behind a table covered in a red-and-white-checked cloth, manning a deep fryer from which she pulled golden brown oliebollen—Dutch doughnuts. She placed them on a paper towel–lined plate and sprinkled them with powdered sugar.

A woman with a Dutch accent and blond hair sprinkled with gray grabbed her companion's arm and pulled her over to Rieka's booth. "Look, Anneke. Oliebollen, still warm from the fryer."

Monica was tempted, but she was saving room for the many delights of the rijsttafel first.

A young man, dressed as a clown and maneuvering down the sidewalk on a pair of tall stilts, had the children squealing with delight. Music drifted from the far end of the path, where an old-fashioned carousel had been trucked in for the day.

Monica passed another stall where unusual looking frying pans with dimpled bottoms sat warming over a burner.

A woman in traditional Dutch dress with a lace apron, lace cap and sturdy wooden shoes was pouring batter into the hot pans.

"What are you making?" Monica asked.

The woman gave her a slightly condescending smile. "These are poffertjes—pancakes made with yeast and buckwheat flour. You watch—they're going to puff up like balloons."

As Monica watched, the batter did puff up into round fluffy balls that the woman placed on a plate. She grabbed a shaker and liberally dusted them with powdered sugar.

Again, Monica was tempted, but she moved on. There would be time enough to come back to sample the poffertjes.

It was time to try the rijsttafel. She turned around and headed back toward the Yacht Club.

The smells were so tantalizing Monica found her mouth watering as she approached the table where the food was displayed in large warming trays.

"Can I help you?" A young man smiled at Monica. He had blond hair and very blue eyes.

"It's overwhelming," Monica admitted.

"I suggest you start with some rice—we have plain

nasi goreng, which is fried rice, or nasi kuning, which is yellow Indonesian rice. A rijsttafel is meant to offer an array of tastes, textures and spices such as hot, cold, sweet, salty, sour, bitter, crispy, chewy, slippery and so on. Rice makes a perfect base for all the other dishes."

"What's that?" Monica pointed at a tray filled with skewered barbecued meats.

"That's satay. It's served with sambal kacang, or peanut sauce. You should try it."

"Okay."

He reached for a plate, added a spoonful of yellow rice and a skewer of meat, then drizzled sauce over the meat.

"I'd suggest some of the opor ayam—chicken coconut curry." He added a spoonful of that to her plate.

Monica added a few more things to her now heaping dish and went in search of a place to sit. She found a shaded spot on the rock wall that bordered the Yacht Club and sat down.

The food was delicious—the myriad of tastes was like an explosion of flavor in her mouth. She hoped Greg would have a chance to sample some of the food before it was gone. There was a long line of people waiting to fill their plates.

Monica finished her meal and sat for a moment, watching the crowd and enjoying the fresh air. She thought she had some room left for dessert—she had decided she wanted to try a poffertje.

The woman behind the food stall had just finished making a fresh batch when Monica got there. She accepted the warm, powdered sugar–covered pancake the

woman handed her and took a bite. She closed her eyes—
it was the perfect end to a delicious meal.

She finished the poffertje and contemplated having
another one, but thought better of it. She wiped her hands
on her paper napkin, dropped it in a wastebasket and
continued down the path. Despite already being full with
delicious food, tantalizing aromas of garlic and herbs and
spices drew Monica forward.

She rounded a slight bend to find Gus manning a food
stall festooned with fluttering blue-and-white Greek flags.
His usual grimace had temporarily been replaced by a
stiff and painful looking smile. He was wearing white
pants, a navy-and-white-striped T-shirt and a black fisherman's cap. He gave Monica an almost imperceptible nod.

Skewers of meat sizzled on the grill in front of him
and a tiered stand held bites of pastry that looked as if
they'd been drenched in honey. The smells were tantalizing, and Monica's mouth watered in spite of having already finished a fairly large meal.

She continued on until she came to a table loaded with
books standing on end so their spines were facing up. A
hand-lettered sign stuck between the rows of volumes
read *Library Book Sale. All Proceeds Benefit the Cranberry Cove Library.* Behind the table was Phyllis Bouma,
wearing a blue visor with *Save the Animals* written on it.

"I didn't know the library was going to have a sale,"
Monica said as she approached the table.

Phyllis grunted and waved her hand over the books.
"Time to clean out the collection. If we make a little
money, too, that's all the better."

"Do you have any mysteries?"

Phyllis ran a hand over the spines of the books. "You want this section over here."

Monica scanned the titles. Nothing really caught her interest. She saw a book on ships that made her think of Xavier Cabot. There were a number of unusual titles including one on the mating habits of bees. It brought Lori's murder to mind, and Monica shivered.

Phyllis noticed Monica's hand lingering on the book.

"I'll never look at bees the same way again," Phyllis said, retrieving a cloth from under the table and swiping it over the covers of the books. "Been stung more than a few times myself and while it wasn't pleasant, at least it didn't kill me."

Monica was about to tell Phyllis that it wasn't the bees that had killed Lori but then changed her mind. It might be a detail the police were withholding from the public.

"I never had any idea how important bees are—a major number of our crops depend on bees for pollination."

Phyllis raised her eyebrows.

"I know cranberries do," Monica said.

"Is that why Jeff had all those bees out at the farm that day?"

"Yes. Apparently there aren't enough native bees to do the job effectively."

"It seems like there are plenty of them around to me, especially when I'm out trying to do some work in my garden, but I don't pretend to understand it. That reminds me. You know that woman who works for you?"

"Nora?"

Phyllis shook her head. "No, the other one. The one who helps you with the baking."

"Arline?"

"Yes, that's the one. I'd forgotten all about it until right now, but shortly before the death out at your farm, she took out a book on bees. A big volume—*The Beekeeper's Bible*. And it's overdue," Phyllis grumbled.

"That's odd."

"It's certainly a coincidence." Phyllis straightened a row of books that were threatening to topple off the table like dominoes. "She said Lori was always talking about bees and all the things she'd learned working with them, and it made her feel like she didn't know anything."

Phyllis leaned across the table toward Monica. "Some people may think being a librarian is dull work, but they have no idea. Of course the minute we go to one of those systems where the patrons check the books out themselves, I'm retiring. Where's the fun in that?"

Monica shrugged her shoulders. *Indeed,* she thought.

"You can learn a lot about a person by the books they take out. People think I don't notice, but I do. I know that Dirk VanHuizen likes to bird watch and old Mr. Voorhees grows orchids. Or at least he likes to read about growing them. Mildred Victory likes those romance novels with the half-naked men and women on the front. Oh, she always hands me the books with the cover side down, but I know what she's up to. And get this." Phyllis leaned farther across the table and lowered her voice to a near whisper. "The pastor's wife checked out one of those books about *you-know-what*. What used to be called a marriage manual. She didn't even have the grace to blush when she handed it over!"

Monica was at a loss for words, but right then a

gentleman with tousled white hair, wearing a cardigan sweater despite the pleasant warmth of the day, approached the library's table.

He smoothed his mustache with his finger. "Do you have any books on local history, perhaps?"

Monica waved good-bye to Phyllis and hurried off. She needed to think. Why had Arline borrowed a book on bees? Her explanation to Phyllis didn't ring true. Arline was hardworking and a good baker but she'd never seemed interested in anything more intellectual than what was happening on her favorite television programs and gossip about movie stars.

Monica was so engrossed in her thoughts she nearly collided with a woman in denim capris and a tank top who was eating an ice cream cone that Monica nearly toppled from her hand.

"Excuse me. I'm so sorry," Monica said.

The woman smiled at her. "Oh, no, that's okay, you're fine."

Thoughts collided in Monica's head like pinballs. For some reason thoughts of the story Xavier Cabot had told about the sailor who had sent his captain and the rest of the crew into that deadly storm suddenly surfaced.

Hadn't Arline said that Rick had been calling for Lori's help right before Lori had walked out of the farm kitchen and into the swarm of bees? But Rick's truck hadn't been there at the time—he'd already left for his aborted trip to the lawyer in town. Which meant Rick couldn't possibly have summoned Lori.

Had Arline been like that sailor in Xavier's story—

sending Lori into a deadly swarm of bees to cover up the nearly invisible mark from the hypodermic needle?

But why would Arline want to kill Lori? They seemed to have gotten along okay. Was she looking at things from the wrong angle? Monica wondered was Dale the killer after all and there was a perfectly innocent explanation for Arline taking a book on bees out of the library.

She continued walking along the path that ran alongside the harbor. Sailboats and motorboats were moored in the channel, their occupants sprawled on the prow, soaking up the sun or lounging in deck chairs with cold drinks. A girl with her bikini top untied was stretched out facedown on a striped beach towel, an old-fashioned radio propped next to her. Music drifted from the boat—"Can't Buy Me Love" by the Beatles.

Monica was barely aware of her surroundings as she walked along, and several times she earned dirty looks from people she nearly collided with. Right now she had a random handful of jigsaw puzzle pieces and the trick was going to be to put them together. But every time she thought she'd completed the puzzle, the last piece would refuse to fit.

By now she'd reached the end of the path, where the crowds were sparser and the delicious food smells considerably fainter. She turned around and started back, putting up a hand to ward off the sun that was shining in her eyes. She could feel the warmth of it on her arms and legs and thought it looked as if her skin was getting a bit pink. Monica didn't tan easily—her fair skin usually turned red and then peeled before ever achieving the golden brown look that came so easily to other people.

She passed Gus's stall again. He was counting a stack of bills before tucking them into a green canvas zippered pouch that hung from the belt around his waist.

Money! Monica stopped so short that the person behind her slammed into her, nearly knocking her off balance.

"What do you mean stopping like that?"

He was wearing plaid Bermuda shorts and a yellow polo shirt that matched the stripe in his shorts. Both were festooned with well-known logos of expensive brands.

Monica immediately labeled him as a tourist—an entitled one who probably had a yacht anchored in the Cranberry Cove Yacht Club marina.

She made profuse apologies, smiled sweetly and went on her way. She imagined she could hear him continuing to fume in back of her.

She didn't care. She thought she'd found a way to fit the final puzzle piece into place.

Chapter 24

Monica tried to pay closer attention to where she was going as she walked along. She had no particular destination in mind, but walking helped her think.

Maybe the withdrawal slip for Mrs. Wenk's bank account hadn't fallen out of Lori's pocket. Maybe it had fallen out of Arline's instead.

The faster Monica walked, the more things came into focus. Mrs. Wenk had signed some papers that gave another person access to her bank account but couldn't remember who it was. Monica had assumed that that person must have been her daughter, Lori. But what if Arline had convinced Mrs. Wenk to sign the paper—perhaps saying she wanted to help her because her daughter was obviously not interested. The woman was easily confused—it would have been child's play to pressure her into signing.

Money had gone missing from Mrs. Wenk's account—money she insisted she hadn't withdrawn. Had Arline used the money to line her own pockets?

But why kill Lori then? Unless Lori had found out and confronted Arline with the evidence.

Once again, Monica stopped short. But mercifully no one was behind her this time.

The argument the neighbor had overheard between Lori and Arline—it wasn't long afterward that Lori was killed. If Lori had threatened to go to the police, Arline might have been desperate to stop her—desperate enough to kill.

Monica pulled her cell phone from her pocket and hesitated. Detective Stevens needed to know about this, but she didn't want to believe that Arline would kill anyone. She would have to let Stevens decide if it was important or not. She punched in the detective's cell phone number and waited for the call to connect.

It rang multiple times before going to voicemail. Monica hesitated—should she leave a message or call back later? She finally decided to leave a brief message asking Stevens to call her. She stuffed the phone back in her pocket and began walking again.

By now she was beyond the food stalls. The crowd had thinned out and she only passed one or two people on the path. She still had no particular destination in mind, but the walking was helping to dispel some of the anxiety she'd felt ever since finding the farm kitchen filled with gas.

Another thought struck her—the story Arline had told about the jealous boyfriend out to get her didn't ring true. Monica had been upset and flustered at the time and had merely accepted Arline's explanation. Arline had a key to the farm kitchen—she could easily have turned on all the gas herself and then fled, only to arrive back after the damage had been done.

Monica pulled her cell from her pocket and tried Detective Stevens again, to no avail. She ended the call without leaving a message then dialed Jeff's number. Again the phone rang and rang before going to voicemail, which wasn't surprising. Jeff was probably out in the bogs. She wasn't sure why she'd called Jeff anyway— except that it had been instinct to want to talk to her brother.

By now Monica had reached the end of the path. She turned around and began to head back the way she had come. She passed several people she knew enough to wave to, which made her feel curiously at home.

She was rounding a bend when she saw Hennie and Gerda perched decorously on a park bench, balancing paper plates on their laps. They were dressed in matching lavender cotton slacks and white blouses printed with lavender flowers. Monica couldn't remember ever having seen them in anything but a dress or skirt before.

"Good morning," Monica called as she approached the two ladies.

"Good morning, dear. Splendid day, isn't it?" Hennie said, patting her lips with a paper napkin. "We got a helper in for a couple of hours to take care of Gumdrops so we could sneak away and enjoy the celebration."

Monica was pleased to see Gerda looking much stronger, with some good color in her cheeks.

"Everything is so delicious, isn't it?" Gerda said.

"We've even tried some of Gus's Greek food, and I quite like it."

"We grew up eating Dutch food." Hennie crumpled her used napkin in her hand. "So why not try something new?"

"Why not?" Monica said.

They chatted for a few more minutes then Monica said good-bye and continued on her way. She still hadn't heard from Detective Stevens and was wondering if it was worth stopping at the police station to talk to someone. But would they even believe her?

Maybe she hadn't heard her phone ring? Monica pulled it from her pocket but there were no missed calls and no messages.

She looked up to see Gina walking toward her in a Hawaiian-print strapless sundress and strappy high-heeled sandals. It made Monica's feet hurt to look at them.

"Monica!" Gina exclaimed, grabbing Monica's arm. "I'm so angry I could spit."

Gina did look angry, with her carefully casual updo hanging precariously from one pin and her cheeks flushed and red.

"What's the matter?"

Gina's face crumpled and her lower lip quivered. "It's Xavier." She balled her hands into fists at her sides. "And that woman."

"What woman?"

"Tempest! I saw them walking arm in arm past that stall where they're selling those pancakes."

"The poffertjes?"

"I suppose that's what they're called. They look like puffy pancakes to me. The bastard," Gina added.

"Did you and Xavier have some sort of understanding?" Monica said gently.

Gina sniffed. "Not exactly. But we were getting along so well and I thought . . ." Gina pulled a tissue from her purse and blew her nose. "That's it. No more men for me. I'm going to . . . join a convent or something."

The thought of Gina as a nun made Monica laugh. Gina shot her a quelling look.

"It's not funny." She put a hand over her chest. "My heart is broken."

"Do you remember that story Xavier told us when we had dinner at the Pepper Pot? About the sailor sending his captain and the crew into that huge storm?"

Gina frowned. "Yes. But what does that have to do with anything?"

Monica explained her thoughts about the murder and her conviction that Arline had been responsible.

"How terrible," Gina said. "How could someone do something like that? Of course, I've had some pretty murderous thoughts about Tempest myself."

"Yes. But you would never act on them."

Gina looked doubtful. She linked her arm through Monica's.

"Come on. Let's walk over to the Yacht Club and see if there are any eligible men about."

Monica was about to protest but thought better of it. Gina needed some cheering up, so why not?

As they neared the Yacht Club the soft murmur of

voices floated on the air, interspersed with the clinking
of ice against glasses and the ping of silverware on china.
The lines at the food stalls on the club lawn had dimin-
ished but the seductive aroma of delicious food lingered
behind.

Suddenly Monica stopped short. She grabbed Gina's arm.

"What's the matter?" Gina said.

"It's Arline," Monica hissed under her breath. "Right
there, coming toward us."

"Don't be silly," Gina said. "We don't have a thing to
worry about. What is she going to do to us out in the open
like this? Besides, she has no idea you've figured out that
she's the one who killed that woman."

"Hey," Arline called when she saw them. Her short,
dark hair was ruffled by the breeze off the lake and her
nose was freckling in the sun.

"Arline," Monica said, and even to her own ears her
voice sounded stilted and awkward. "Are you . . . are you
enjoying the celebration?"

Her palms had begun to sweat, and she felt a trickle
of moisture make its way down her back.

Arline studied Monica's face like someone prepping
to give a description to a police sketch artist.

Monica tried to smile but it felt forced, and she could
tell it didn't look natural. She had to remind herself that
Arline had no idea what she'd figured out about the murder. Besides, there were plenty of people about—Arline
would hardly risk doing anything in public.

There was no reason to feel so uneasy.

Except for the way Arline's face hardened into lines

Monica had never noticed before. Her eyes had taken on a reptilian look, wary and unblinking—like a snake on the verge of striking.

Monica took a step backward and grabbed Gina's arm. Gina didn't protest. She'd obviously picked up on the same signals Monica had.

They had nearly turned to run when Arline spoke.

"We're going to keep walking. Together. And you're going to make it look as if we're the best of friends.

Monica was about to protest when she noticed a small gun in Arline's hand—no less deadly looking because of its diminutive size.

"But why? We haven't—"

Arline cut her off abruptly. "You've guessed. I could tell by your face immediately. You're not very good at hiding your thoughts, are you?"

"Where are we going?" Gina asked as Arline urged them along the path.

"You'll find out soon enough." Arline gave Gina a shove. "Get moving."

A sense of unreality descended on Monica. She heard the animated chatter of the crowd and saw the brightly decorated boats drifting up and down with the rhythm of the waves. There were people everywhere enjoying themselves and no one noticed that she and Gina were at the mercy of a homicidal maniac.

It was the same feeling she'd had after her fiancé had died—she was grieving but the rest of the world was going about its business as usual.

As they walked along, the heel of one of Gina's sandals caught in a crack in the macadam and she nearly pitched forward. She only stopped herself by grabbing onto Monica, and for a moment, Monica thought they were both going to go down.

"If you're trying to trip me, it's not going to work," Arline said, pushing the gun into Gina's back.

Gina gave a squeak like a cornered mouse and put up a hand to steady her French twist, which was hanging by a pin.

"Where are you taking us?" Gina asked.

"Like I told your friend here. You'll find out. Meanwhile, keep going."

The noise of the crowd at the Yacht Club receded to a murmur as they walked farther along the path. Monica glanced over her shoulder but no one was coming up behind them. There was no one in front of them, either.

They were passing the Yacht Club marina now. Few boats were anchored there—most of them had joined the armada celebrating out on the lake.

A couple of hundred yards beyond the Yacht Club marina was a public marina with wooden docks weathered by sun, harsh winters and brutal storms. The wood was rough and splintered and cracked through in spots.

"Keep moving," Arline barked when Monica stopped briefly to take stock of her surroundings.

They were alone and the only sound was the slapping of the waves against the shore. Screaming would be useless—there was no one close enough to hear. They had to find a way to disarm Arline. Monica looked around, but she was careful not to stop this time. There was an occasional rock alongside the path. Could she grab one of those and lob it at Arline? Her aim had never been that good, but surely at such close quarters she could manage to hit her target. It might stun Arline long enough for one of them to grab the gun.

She'd have to pretend to fall in order to pick up one of the stones. And she'd have to make it look realistic enough to fool Arline.

Monica soon discovered it was harder to make yourself fall than she realized. The human brain automatically recoiled from the idea of throwing your body on the ground on purpose. In the end, providence intervened and the toe of Monica's sandal caught in a small crack in the macadam and she pitched forward, landing on her hands and knees.

Pain set in immediately and she looked down to see she'd skinned her knees—and the palms of her hands as well. But she managed to ignore the intense stinging long enough to stretch out an arm and grab a rock. She wished it was bigger, but it would have to do.

"Are you hurt?" Gina cried.

"I'm fine," Monica mumbled as she struggled to her feet. She held the stone close against her body, hoping Arline wouldn't see it.

"Your knees," Gina exclaimed.

Monica looked down. Both knees were scraped raw and blood trickled slowly down her legs.

Gina began digging in her designer handbag. She pulled out a wad of tissues. "Here." She handed them to Monica. "Use these to stop the bleeding."

Arline had become edgier and edgier as they walked along. Her movements were jerky, and her glance kept darting over her shoulder, although no one was in sight.

"Get moving." She poked the gun into Monica's ribs.

With the help of Gina's tissues, Monica had managed to staunch the flow of blood from her knees. She straightened up, the rock hidden in her right hand. Arline was next to her—perhaps there would be no need to actually throw the rock.

Monica took a deep breath, swung her arm around and smashed the rock into Arline's temple. It wasn't a terrific blow, but it was enough to put Arline off balance. She dropped the gun and grabbed her head with both hands.

Monica kicked the gun away, but the blow had merely stunned Arline, who dove after the gun and managed to grab it before Monica or Gina could get to it.

A thin trickle of blood was coming from the side of Arline's head. She felt the spot and winced.

"You think you're so clever, don't you?" She waved the gun at Monica. "We'll see just how clever you are. Now move," she barked.

Monica and Gina hastened to do as they were told. They walked until they came to the last dock. A small boat with an outboard motor bobbed gently in the water, occasionally thudding against the dock.

Arline motioned to it. "Get in."

Chapter 25

Gina balked at the sight of the small boat.

"How am I supposed to get into that thing?" She tugged at her dress. "My skirt's too tight. Besides, I get seasick."

"I don't care what you have to do or how you do it, just get in." Arline motioned toward the boat with the gun.

"I'll go first and help you in," Monica said.

She hiked up her sundress, sat down on the dock alongside the boat and then shoved off and jumped in. The small craft rocked wildly under Monica's feet and she struggled to maintain her balance.

"Now you," Arline said, pointing the gun at Gina.

Gina hesitated, and Arline stuck a hand between Gina's shoulder blades and pushed. Gina quickly sat on the edge of the dock as Monica had done. Monica looked up at Gina's frightened face as she grabbed Gina's hands.

Gina continued to hesitate but when Arline once again stuck the gun in her back she pushed off and jumped the short distance into the boat. There was the sound of fabric tearing.

Gina quickly sat down opposite Monica on one of the three rough wooden planks that functioned as seats. "Now look what you've made me do. A perfectly good Oscar de la Renta sundress ruined." Her look of fear had turned to one of outrage.

Arline laughed. "Ask me if I care."

The boat rocked wildly again as Arline jumped in, and Monica grabbed the sides to keep from sliding off the seat. She winced as the rough wood came in contact with her abraded palms.

Arline held the gun in one hand while she pulled the cord on the motor with the other hand. The engine caught on the third try and Arline guided the boat past the docks, out of the harbor and into open water.

Monica watched as the shore gradually receded. The lake was fairly calm, but the ride was choppy in the small boat, which pitched from side to side, the hull slapping the water as they crested each wave.

"Was I right that you were taking Mrs. Wenk's social security money out of her bank account?" Monica asked Arline as they skimmed along the shoreline, heading north.

"Yes. It was so easy, it was ridiculous. The woman has no idea what she's doing, and that daughter of hers couldn't have cared less about her mother. I got some papers from the bank authorizing me to have access to Mrs. Wenk's account, and she signed them without a whimper—just like I thought she would."

"But Lori figured it out?"

"Yes. She said she was going to go to the police. I couldn't let her do that. I've been accepted to the University of Michigan, and the tuition isn't cheap. My family might not have amounted to much, but I plan to do better for myself."

Arline managed to make it sound like a perfectly reasonable explanation.

"So you killed Lori to keep her from talking?"

"Yes. She would have ruined everything."

Monica was speechless. How could Arline think that that was justification for taking a life?

"You told Lori that Rick wanted her to come out and check on the bees. That wasn't true, was it?"

Arline laughed. "No, but she fell for it. Meanwhile I'd let the bees out and gotten them riled up."

Monica thought back to that morning in the kitchen. Arline had been scratching at a red spot on her hand. Monica had assumed it was a mosquito bite but it must have been a bee sting.

A large cabin cruiser crossed their path, and Monica was tempted to call out, but she doubted anyone would hear her. Their small boat rocked precariously in the wake of the larger one and water splashed over the side, nearly drenching them.

"Now look what's happened to my dress," Gina wailed.

"I don't think this is the time to be worrying about that," Monica hissed at her stepmother.

"Although the bee stings weren't what killed Lori, were they?" she asked Arline, more loudly.

Arline laughed. "No. Unless a person is allergic, you

can't count on bee stings doing the job. The stings were to cover up for something else."

"Injection with ricin?" Monica grabbed for the side of the boat as they made a sharp turn, causing it to list to one side. "How did you get hold of ricin? I imagine it's not something you can pick up at the corner drugstore."

Arline looked smug. "I lied when I said I was having trouble with chemistry. I'm planning on majoring in it at the University of Michigan. It's a relatively simple process to extract ricin from castor beans—if you know what you're doing."

"Castor beans!" Gina exclaimed. "My mother made me drink a spoonful of castor oil every day—said it was good for my constitution, whatever that is. How come I wasn't poisoned?"

Arline rolled her eyes. "The beans themselves aren't poisonous and neither is the oil that your mother gave you."

By now the shore had receded even further and their small craft was being tossed around as if it was a toy boat. Waves repeatedly washed over the sides and an inch of water had collected on the bottom. Monica was worried that they would soon have to start bailing.

Arline had one hand on the rudder and was scanning the shore and the water around them. Monica wondered if they could take advantage of the opportunity to try to grab the gun. But if Arline pulled the trigger, it was unlikely she would miss in such close quarters.

Suddenly Arline cut the engine and the boat slowly came to a halt, the only movement now caused by the buffeting of the waves.

"Why are you stopping?" Gina asked.

Arline turned to them, her face set in hard lines. "This is where you two are getting off."

Gina looked around as if she expected a dock to suddenly materialize. "You've got to be kidding."

Arline leveled the gun at her. "I'm not."

"But why . . . ?" Monica said.

"I couldn't have Lori going to the police, and I can't have you two going, either. And don't bother telling me you won't because I would never believe you."

A wave slapped the small boat, putting everyone off balance. For a second Monica thought she might be able to take advantage of the moment to grab the gun. She lunged toward Arline but Arline raised the gun in the air, and Monica couldn't reach it. She landed on her knees in the well of the boat, the water they'd taken on soaking the hem of her dress.

Monica scrambled back to her seat and tried to ring out the water.

Arline laughed. "I wouldn't bother with that if I were you. You're going to be going for a swim in a minute." She leveled the gun at them again. "Over the side you go. I don't care which one of you goes first."

Neither Monica nor Gina moved. Monica stared at the dark gray water of the lake and shivered. She knew how to swim, but she wasn't a particularly strong swimmer. And having lost her fiancé, who had at one time been considered for an Olympic team, to a swimming accident had made her especially leery of the water.

Monica and Gina continued to sit and stare at Arline, not quite believing she meant what she said.

"Get going now!" Arline raised the gun and fired into the air.

Monica and Gina jumped and Gina gave a little cry. Monica wondered if anyone had heard the shot? If so, had they assumed it was a car backfiring or someone shooting off fireworks?

Monica suddenly found herself staring down the barrel of Arline's gun. She had a choice—certain death by a gunshot to the head or take a chance that she could stay afloat long enough to reach shore or another boat. She looked around. There were no other crafts nearby and the banks of the lake seemed impossibly far away.

When Arline's finger began twitching on the trigger of the gun, Monica took a deep breath and hurled herself over the side of the boat.

The cold water made her gasp and she swallowed a mouthful as she rose to the surface, choking and sputtering. She reached out an arm and grabbed for the boat. The first time she missed, and she felt panic seize her before reason and instinct set in and she began treading water.

She reached again for the boat, and this time she grasped the side with her fingertips. Gina's white face loomed over her as she pulled herself closer.

"You've got to let her back in the boat," Gina said, a sob catching in her throat.

"Let her back in?" Arline sneered. "You're about to keep her company."

A look of fury tinged with determination came over Gina's face. With lightning speed, she ripped off her stiletto-heeled sandal and brought the business end down sharply on Arline's wrist.

Arline yowled in pain and dropped the gun. The point

of Gina's shoe had punctured the skin and her wrist was bleeding. She grabbed her wrist with her other hand.

Gina, meanwhile, took control of the gun and with a quivering hand pointed it at Arline.

None of them saw the wave that had been gathering steam and was now bearing down upon them. It hit like a slap and washed over them, losing power as it rushed toward shore.

Monica lost her grip on the boat and for a terrifying moment, went under, turning head over heels until she didn't know which way was up and which way was down. She finally broke the surface, took a shuddering breath and spit out a mouthful of water.

The boat had drifted several feet away and Monica struck out toward it, thankful she was wearing only a light sundress and not her usual jeans. A lock of hair had been washed across her face, covering her eyes, and she could barely see.

The capsized boat seemed to drift farther away with each stroke she took toward it, but finally she reached it. She held on for a few moments, trying to catch her breath, which was coming in ragged gasps.

Arline had struck out toward shore, her strokes strong and assured. Gina was flailing in the water several yards away.

"Help," Gina yelled.

Monica reluctantly let go of the boat and set out toward Gina. She was beginning to tire and her breathing was labored. She stopped for a moment to tread water. She brushed the water from her eyes and looked around. There were no other boats nearby—they'd have to get back to their boat and hang on until, hopefully, someone saw them and rescued them.

Monica set off again and with a few more strokes reached Gina.

"Can you tread water?" Monica said.

"I'm trying. Now I'm sorry I skipped gym when we had swimming in high school. I didn't want to get my hair wet or ruin my makeup."

Trust Gina to make her laugh even at a time like this, Monica thought.

"You're going to have to swim to the boat." Monica pointed toward the overturned vessel. She devoutly hoped that Gina's swimming went beyond the doggy paddle, although it really didn't matter how she got there—just that she did.

Gina's teeth were chattering and her updo had come down completely. Her hair hung lankly on either side of her face, with one long strand plastered to her cheek. The sash of her expensive sundress floated behind her like a piece of seaweed.

"I'm not much of a swimmer, but under the circumstances, I don't imagine I have much choice, do I?"

Monica shook her head. "I'm afraid not. If you get tired we can stop and tread water or float on our backs."

Gina looked doubtful, but she dutifully struck out, her strokes tentative at first but growing stronger as she moved through the water. Monica stayed behind her. If Gina got in trouble, she would do what she could.

Monica could have sworn that they were making no progress whatsoever, but eventually they did reach the boat, and clung to the rough bottom stained green by algae. Neither said anything for several minutes as they struggled to catch their breath.

"What do we do now?" Gina finally asked. "The boat is too heavy to turn it back over."

"I suppose we can use it as a paddleboard and hang on and kick toward shore."

"I don't think I have enough energy left to bat my eyelashes if a cute guy came along, let alone kick," Gina said.

Monica started to laugh, but water got in her mouth and she sputtered instead.

"We can rest for a few more minutes, then we have to start kicking, okay?" She glanced toward the sun, which was getting lower on the horizon. "We have to get to shore before the sun sets."

Monica was anxious to get going—she was chilled to the bone and the kicking would warm them up—but she waited a few more minutes to give Gina a chance to rest. She needed to catch her own breath as well, but finally she decided they would have to move.

"Okay, let's get started. We need to kick together and keep the boat going in the direction of the shore. If you need to take a break, say so and we'll stop for a few minutes."

They set off, but it was slow going and within minutes they were exhausted.

"I can't do it," Gina cried, sniffing back tears. "You go ahead. You'll be faster on your own."

"I'm not leaving you here," Monica said in a stern voice. "We're in this together. And we can do it. I know we can. You just have to put your mind to it."

"Alright," Gina said, her voice sounding stronger and

more determined. "You're right. We can't let that miserable Arline win. Let's go."

They resumed kicking and actually began to make some progress. Monica was feeling hopeful when another rogue wave washed over them, tearing the boat from their grasp.

"No!" Gina called after it.

"Wait here. I'll get it."

It took Monica longer than she'd anticipated to capture the runaway craft but she finally reached it and steered it back toward where Gina was treading water frantically.

Gina grasped the side. "Thank goodness. I don't think I would have lasted much longer. You rest for a bit, and then we'll get going again."

"I'm fine. Let's go."

They resumed their journey toward shore, holding onto the boat even more tightly this time. Their knuckles were blanched white from the effort of clinging to the rough wood.

They finally began making some progress when the wake from a larger boat sent them bobbing furiously and once again they were in danger of losing their grasp on the boat. The noise of the larger craft's engine got louder and louder.

Monica glanced over her shoulder. Bearing down upon them was a good-sized yacht. It had a sharp prow—like a swordfish—and its white paint looked fresh and gleaming. *The Yooper II* was written on the side in fancy black script.

The skipper cut the engine.

Gina turned around, too. "It's a yacht. Oh my goodness, and here I look a complete mess. I'm sure my mascara's run and my poor dress is completely ruined."

"I don't think that matters at the moment," Monica said dryly. "Besides, the owner might be a ninety-year-old fat, bald man who smokes cigars."

"Yes, but honey, that doesn't matter if he owns a yacht. Money makes all men handsome, don't you think?"

Monica didn't happen to agree, but she kept her mouth shut.

"Having some trouble?" someone called from the deck of the other boat.

A gray-haired gentleman in white pants and a navy blue polo shirt leaned casually over the deck railing, his hands cupped to his mouth.

"Can we help?" he called again.

"Yes," Monica spluttered, waving her arms in the air. "Yes, please. Help."

Gina was attempting to bring some order to her hair but her efforts only succeeded in dunking her and she came up gasping and spitting out water. She dashed at her eyes and looked over at the yacht.

"Not fat and bald at all," she purred. "Very distinguished, actually."

Monica had to agree. Although all she cared about at the moment was the fact that the gentleman was offering to rescue them. She'd gone from being cold to being numb, and she was exhausted from trying to stay afloat in the water.

Another man appeared on deck. He was wearing navy blue shorts, navy deck shoes and a white T-shirt with *The Yooper II* printed on the back. The two men put their heads together for a moment before the fellow in the T-shirt disappeared briefly, returning with two life preservers.

He uncoiled two lengths of rope and tied one end to each of the flotation devices before tossing them into the water to Monica and Gina.

They landed a bit shy of Monica's position, but with two strokes, she was able to reach them both. She handed one to Gina and just in time. Gina was barely keeping her head above water—her face was pale with exhaustion and her teeth were chattering.

"Hold on, and we'll reel you in," the gentleman on the deck yelled.

Monica was more than happy to do as she was told. She made sure Gina had a good grasp on the life preserver then gave the signal for the men to start pulling.

In moments they were being helped onto the boat, where a very young woman in a bikini and a brightly colored, gauzy cover-up appeared with two thick, plush terrycloth towels.

Monica accepted one of them gratefully and wrapped it around herself securely. The gentleman in the polo shirt—who they assumed was the owner of the yacht—led them to two deck chairs.

Monica collapsed as gracefully as possible onto one of them—and in the nick of time. Her legs were about to give out from strain and fatigue.

"Do you suppose that's his daughter?" Gina whispered to Monica as the owner conferred with the young man in the T-shirt.

"I would hope so. He's certainly old enough to be her father. More likely even her grandfather."

"He is handsome, don't you think?"

Monica mumbled agreement and sank back against the chair, her eyes closing. When she opened them again, the young man in the T-shirt had reappeared with a tray, two cups and saucers and a pot of hot tea.

"This is the life," Gina murmured as she stirred a spoonful of sugar into her cup.

"Don't get too used to it. It's back to reality shortly," Monica said.

"Speak for yourself," Gina said with a mischievous smile.

"I should introduce myself." The man in the navy polo shirt pulled up a chair and sat down opposite Monica and Gina. "I'm George Chadwick."

"Gina Albertson."

"Monica Albertson."

"Your daughter?" he said to Gina.

Gina scowled. "My stepdaughter. I'm hardly old enough—"

"Of course not," he said smoothly. He smiled at them. "Do you want to tell me what happened? How you ended up clinging to that piece of scrap wood?"

He had a glass of amber-colored liquid in his hand, which he agitated occasionally so that the ice cubes pinged back and forth against the sides of the glass.

"Is that whiskey?" Gina asked with one eyebrow raised. "I'll tell you all about it as soon as you bring me a drink."

"Well the sun is over the yardarm and has been for quite a while," George said with a smile. "I'd be happy to oblige."

He looked at Monica and raised an eyebrow.

"No, thank you. I'll stick with the tea."

"Party pooper," Gina said as she watched him walk toward the boat's cabin. She twisted around in her seat so she was facing Monica. "I think I'd better book an appointment with Dr. Dixon back in Chicago for some Botox and maybe some filler." She put her hands on either side of her face and pulled her skin back. "Is this better?"

"You look fine the way you are," Monica said, although she knew Gina wouldn't believe her.

"I can't possibly look fine if that man thought you were my daughter."

"Here you go." George came out of the cabin with a drink in one hand and a white paper napkin with *The Yooper II* written on it in navy blue. "Cheers." He handed the glass to Gina.

"You still haven't told me how you ended up in the water clinging to that very unseaworthy looking boat, but I imagine you ladies are anxious to get home and into some dry duds. This evening I have a reservation at the Yacht Club for eight o'clock, and I'd love to have you join me. You can tell me all about it then."

He turned around and beckoned to the young man in the T-shirt, who was standing at a discreet distance, his arms folded across his chest. "I'll have my man take you ashore, and I'll meet you at the Club at eight o'clock."

Monica opened her mouth to protest, but George was already discussing arrangements with the young man. She would have to ask Gina to make her apologies for her.

Gina was finishing her drink when they heard their names being called through a bullhorn.

"What the . . ." Gina said, spinning around in her seat.

A small motorboat with *Cranberry Cove Police Dept.* stenciled on the side in red pulled up alongside the *Yooper II*. Detective Stevens, her blond hair blowing in the breeze, stood at the helm, a bullhorn held at her side.

Gina frowned. "Trust that woman to ruin everything!"

Chapter 26

"Arline Loomis is the killer," Monica said as soon as she and Gina were safely on board the police cruiser with Detective Stevens.

Stevens tucked an errant strand of blond hair behind her ear, but the minute the boat began to pick up speed as it headed toward shore, the piece came untucked and flew across her face again.

She brushed it out of the way. "We'd reached the same conclusion. My men are out searching for her now." She shielded her eyes and looked toward shore before turning back to Monica and Gina. "Do you two want to tell me what you were doing out on the lake in a stolen boat? The owner reported it missing an hour ago. Then we had a call come in from *The Yooper II* that they had picked up two women clinging to an overturned boat. The skipper found it odd that two women would be out in such a small craft dressed as if they were on their way to a garden party."

Gina looked down at her dress and frowned. "If you think we stole that wretched motorboat, you're crazy. I'm sure I have splinters from those rotting wooden seats."

"If you didn't—"

Monica cut in. "Arline Loomis stole the boat. She took us out into the middle of the lake and dumped us."

"Where is she now?"

"The last we saw of her, she'd struck out toward shore."

"Swimming?"

"Yes."

"Then we may be looking in the wrong places. We should be combing the shoreline. She can't have gotten too far."

Monica hoped Stevens wasn't going to ask too many more questions. The sun was getting lower in the sky and a cool breeze had picked up. Goose bumps were forming on her bare arms and legs and all she could think about was getting into a pair of jeans and one of her old sweatshirts.

Gina stopped attempting to pin up her hair. Her eyes got wide. "You mean you haven't caught her yet?" She turned to Monica with a panicked look on her face.

"Don't worry, we will," Stevens said, her mouth set in a line of grim determination.

"Of course, she might have drowned," Gina said, inserting the last pin into her hair, which was now swept up into an approximation of a twist.

"I hope not," Monica said.

Gina frowned at her. "How can you say that? After she tried to kill us by throwing us in the lake?"

"No reports of drownings," Stevens cut in brusquely. "Of course it might have gone unnoticed. People always assume a drowning person will flail around splashing and yelling for help, but in reality, drowning victims make hardly any noise at all. They simply slip beneath the water when their energy gives out. If we don't find her hiding somewhere, we'll send some divers out to look."

Monica shivered. "I hope it doesn't come to that."

When Monica got home, Mittens greeted her as if she'd been gone for days and not just a few hours. She picked the kitten up in her arms and cuddled her close, feeling Mittens's soft fur against her face and the thrum of her excited purring.

Suddenly the tears started. Monica swiped a hand across her eyes and tried to stem the tide of emotion that threatened to engulf her. She'd had to be brave for Gina's sake and hadn't wanted to let her guard down in front of the men on the yacht or in front of Detective Stevens, but now that she was alone, it was impossible to keep from crying.

Monica was reaching for a tissue when the landline rang. It was Greg.

"Are you okay? I looked all over for you at the celebration but couldn't find you. Phyllis Bouma said she'd talked to you earlier in the afternoon but hadn't seen you since."

"I'm fine."

"You sound like you've been crying. Is something wrong?"

Monica explained about Arline, the stolen boat and being forced into the lake so far from shore.

"And the police haven't caught her?" Greg sounded alarmed. "I don't like that. You could still be in danger. I'm on my way over."

Before Monica could protest, Greg hung up.

She hadn't thought about the possibility that Arline might still come after her. She quickly checked the locks on the front and back doors and went upstairs to change.

It felt good to peel off her wet sundress and wrap up in her terrycloth robe. She hung the dress over the shower rod to dry—hoping it wasn't ruined—and went into her bedroom to get dressed.

Since Greg was coming over, she chose her best pair of jeans—the ones without any holes, although there was a small but hardly noticeable bleach spot on the back pocket.

She automatically reached for her favorite sweatshirt but then decided it was too ratty for public consumption and chose a white cotton sweater instead.

She tried not to jump at every sound she heard—the tree branch outside her window that needed trimming and was scraping across the glass, the settling noises the old house regularly made, Mittens's irritated squeal when her claws got caught in the bedspread.

She didn't want to admit how relieved she was when the front doorbell rang. As she descended the stairs she could see the top of Greg's head through the small window set high in the door.

It was all she could do to restrain herself from throwing herself into his arms when she opened the door.

"Whoa," Greg said, enfolding Monica in a strong hug. "Everything is going to be okay now."

"I know," Monica said, sniffing back the tears that were threatening to resurface.

She rested her head against Greg's shoulder, enjoying the warmth and security of his embrace. He smelled like a mixture of citrus and old books—it was very soothing.

"I noticed a number of police cars out and about on my way here, and that's unusual. Normally the only time I ever see a patrol car is when one of them is parked outside the Cranberry Cove Diner on a food run. But from what you just told me, I imagine they're out looking for Arline. I'm sure they're bound to find her soon."

"I hope so." Monica shivered.

"Don't worry, because I'm not leaving you alone." Greg pulled Monica to him.

Again, she rested her head on his shoulder and allowed herself to relax in his embrace. She felt the worry and fear of the last few hours slowly drain away.

She drew back slightly, looked up at Greg and smiled. "I have some white wine chilling in the refrigerator."

He tightened his arm around her. "That sounds great."

Greg was wrestling with the cork in the wine bottle and Monica was fetching glasses when the telephone rang.

"Hello?"

Monica listened for a moment. "That is good news." She sagged against the counter in relief. "Thanks for calling." She hung up the phone and let out a deep sigh.

"Good news, I gather?" Greg poured a measure of wine into each of their glasses.

"The police caught Arline. A couple of fishermen saw her struggling and picked her up and took her to shore. She told them that she'd taken her little boat out to join the Flag Day celebration but that she'd taken on water and started to sink. A reasonable explanation—she is a quick thinker."

"And a good liar," Greg said. He handed the glass of wine to Monica.

"But apparently she made the mistake of going back to Mrs. Wenk's house, where the police were waiting for her. I guess she had some cash hidden in her room somewhere and wanted to retrieve it before she bolted."

"I wonder where she planned to go?"

"Detective Stevens said they ran her fingerprints, and she'd been involved in a couple of scams before—nothing on this scale though."

Greg shook his head. "Some people will insist on trying to make a fast buck. Unfortunately there is no such thing unless you win the lottery or have rich ancestors. And, let's face it, most of us don't. It takes hard work. I feel extremely lucky that I get to work hard at something I enjoy immensely."

"Me, too."

Monica realized that she did indeed relish each day on the farm, and woke to greet it with enthusiasm. She was lucky indeed.

"Are you hungry?" Monica opened the door to the refrigerator.

"Yes, actually I am. I was too distracted looking for you at the celebration to sample any of the food."

Monica paused with her hand on the refrigerator handle. "I'm sorry."

"Don't be. You're worth it."

She quickly stuck her head in the refrigerator, pretending to examine the contents, so Greg wouldn't see her blush.

"I'm sure I can rustle up something."

Greg peered over Monica's shoulder. "You've got eggs and bacon. Do you have any Parmesan cheese?"

"I've got a small piece I picked up at Fresh Gourmet."

"How about spaghetti?"

Monica opened the pantry door. "You're in luck. What are you thinking of concocting?"

"Pasta carbonara. Assuming you don't mind if I take over your kitchen."

Before Monica could answer, there was a brisk knock on the back door and then it opened.

"Hey." Jeff was standing on the doorstep, and Lauren was right behind him.

"Surprise." He motioned to Lauren. "Lauren's home for a few days."

"Come in." Monica ushered them into the kitchen. "We were about to make some dinner. Can you join us?"

"Sure," Jeff said enthusiastically.

Monica smiled. She knew that with all the physical labor Jeff did on the farm, he was pretty much always hungry and could easily eat four or five meals a day.

Monica poured Lauren a glass of wine while Jeff opened the refrigerator and helped himself to a beer.

Monica could tell by the expression on Jeff's face—the lines of worry around his eyes and mouth were gone—

and the way he carried himself that he must have good news.

"I guess there was nothing to worry about," Monica said, cocking her head toward Lauren.

"What do you mean?" Lauren looked from Monica to Jeff and back again.

Jeff colored slightly. "I was worried when I couldn't reach you on the phone. I was afraid you were trying to ditch me."

"I'm sorry." Lauren put an arm around Jeff. "My phone was stolen and it took several days to get it replaced. I didn't realize you'd be worried. And I certainly wasn't planning on ditching you." She squeezed his shoulders.

"It looks like everything is okay now," Monica said as she put a pot of water on the stove.

"More than okay."

Monica turned around just in time to see the twinkle in Jeff's eye. He put his beer on the table and took Lauren's hand.

"Lauren," Jeff held up their linked hands, "has decided to stay in Cranberry Cove. The company she's interning with has offered her a job when she graduates. Fortunately they allow employees to work off-site. It will mean frequent trips to Chicago but at least she won't have to live there."

Lauren answered Jeff's smile with one of her own.

"That's wonderful," Greg said. "We should have a toast." He opened the cupboard, retrieved a wineglass and filled it. He handed it to Lauren.

"Wait," Jeff said. "We have something else to celebrate as well." He exchanged glances with Lauren, who broke into a grin as large as Jeff's. "Lauren has agreed to become my wife."

"That definitely calls for a toast," Greg said, raising his glass. "To Jeff and Lauren."

"To Jeff and Lauren," Monica repeated, raising her own glass. "I'm so happy for you both." She gave Jeff a hug and then Lauren. "Have you set a date?" She laughed. "I don't imagine you've had the chance to figure out the details yet. I'm just so excited."

"We do plan to be married here on the farm." Jeff glanced at Lauren and smiled. "We thought we could set up a tent on one of the fields by the bogs."

"That would be lovely!" Monica exclaimed, picturing the scene in her head.

"We thought about having a wedding brunch," Lauren said, glancing at Jeff. "With plenty of your cranberry baked goods to eat."

"If you wouldn't mind," Jeff hastened to add.

"It would be my pleasure."

Over dinner, Monica told Jeff and Lauren about what had happened that afternoon.

"Thank goodness you're okay!" Lauren said.

Jeff looked horrified—his face had gone as white as his napkin. "You and Mother could have been killed."

"Let's not talk about it anymore," Monica said briskly. "I'd much rather talk about your wedding."

"Speaking of which, we still have to tell Lauren's parents our news before it gets too late. They go to bed pretty early."

"Of course," Monica said, getting up to clear the table.

Lauren jumped up to help, but Monica shooed her away. "You get going. I'll take care of this."

Lauren opened the door and took Jeff's hand.

"Good luck," Monica called after them as they left.

"Why good luck?" Greg asked with a puzzled look on his face.

Monica shut the back door. "I don't know. I suppose because Jeff's concerned that Lauren's parents don't approve of him."

"Why ever not? He's a fine young man."

"He is. But Jeff thinks they wanted someone different for Lauren—someone with a high-powered job and the income to go with it."

"Is that what you're looking for in a man?" Greg asked with a laugh, although his expression was serious.

"Not in the least," Monica reassured him. "Been there, done that. And it was a mistake."

Greg looked relieved. "I have an idea," he said, coming up behind Monica and putting an arm around her waist. "Let's leave the dishes and take our wine into the living room and relax for a bit. You must be beat."

"I am," Monica admitted.

She picked up their two glasses and followed Greg into the living room. They sat on the sofa and he poured them each more wine.

Mittens jumped onto the coffee table, knocked the wine cork off and began batting it around the living room floor. Monica watched her fondly. It was hard to imagine life before Mittens arrived.

Monica took a sip of her wine and sighed contentedly,

snuggling back against the cushions of her old sofa. "I'm so happy for Jeff and Lauren. I was worried for a while—that Lauren was going to find life in the big city more enticing than the slow pace here in Cranberry Cove."

"I'm happy for them, too. They'll make a great couple."

"Jeff has had a spot picked out for a house for quite a while now. If the farm continues to do well, he should be able to start building soon." Monica plucked at the fringe on the afghan tossed over the arm of the sofa. "He wants an updated version of a traditional farmhouse with a big wraparound porch. A perfect place for children to play."

"Whoa. Aren't you getting a bit ahead of yourself?" Greg laughed. "They're not even married yet."

"True. I don't even know if they want children. I think Jeff does, but I don't know about Lauren."

Monica noticed Greg was looking at her very intently. She began to chatter nervously.

"I'm so excited for there to be a wedding here at Sassamanash Farm. I can picture the tent and the tables set with white tablecloths and cranberry-colored overlays." Monica stopped abruptly. "I think I'm getting a little carried away. Of course it will be up to Lauren and her mother to plan the wedding, not me." She laughed.

Greg cleared his throat. "Speaking of weddings . . ."

Monica felt her breath catch.

Greg intertwined his fingers with Monica's and gave them a squeeze.

"I'm hoping there will be another wedding here at the farm." Greg turned toward Monica and took her chin in his hand, tilting her face up to his. "Ours. Monica Albertson, will you marry me?"

A million thoughts ran through Monica's mind. *Was this too soon? Did she know Greg well enough? Was she ready for this?*

But the only word that came out was, *Yes*.

Later, as Monica was getting ready for bed, she reflected on her day. It had been like Michigan weather, where you could have sun, rain and snow all on the same day. She'd had fun at the Flag Day celebration, uncovered a killer, been nearly drowned, learned of Jeff and Lauren's splendid news and said yes to a marriage proposal.

She fell asleep dreaming about weddings under a tent out by the cranberry bogs.

Recipes

Cranberry Cobbler

4 cups fresh cranberries
1½ cups sugar
1 cup all-purpose flour
½ teaspoon baking powder
1 egg, beaten
¼ cup butter cut in small cubes

Preheat oven to 375 degrees.

Toss cranberries with ¾ cup sugar and spread in a greased 8- or 9-inch square baking dish.

Mix flour, baking powder and ¾ cup sugar. Add egg and mix until incorporated. Spread over berries.

Dot with butter cubes and bake for approximately 45 minutes until top is golden brown and filling is bubbling.

Cranberry Walnut
Chocolate Chunk Cookies

1 cup butter, softened
½ cup granulated white sugar
1½ cups brown sugar, packed
2 eggs
2 teaspoons vanilla extract
1 teaspoon baking soda
2 teaspoons hot water
½ teaspoon salt
2½ cups all-purpose flour
2 cups semisweet chocolate chunks
1 cup dried cranberries, chopped
1 cup walnuts, chopped

Preheat oven to 325 degrees.

Cream softened butter, white sugar and brown sugar until light and smooth. Beat in eggs one at a time along with vanilla extract.

Dissolve baking soda in hot water and add to batter along with salt. Mix in flour. Stir in chocolate chips, cranberries and walnuts. Chill batter for 1 hour.

Drop by tablespoons onto cookie sheet, leaving room for cookies to expand. Bake for approximately 10 to 12 minutes. Cool on a rack.

Quinoa with
Dried Cranberries and Walnuts

1 cup uncooked quinoa
2 teaspoons olive oil
3 tablespoons shallot, chopped
1 cup water
¼ cup white wine
½ teaspoon salt
2 tablespoons olive oil
3 tablespoons fresh lemon juice
freshly ground pepper to taste
½ cup dried cranberries, chopped
½ cup walnuts, chopped
¼ cup fresh mint, chopped

Rinse quinoa according to package directions.

Heat 2 teaspoons olive oil in a saucepan over medium heat. Add shallots and cook, stirring, until tender—approximately 2 minutes. Add water, wine and salt to pan and bring to a boil.

Add quinoa, cover and reduce heat. Simmer for approximately 15 minutes or until liquid is absorbed. Remove from heat and let cool.

Combine 2 tablespoons olive oil, lemon juice and pepper and whisk until emulsified. Place quinoa in bowl, mix in cranberries, walnuts and mint and stir. Add dressing and toss until combined.

The
Cranberry Cove
Mysteries
by Peg Cochran

**Cranberry farm owner Monica Albertson can
pick out killers faster than she can harvest berries
in quaint Cranberry Cove, Michigan.**

Find more books by Peg Cochran
by visiting prh.com/nextread

"A fun whodunnit with quirky characters and a
satisfying mystery... As sweet and sharp as the heroine's
cranberry salsa."—**Sofie Kelly**, *New York Times* **bestselling
author of the Magical Cats Mysteries**

pegcochran.com
 PegCochran